THE AMATEURS

SARA SHEPARD

FREEFORM BOOKS

LOS ANGELES   NEW YORK

alloyentertainment

Produced by Alloy Entertainment
1325 Avenue of the Americas
New York, NY 10019

First Edition, November 2016
10 9 8 7 6 5 4 3 2 1
FAC-0020093-16260

Printed in the United States of America

Library of Congress Cataloging-in-Publication Data
Names: Shepard, Sara, 1977– author.
Title: The amateurs / Sara Shepard.
Description: First edition. | Los Angeles ; New York : Freeform Books,
    2016. | Summary: "Four teens who met on an online cold-case solving
    forum attempt to solve another teen's murder"—Provided by publisher.
Identifiers: LCCN 2015044197| ISBN 9781484742273
    (hardback) | ISBN 1484742273
Subjects: | CYAC: Mystery and detective stories. | Murder—Fiction. |
    Love—Fiction. | BISAC: JUVENILE FICTION / Mysteries & Detective
    Stories. | JUVENILE FICTION / Love & Romance. | JUVENILE
    FICTION / Social Issues / Death & Dying.
Classification: LCC PZ7.S54324 Am 2016 | DDC [Fic]—dc23
LC record available at https://lccn.loc.gov/2015044197

Reinforced binding
Visit freeform.com/books

SUSTAINABLE Certified Sourcing
FORESTRY
INITIATIVE www.sfiprogram.org
SFI-00993

THIS LABEL APPLIES TO TEXT STOCK

To Kristian and Henry

BEFORE

THE SNOW FELL all night, transforming the world by morning. It was crystal snow, magical snow, creating a perfect, uniform blanket that concealed everything underneath.

Eleven-year-old Aerin Kelly scrambled down the three-tiered back patio, her boots sinking into the sparkling fluff. She fell forward and laughed, rolling onto her back and staring at the white sky. A figure appeared over her. It was her seventeen-year-old sister, Helena, wearing a fitted white overcoat with a fur collar, fur boots, and a brown fedora. Her eyes looked extra blue. Her newly short platinum-blond hair framed her face. Helena looked more beautiful than ever that day, Aerin would think later.

Aerin scrambled to her feet just as Helena tipped her face upward. "Isn't it funny how snow has a smell?" Helena mused.

"I think we're supposed to get more," Aerin said eagerly.

Helena pressed a fur boot into a snowdrift. "Got your phone? Can I check Weather.com?"

"You're always losing yours," Aerin said good-naturedly, lobbing her iPhone, which she'd talked her mother into buying for her last summer, to her sister.

Helena caught it between her red leather gloves, pulled them off, and tapped on the screen. "Six more inches today." She grinned. "We really should make our inaugural snowman *tomorrow*, but I bet you'll be on the slopes all day. You up for it now?"

"Sure." The girls tramped toward the middle of their vast six-acre property, where they'd been building the first snowman of each season since they were little. Helena started rolling a snowball, her hat tilting across her eyes.

"I think this year's should be a snow-*woman*," Helena decided. "With big boobs."

"And a badonka butt," Aerin added, still breathless.

Helena smirked. "And maybe a vagina. Make her totally anatomically correct."

Aerin giggled. But what she really wanted to do was throw her arms around her sister. Helena was downplaying it, but it was weird they were hanging out again. Laughing.

There was a time when Helena and Aerin had been inseparable. They made tents out of blankets and told ghost stories. They dreamed up new, better uniforms to propose to Windemere-Carruthers, the private school they attended in Dexby, Connecticut. They invented new ice cream flavors like strawberry jalapeño for their mother to make in her ice cream machine, crazy ones they both admitted they would *never* try themselves.

At the beginning of last summer, though, Helena had . . . changed. She'd holed up in her room, chopped off her signature long hair, and stopped talking to her family, even Aerin. "She's a teenager," their mother had told Aerin absently. "She has her first boyfriend. Give her space to figure it out."

But Aerin had needed her more than ever. Their parents, who had always seemed so in love, were fighting nonstop. Aerin knew Helena heard the fights through her thin bedroom walls, too, but whenever Aerin tried to talk to her about it, Helena always changed the subject.

But now Helena was piling snow together for the torso, smiling like things were totally normal. She even started chattering about how Aerin should join the junior ski team—she was so talented. Suddenly, Aerin blurted, "I guess Kevin didn't want to make a snowman?"

Helena stopped and looked at her. "I didn't ask him."

"Do you guys, like, do it?" Aerin asked quickly.

Helena's brow furrowed. *"Do it?"*

Aerin had thought asking would make her seem older, like a girl her sister still wanted to hang out with. Helena would probably go inside and slam her door, and that would be that.

Helena cupped Aerin's shoulder instead, the way she used to at swim meets when Aerin would climb out of the water after coming in last. The gesture was so tender and familiar that Aerin felt a rush of tears. "It's just that I *miss* you."

Helena squeezed hard. "We'll talk more. But . . . some of it will have to be under wraps."

Aerin blinked. "Huh?"

"Like on our phones."

"Like . . . texts?"

Helena looked at her as if she wanted to say something more, but then cocked her head toward the woods like she'd heard something. Aerin followed her gaze but only saw the same trees that had always been there. When she peered at Helena again, her sister was scooping up a ball of snow and smashing it into Aerin's head. Aerin squealed. "Let's find sticks for her arms," Helena said. "I'm freezing my butt off."

They built the head and shaped the hair. Chatted about getting a new puppy. Aerin voted for a golden; she thought they could name him Cap'n Crunch.

"That's a good name," Helena said softly.

Aerin looked up, even more puzzled. It was a dumb name, and they both knew it. Why was Helena being so nice? Aerin felt self-conscious. What if she knew something about their parents Aerin didn't—like they were getting a divorce? Aerin wasn't sure she was ready for that conversation.

But Helena said nothing about that, and then the snow-woman was finished. Both girls stepped back a few feet. Aerin smiled at their work. "She's our best one yet."

When she looked at Helena, her sister's head was turned toward the woods again. "Totally," she said softly. For a moment, she looked like she might cry, but then she focused on the snow-woman and smiled cheerfully. "She needs something else, don't you think?"

"Like what?"

"Like . . ." Helena put a hand to her mouth. "A purse, maybe. I found a brown vinyl one at Goodwill a few days ago. It's on my bed. Wanna grab it?"

Aerin was certain she'd heard her wrong. Helena's room was off-limits. Maybe this was some kind of test? "O-okay."

Aerin opened the sliding door and padded through the living room, leaving wet tracks on the handwoven rug. The house was quiet, her parents absent. She smiled at her reflection in the giant hallway mirror. She had the same blond hair as Helena, but her features were more muddled, her shoulders broader, her face more masculine. Still, it was clear they were sisters.

Maybe they would get pizza later. Maybe Helena would drive her somewhere in her VW Bug. Maybe they'd figure out some way to get their parents to stop arguing.

Helena's bedroom door was closed. Aerin turned the knob. Inside, she breathed in patchouli oil and jasmine—heady scents that seemed mysterious and grown-up. She surveyed a desk full of art supplies, posters of bands Aerin had never heard of, an iPhone on a heart-shaped pillow on the bed, the brown vinyl purse. Helena's closet doors were flung open, revealing the flamboyant clothes she'd been wearing lately— feathers and silk, swirl prints and fringe. Aerin's gaze moved to the dresser. A crane, folded out of slick red paper, stood like a sentinel.

A shiver went through her body. It seemed to be staring at her.

She walked closer, touched its wing. A cloth-covered journal lay next to it. Aerin lifted the cover and looked at her sister's name written on the front page in her spiky scrawl.

There was a *creak*, and Aerin stiffened. She grabbed the purse from Helena's bed, slung it around her elbow, and ran into the hall. The giant kitchen was still empty. She peeked into the backyard. Helena was gone. The snow-woman stood, arms akimbo, in the middle of the yard.

"Helena?" Aerin called out, taking a few steps onto the patio.

A bird called from a high branch. The wind was still. The yard was a blank, open, lonely square.

"Helena?" Aerin cried again, clomping down the steps. "Where are you?"

Her voice echoed in the stillness. Her heart thudded. *She left because I spied.*

She ran around to the front. Helena's car sat in the driveway. No one was in the driver's seat. Aerin flashed on the image of Helena's phone, still inside the house. Her sister would never leave without it.

Something flickered at the tree line, and Aerin turned. "Helena?"

Then she noticed something in the snow. The fallen berries from the bushes that lined the back of the property looked like smeared blood against white. In their midst, Aerin almost hadn't seen the red leather gloves Helena had been wearing, in the snow next to them, palms up.

Aerin ran to them, heart pounding hard. "Helena?" she called out. *"Helena!"*

Helena would never answer again.

FIVE YEARS AND
FOUR MONTHS
LATER

Welcome to CASE NOT CLOSED, the #1 cold-case web community

AKellyReal: I need some answers about my sister. Help . . .

ONE

ON THURSDAY NIGHT, just before school was off for spring break, Seneca Frazier sat cross-legged on her bed in her small dorm room at the University of Maryland. It was after 11:00 p.m., and the dorm was quiet because everyone was out partying at the frats or in upperclassmen houses. Tove Lo played through her laptop's speakers. Packed boxes sat around her bed. She'd shut off the overhead light, and the glow from her computer turned her tawny skin a brassy gold. The perfume her roommate, Eve, had sprayed on before she went out kept making Seneca sneeze, and pieces of her wiry ponytail kept falling out and tickling her cheeks. But when she saw the post Maddy had just written on the chat feature of Case Not Closed, a crime-solving forum Seneca was a little bit addicted to, those small aggravations fell away. Her gaze tunneled in on the words on the screen.

MBM0815: *Do you know this case?*

Below was a screen grab of a post written just hours before by someone called AKellyReal. Seneca's stomach flipped at the name in the thread's title: Helena Kelly. *Yeah, Maddy. I have every last detail of that case memorized.*

But she couldn't tell Maddy that. She wiggled her fingers over the keyboard.

TheMighty: *Rich girl goes missing about five years ago? Body found in a park?*

MBM0815: *Yep. It happened in my town. I'm thinking about looking into it.*

Seneca pulled at the chunky-knit infinity scarf around her neck and looked again at the screen grab. Was the poster, AKellyReal, *Aerin Kelly,* Helena's sister? How had Aerin heard about Case Not Closed? Maybe the same way Seneca had—by accident. Ashton, one of her friends at college who she'd swapped dog-eared Agatha Christie paperbacks with, mentioned it in the dining hall: "Did you know there's a website where amateur sleuths solve crimes?" he said excitedly. "It's, like, part video game, part *Bones.* It's totally eating into my homework time." Seneca had given him an apathetic shrug and pushed around her concoction of strawberry froyo and Cocoa Krispies. "Sounds fun." The first moment she could, however, she'd bolted up to her room, pounced on her laptop, and typed *Case Not Closed* into the browser.

It was easy to lose hours on the message boards of CNC. She'd bring her laptop to class, pretending to take notes but instead weighing in on cold-case murders and abductions. Some days she skipped class altogether—the course videos went online later anyway. She didn't want to miss any new developments on her cases. Some of the posters were morons or rubberneckers, but others had smart input and practical knowledge: MizMaizie used to work for the Seattle PD. UnicornHorn had a background in forensics. BMoney60 always chimed in with a one-sentence proclamation like *Spoiler alert: The mom did it.* He was often right.

It was like Seneca had her own little CSI unit inside her computer.

And then there was her friend Maddy—or MBM0815, or Madison Wright from Connecticut. On Facebook, Maddy was a smiley cheer-leader type with perfect Asian skin and hair and a penchant for pink, but her posts on Case Not Closed were witty and insightful. When they'd graduated to Gchat, they talked about silly, personal things and made up a game where they compared people they knew to types of candy. Seneca had admitted lots to Maddy, but not everything. She never told *anyone* everything if she didn't have to.

Temptation stirred inside Seneca, and she started a new message.

TheMighty: *Crazy idea. I'm on spring break starting tomorrow, and I'm going to be super bored. I could come see you. We could check out the Helena stuff together.*

She added a surprised-face emoji and pressed SEND, anxiously tap-ping her nails against the bedpost. It would be amazing to meet up with a new friend. She had a group of kids she hung around with at college, but they all still felt like acquaintances.

And Helena Kelly . . . well. That was the Holy Grail of cases for her. She was dying to dig in.

Five and a half years ago, right around when Helena disappeared, Seneca had watched CNN religiously. The news wouldn't shut up about the story. Valiant search parties went out every day, the whole town was interviewed, and even the governor of Connecticut gave a speech about bringing Helena home safely. At first, it disgusted Seneca, leaving her empty, but as the months passed and Helena still hadn't been found, her feelings began to shift. When Seneca saw a Helena report on the news, she dropped everything to watch. She read every Helena investigative story over and over. She trolled her memorial page, inadvertently memorizing her friends' names. She searched the family's Facebook pages for months, discovering that the Kelly parents were separating and that Mrs. Kelly was reviving an ice cream business in town, supported heavily by the Dexby community "in the family's time of need." Seneca had held her breath, hoping for Helena's safe return. She understood that the universe didn't dole out happy endings, but she thought, just maybe, Helena would beat the odds.

Then, four years later, Helena's body was found. Seneca watched in horror as the Dexby police admitted that they doubted they'd ever find who'd done it. *But there's so much more to look into!* she'd thought. Why hadn't they tried harder to prove the boyfriend's alibi? Couldn't they send more dogs into that upstate park? Was every moment of Helena's life accounted for?

Seneca's computer pinged again. She clicked the message.

MBM0815: You must have ESP. I was thinking the same thing. You can stay with me. Amtrak to Metro-North will get you here—there's a train station in Dexby.

Seneca sat back, knocking into her packed box labeled *Mysteries, A–L.* Excitement flooded her body, followed by a chilly grip of fear. She was actually going to do it. Travel to the place that had consumed her thoughts, question the people she already knew so much about. It would bring up a lot of memories she'd long tried to ignore.

Yet she couldn't help but feel galvanized by the challenge. She knew more about this case than most of the cops who'd worked it. Maddy *needed* her. Hell, *Helena* needed her, and Aerin, too. Seneca could just picture Aerin logging on to Case Not Closed just like she did, desperate for answers. Maybe if Seneca figured it out, everything else in her life that was spinning out of control would fall into place, too. All right, then: She was going. She was going to figure out what happened.

It wouldn't solve all her problems. It wouldn't solve all her mysteries. But it was a start.

TWO

AERIN KELLY SANK into an uncomfortable wicker love seat in her friend Tori's sunporch, crossed her legs provocatively, and gazed at the guy next to her. Oliver. No, Owen. Shit. It was definitely Owen.

"Some party, huh?" She sipped the Mike's Hard Lemonade she'd grabbed from the ice chest, wincing at its sickly sweet flavor. She should have gone for a Corona.

Owen's fingers twitched around his beer. "I wish I lived in Dexby. This place rocks."

"Not if you live here," Aerin said with a shrug.

She gazed out the screened windows at Tori's immense backyard. Even though Mr. and Mrs. Gates had explicitly told Tori to stay away from the fire pit when they were out of town, there was a big bonfire blazing. A bunch of kids were dancing tribally around it, drunk or stoned or both. On the court, guys from Windemere, Aerin's stuffy prep school, were playing basketball, tripping over three cackling girls who'd decided to lie down and stargaze. Pitbull was blaring, someone was throwing up in the bushes, and Aerin was pretty sure she'd seen

Kurt Schultz back Mr. Gates's Porsche out of the driveway. A typical night in Dexby, Aerin thought wryly. People here did everything to excess—especially parties.

She gave Owen her sexiest smile. He was an out-of-town cousin of Cooper Templeton, who was probably smoking out of the gravity bong he'd brought with him because that was what Cooper *always* did at parties. Earlier, Aerin had noticed Owen across the crowded, trashed great room. He'd looked kind of adrift, so she'd sidled over. "Let's find somewhere quiet to talk," she'd said, taking his hand. On her way out, Quinn McNulty, Aerin's friend from homeroom, had given her a thumbs-up. "He's cute," Quinn had murmured, but Aerin had chosen Owen mostly because he didn't know her . . . or her baggage.

Owen's gaze drifted to Aerin's fingers, which were tiptoeing up his arm. He laughed nervously. "What do kids do around here? I saw there's a ski slope close by. You into that?"

"I used to be," Aerin said, "but I got bored." It was the same lie she'd told her parents.

She wasn't in the mood to talk, so she stood up and pulled her T-shirt over her head, revealing a pale purple lace bra. The sunporch was empty and private. Sort of. Though plenty of guys here had already seen her bra anyway. Owen's jaw dropped. "Whoa."

"Your turn," she demanded, pointing at him and lowering her lashes.

Owen pulled his oversized Sunkist T-shirt over his head and dropped it to the floor, too. It was so easy to divert a guy's attention.

Aerin looked him up and down. He had tanned skin and tight abs. The bright yellow waistband of his boxers peeked out over his shorts. There was a quarter-sized scar to the right of his belly button. All details she'd forget within the hour. He reached out his hands and pulled her close. *"Mmm,"* he groaned, pressing his lips to her clavicle. "Wow."

Aerin made a *hmm* sound, too, trying to feel a flutter of . . . well, something. But really, Owen could have been anyone. She just needed an outlet to forget about posting that crazy-ass thing on that crazy-ass crime-solving website.

They made out for a while, Owen's hands moving to the clasp of her bra. Aerin gave him a few attentive kisses and pressed her hands against his smooth, bare chest. His fingers moved down to the waistband of her skirt. She felt him fumble for the button and popped up.

"Wait. No," she said, moving backward.

Owen stared at her. His hair was mussed, and his lips were parted. Then he smiled. "C'mon," he urged, kissing her neck.

His hands eased toward her waistband again. Aerin felt the old panic, and she heard that familiar voice. *Don't.* "I said *no*," she said, lurching away from him.

He sat back, hands on his knees. Someone let out a scream from the party. The basketball loudly thumped against the pavement. Owen looked stunned. "Seriously?"

Aerin stood and almost tripped over her shoes, which she'd kicked off. Owen's eyes searched for an answer as she tugged on her shirt. "Did I miss something?"

She stiffened. "I changed my mind."

He grabbed his T-shirt from the carpet and put it back on. He drained the rest of his Coors Light in one gulp. "Psycho."

She watched as he slammed off the porch to the backyard, wove toward the fire pit, and plopped sulkily on one of the wooden chairs. *You are such a freak,* she said to herself.

Sighing, she walked into Tori's downstairs powder room, which was littered with toilet paper and had a condom wrapper in the sink. She turned on the tap anyway and splashed water on her face. Her reflection stared back at her from the mirror, mascara streaky, lipstick smudged. Her highlighted blond hair was straight, thanks to a hot iron, and her skin was flawless from her forty-five-minute makeup routine. Her boobs, which had grown significantly in the past five years, looked extra voluptuous in her V-neck blouse. What had gotten into her, seducing that poor kid and then blowing him off? It wasn't just that today was the anniversary of her sister's bones being found. It wasn't just about that post she'd put up on that site. This had happened many times before.

The first time had been on the two-year anniversary of her sister's disappearance. She'd been thirteen. She and James Ladd were in line for morning chapel at school, and he'd been looking at her, probably feeling sorry for her. "Want me to take my top off?" she'd blurted.

They'd snuck into the school's theater and hid behind the big Christmas tree on the stage. There, she'd pulled up her shirt. James had looked at her with such . . . appreciation. It felt good to be in control of a situation instead of the other way around. It felt good to feel something after two years of numbness.

So she kept going. There was Kennett McKenzie, the boy she kissed at an Upper West Side town-house party when she was supposed to be visiting her dad. And Landon Howe, the boy she showed her panties to at a garden brunch. Or that time exactly a year ago when Aerin made out with Brayden Shapiro on the ninth tee at the Dexby Country Club. That same day, her mom had gotten the call about her sister's remains in that park in Charles County, two hours away. Aerin had tried hard not to faint when the CSI people spoke of the blunt-force trauma to Helena's pelvis, still apparent after almost five years of decomposition.

Suddenly, there was commotion outside. Aerin peered through the window. Blue and red police lights whirled in the front yard. A siren's whoop pierced the air. As she opened the powder room door, kids stampeded past, tossing beer cans and plastic cups over their shoulders. "The woods!" Ben Wilder yelled. "Grab your purse!" Rebecca Hodges hissed to Greta Attkinson. "Otherwise they'll find your license and know you were here!"

Aerin grabbed a Dorito from a bowl in the foyer and walked calmly into the front yard. She'd had one sip of Mike's. Let the cops bust her. She didn't care.

Police officers were giving Breathalyzers. Tori was crying on the porch. Aerin considered consoling her, but it wasn't like it would solve anything. "You can't leave!" a gruff voice shouted at Aerin. A cop shone a harsh light in her face, but after a moment, he lowered the light to the grass. "Aerin *Kelly*?"

The young officer stepped toward her. He had such smooth, pale skin; Aerin wondered if he even shaved yet. His uniform hung on his skinny frame.

"It's Thomas." There was a slight tremor in his voice. "Thomas Grove? We met at the, um, Easter Bunny party last year?"

Aerin looked closer. "Oh shit."

The Easter Bunny party was an annual thing in Dexby. It was held on the Chester Morgenthau estate on Easter Sunday night—in fact, this year's Easter Bunny party was next weekend. The adults dressed up, schmoozed, bragged about their net worth, bid on stuff in the silent auction, blah-di-blah. One of the traditions was that it was totally appropriate for girls to show up dressed as half hooker, half Easter Bunny, complete with a woven basket.

Last year had been Aerin's first foray into the Easter Bunny party world, and she hadn't been surprised to see fistfights in the wine cellar and people practically having sex on the cashmere rugs. Not one to be left out, Aerin dragged a random Windemere senior into the walk-in pantry. Not that she ever really had to drag anyone.

And here he was: Thomas Grove. If she'd had a million chances to guess his name, she never would have picked it.

Thomas stepped toward her, but not in a menacing way. His smile was surprisingly sweet and shy, and he was the first guy in a while, Aerin noticed, who was *not* staring at her chest. "You're a cop now?"

"Yeah, can you believe it?" Thomas said in a conspiratorial tone, as if he'd pulled something over on his superiors. "I've been on the force for a couple months. It's a huge score to get a job here. Most guys start out in Clearview or Rhode. I didn't even have to move."

Aerin was still thinking about the Easter Bunny party. After making out—he hadn't pushed any further—she and Thomas had sat in the guesthouse's pantry, looking around. There were a dozen tins of Spam, whole pallets of SpaghettiOs, and boxes of Cream of Wheat. The idea of Mr. and Mrs. Morgenthau eating gruel was hilarious, and she and Thomas had laughed together, picturing it. For a few minutes, Aerin had felt almost . . . *normal*, like a regular, tipsy Easter Bunny party attendee.

But then Thomas had taken her hand and said something about how pretty she was and then something about her sister—that he'd always thought Helena was nice. He'd had a study hall with her when he was in ninth and she was in twelfth, or something. Aerin had bolted.

Aerin blinked away the memory and stood up straighter. Thomas was a cop now. She *hated* cops, especially Dexby cops. "So are you going to arrest me or what?" she challenged.

Thomas tugged at his collar, then glanced surreptitiously at a cop to the right who was cuffing Cooper Templeton. "Go. I'd hate for this to go on your record."

Aerin eyed him suspiciously. Why was he being so nice? Maybe it didn't matter. She certainly didn't want to hang around this clusterfuck. "Thanks," she said breezily, tossing her hair. "I owe you one."

"See you around?" Thomas said, but Aerin didn't answer.

Safely inside her Audi, she counted the number of squad cars on Tori's driveway. Four—no, *five*. Practically the whole Dexby force. Clearly they had nothing better to do on a Thursday night. That was because Dexby was super safe, right? Nothing bad *ever* happened here.

Almost nothing. Sometimes Aerin felt she was the only one who remembered that.

WHEN SHE PULLED into her driveway, the house was dark, and her mother's car was still missing from its spot. No surprise there. She was probably still at one of the three Scoops ice cream stores around Dexby, making sure the Rocky Road tasted rocky enough.

Aerin often wondered how much her mom really knew. About the boys she made out with. How she hadn't quit skiing because she was burned-out. How it felt like she was the only person who thought about Helena anymore.

That she'd put a cry for help on a ridiculous website.

She slammed her car door, opened the garage, and blinked in the humid darkness, thinking. The old karaoke booth was still in the corner. *Contains 1,045 songs!* read big pink letters on the side. Years ago, Aerin and Helena had been obsessed with the karaoke machine at the Dexby benefit carnival, and after enough begging, their dad had bought them one of their own. Not that Aerin asked her dad for anything *these* days. She barely visited him in his stark New York City apartment, where he'd moved after her parents split up. She hated its view of the Statue of Liberty's armpit and its mostly empty fridge.

She kicked aside a box of trash bags and pushed back the little curtain. It was hot and humid inside the karaoke booth, and so dark she could barely see her hand in front of her face. She hadn't turned the machine on in five years, but if she closed her eyes, she could still almost hear the long arpeggios of a Mariah Carey song. The sweetness of "A Whole New World." How Helena sang Bruno Mars in monotone, but Aerin gave it all she had.

Tears threatened to spill down her cheeks, and she sniffed vigorously to stop them. She pulled out her phone. Hating herself, she typed *Case Not Closed* into the browser.

Dedicated to investigating unsolved cases since 2010, read the poorly designed banner. There was a tab marked *Visual aids*; when she'd first visited this site, she'd clicked on it, finding thumbnails of drawings titled *The killer's path* and *Knife angles* and *Marks on the body = Satanic ritual?* A blinking message that said *videos* contained gems like a video of a body, bruised and totally naked, lying in a parking lot; a slow pan of a crime scene, bloody handprint smears on the walls; and a coroner standing over a body and blandly describing the cause of death. A link that read, *Media accolades,* listed stories with titles like *Amateur sleuthing group helps find missing girl in Arkansas* and *Cell phone pings tracked by online investigators uncover a murderer in West Virginia.* And there were pages and pages of forums, with categories like *The Rules, Ongoing cases, The Missing, Sex crimes, Webcam feeds,* and even one called *Despicable.*

In *Ongoing cases,* dozens of names popped up. There was Aerin's sister's name among the group: *Helena Kelly, Dexby, CT.* It was shocking to see it, even though Aerin had been the one to put it there. Muscles tensed, she clicked on her message. Her heart leapt. Seven responses!

This is a tough one, XCalibur wrote. *I'm not biting.*

Even the FBI couldn't find a lead, wrote someone named RGR. *I'm out, too.*

Five more messages said the same thing. Aerin drew in a breath, feeling like she'd been stabbed. The joyful feeling she'd had was instantly vacuumed away, leaving her vacant. So there it was. Her big cry for help—and the grim answer by idiotic strangers. She might as well accept it: She was never going to know the truth about Helena. What happened to her sister was going to remain a mystery—and a recurring nightmare—for the rest of her life.

THREE

BY SUNDAY, AFTER a few advisor meetings and an argument with a customer service rep at Storage Lockers 4 U, Seneca sat on a lumpy seat on Metro-North heading toward Dexby. The train car smelled like disinfectant and coffee. She was pretty sure she was in the quiet car, but she had her cell phone pressed to her ear anyway and was trying to calm down her father.

"I really wanted to see you for spring break, too," she murmured. "But Annie went through a crisis at Berkeley and needs my help."

"I just hate the idea of you traveling alone," Seneca's father said.

"*Dad*. I'm nineteen. I can manage Amtrak by myself. Don't worry."

He sighed. "Well, do I need to call Annie's folks and thank them for having you?"

"No!" Seneca yelped, then worried she sounded panicked. "I mean, I'll handle it." She took a breath and looked around. There was a boy in an oversized hoodie, ridiculous-looking puffy gold shoes, and a pulled-down baseball cap a few seats ahead. She kept catching him looking at her. Across the aisle, an overly made-up girl moved her frosted lips as she read *OK!*

"But you'll definitely come home for a bit before you have to go to school, right?" her father asked. "You go back . . . when? A week from Monday?"

"A week from Tuesday." She crossed her fingers behind her back, praying that the University of Maryland advisors didn't call home.

"Have fun with Annie, Tweety Bird," her father said sadly, using Seneca's nickname from when she was little, which gave her another guilty twinge. She hated lying to him. She knew how he stressed over her—it was amazing he'd even let her live in the dorms. He was wary about new people in her life, too, but when she'd told him about Annie Sipowitz, a girl she met at college, he seemed to trust her. How could he not? Annie was a driven musician slash math genius slash youth group leader who never got into trouble. But Seneca wasn't really going to Annie's this time. However, she couldn't tell her dad what she was *really* doing.

She placed her *P* pendant in her mouth and sucked hard, something she did when she was nervous. Once again, she peered at Maddy's text from a few minutes ago. *It's going to be epic. Btw, I said we were friends from track camp, so pretend you're a runner!*

Seneca nodded, recalling how Maddy had mentioned that she was really into running. She typed on the screen. *We just passed Stamford. Got you Krispy Kreme.* She glanced at the box of donuts sitting next to her. She appreciated that Maddy was the type of girl who was okay with indulging in a Krispy Kreme or two.

Sweet, Maddy wrote back. *I've got on a green jacket—I'll be on the platform.*

Seneca smiled, pressed her home button, and called up Google

Chrome. Last night, she'd reread the investigative reports about Helena Kelly's case. Now she clicked a link to Helena's senior-class yearbook from Windemere-Carruthers. There was the photo she used to look long and hard at of Helena walking down the hall in her plaid uniform, a fedora cocked rakishly on her head. She looked so carefree.

On another page, each senior had written dedications beneath their photos. Helena's, which had been submitted shortly before she died, was particularly sappy: *I'll miss Becky-bee, love is strong, you stay cool forever Kaylee, XOXO my ladies, LOL Samurai swordplay late nite.*

Finally, Seneca clicked over to the news blasts from when Helena's remains were found last year. Kids had been playing in a creek in Charles County, Connecticut, when a boy came upon what he thought was a dog bone. His mom realized it wasn't and called the police. It was soon clear that the dental records matched Helena's.

Seneca had to figure out who put her there.

Within a few minutes, the train screeched into the station. Seneca pulled her vintage leather suitcase off the rack. The girl reading *OK!* stood in front of her in the exit line, talking in a syrupy voice on her iPhone. Up ahead, Gold Shoes gazed at Seneca, one eyebrow raised. Seneca glanced at her reflection in the window. With her honey-colored skin, light blue eyes, and wild, dark hair, she knew some guys found her "exotic"—but she also wore little makeup, and her biker boots had steel tips. Wasn't *OK!* girl more his type? When she looked up again, Gold Shoes was gone.

There were swarms of people on the platform, and everyone seemed to be wearing preppy polos. Huge pines shaped like car air fresheners jutted on the horizon, and the crisp air smelled pure and had a chilly bite to it. *So here I am,* Seneca thought. Every news report had stressed Dexby's wealth, so she'd expected castles on hills, Rolls-Royces in the parking lot. There was a small shopping district across the street featuring a Pure Barre, a wine and spirits store, and a Vineyard Vines. A ski lodge–style hotel called Restful Inn was down the block; Seneca couldn't decide if it was a total eyesore or adorably kitsch.

She kept an eye out for an Asian girl in green. Everyone was either streaming toward the stairs or greeting people who'd gotten off Seneca's train. She opened her text thread. *I'm here,* she wrote to Maddy. *Where are you?*

Passengers hurried to find their rides, and the Maddy possibilities dwindled one by one. Seneca looked at her phone; Maddy hadn't responded. After a few minutes, Seneca was the only one left on the platform except for a tall, handsome boy with wavy brown hair, a chiseled jaw, and a T-shirt that said *University of Oregon.* Huh. Maddy had told Seneca she'd just received a scholarship to the University of Oregon for track and field. Maybe this guy was also going there and somehow knew her.

She drifted into the parking lot, wondering if she'd gotten off at the wrong stop. "Excuse me?" University of Oregon had followed her. "Are you Seneca?"

"Yeah . . ."

He grinned and stuck out his hand. "Hey! It's Maddy!"

Seneca stared at his outstretched palm, then at him. In fact, it was kind of hard *not* to look at him. He had piercing eyes that could be described as smoldering and a cleft in his chin. He wore a soft-looking olive jacket over his tee that brought out the green in his eyes. His white-and-orange New Balances were a little scuffed, marring his perfect appearance—as if he'd carefully calculated how to look approachable yet adorable. She found herself playing the game she and Maddy—online Maddy, clearly not this person—had made up, giving him a candy identity that best matched his looks. He was one of those Cadbury delectables she'd bought on a trip to England with her dad last year. The best chocolate ever, but you could buy it at the corner store.

She felt herself blush and wrenched her gaze away. "Wait, you're *who?*"

"Maddy." He pointed to himself with a goofy smile. "From Case Not Closed."

"*You're* MBM0815?" she sputtered.

He cocked his head quizzically. "Yeah . . ." Then he looked down at the donut box she was carrying. "Nice. You're going to help me eat these, right?"

Seneca had no idea what to say. She couldn't imagine eating a donut in front of this guy; she'd be way too self-conscious.

"Who names a guy *Madison*?" she finally said.

"My real name's Maddox." He leaned back. "Did you think . . . holy shit. You thought I was Madison Wright, the girl? She's my sister." He rolled his eyes knowingly. "Did you find her on Facebook? I'm not on it, but my sister is so all over friending people she doesn't know."

Seneca's head felt stuffed with shaving cream—unusual, for her. She hated feeling off-balance, and usually came into every situation having done her research and knowing exactly who and what was in store for her. "Um, no, I knew you were you. I just got your names confused."

It just didn't make sense. Online, Maddy had professed a love for *Antiques Roadshow*. He'd told her he sometimes felt out of place among the rich kids at his school. Yet here he was, standing tall and relaxed and confident, fingers hooked in the belt loops of his expensive-looking jeans. The smile on his face was one of a guy who knew he was attractive and well liked. Even worse: Seneca had confessed in Gchat that she'd never had sex, that she still wore a retainer at night, that she spent more time at the university library than the bar—or, for that matter, in class. She'd told Maddy about her troubles in school. She'd even regaled Maddy with stories about Chad, her ex-sort-of-boyfriend, including one where he'd totally ignored her while watching football during what was supposed to be a romantic dinner in Philly. This person, this Maddy, looked like someone who'd tune her out for football, too.

And good Lord. *She'd* been the one to suggest coming to Dexby. What if he thought she was looking for a hookup?

Then, with an effort, she shrugged away her insecurities. So he was a guy. So he was delicious to look at. So he was a weirdly cool track dude. Who cared? She knew why she was really here.

"So what do you say?" Maddy had that self-assured, easy grin again. "Wanna motor?"

He reached for her suitcase, but Seneca's hand shot forward. "I've got it."

She started to walk. When she finally looked up, Maddy was loping next to her. Even his walk was sexy and athletic. "Hey—it's cool. It's me. You know me." His eyes crinkled when he smiled.

Seneca adjusted her suitcase in her hand. *No I don't,* she wished she could say. "For the record?" she called instead over her shoulder. "Maddy *is* a girl's name. You should probably stick with Maddox."

FOUR

MADDOX WRIGHT OPENED the hatch to his Jeep, his car keys hanging from a long lanyard that read, *Dexby Varsity Track*. "Good train ride?" he asked Seneca, placing the box of Krispy Kremes next to her bag and sliding into the driver's seat.

"Fine," Seneca said coldly. She hesitated outside the passenger door like she wasn't sure about getting in. Maddox wondered what her deal was. *Had* she thought he was going to be a girl? Come on: His posts screamed dude, didn't they? Okay, so maybe Maddy swung either way as a name, and maybe he'd been a little more confessional with Seneca than he was with kids around here. It was easier to say what he was thinking, sometimes, when it was late at night and he knew the person he confided in wouldn't be mocking him in school the next day. But there was no reason for her to be shocked or to be acting so reluctant now. He kind of wanted to tell her that most girls at his school would be pretty freaking psyched to be hanging out with him, but that sounded so arrogant, even in his head.

The thing was, Seneca really didn't seem like any of the girls at school. He peeked at her out of the corner of his eye, taking in her appearance, so different from what he'd expected. Her cheeks were pink, her skin was coppery, and her hair was a pretty almost-black and bunched into a wild, sproingy ponytail. She wore fringed denim shorts, a plaid shirt that looked like it could belong to someone's grandpa, and badass motorcycle boots that showed off her long legs. *Totally* not what he'd expected.

The Internet was weird like that. During all the time they'd talked online—first on the boards, then Gchatting, and then exchanging long e-mails about cases, and other stuff, too—he'd pictured her . . . differently. Mousier, maybe, with bad skin and dark-framed glasses and a less-rocking body. Someone he wouldn't be attracted to. Someone he wouldn't automatically picture in a bikini.

There was a loud rapping on the car. Carson Peters and Archer McFadden, two friends from Maddox's team, appeared. "Yo, man, you doing the Achilles 5K tomorrow?" Archer boomed after Maddox rolled the window down. "You'll totally nab first. And I hear Tara's doing it, too." He punched his arm.

"I know you could chase that hot booty all day," Carson teased.

"I'm too busy chasing your mom's," Maddox quipped, but then he caught Seneca's sour expression in the rearview mirror. "Nah, I got things to do," he said in a lower voice. Archer and Carson noticed Seneca, too, and gave Maddox sly, questioning grins. "This is my buddy Seneca," Maddox told them. "We met at track camp."

"What up," Archer and Carson said, looking her up and down. Seneca politely nodded at both of them, and a weird, awkward silence followed.

Maddox gunned his engine. "We're heading out," he told his

teammates. Archer gave him a creepy grin. Carson was still staring at Seneca's boobs.

At the turn to the road, Maddox glanced at Seneca. "Sorry about that. But they're good guys once you get to know them."

Seneca's face was pinched. She set her jaw and mumbled something under her breath.

"So *anyway*," Maddox said, pretending not to notice, "here we are in Dexby. You know you want a tour."

"Actually, I want to head over to the Kellys'," Seneca said in a prissy voice.

Maddox frowned. "As in Aerin Kelly?"

She looked at him like he was crazy. "Who else?"

"I was thinking we could check out some spots Helena frequented first, like Connecticut Pizza and the ski slope, maybe even Windemere Prep. And then I have this list of her friends we should talk to. Her old best friend, Becky, owns this restaurant that makes awesome chili fries. And she knew this girl Kelsey who works for the Rangers now, and *then* we were going to meet up with—"

"But Aerin wrote us an SOS on the boards," Seneca interrupted.

"We don't *actually* know it was from her. And anyway, Helena's friends might have more insider knowledge than her little kid sister, don't you think?"

"Her *little kid sister* was the last one to see her alive." Seneca stuck her tongue into her cheek. "I mean, correct me if I'm wrong, but isn't that more important than chili fries?"

"That's not what I . . ." Maddox hadn't meant to sound like a tool. Seneca was right about Aerin . . . but he didn't *want* her to be right. "Okay," he surrendered, moving into the right lane toward Aerin's house as if it was totally normal. "I guess we can do that."

He gritted his teeth as he checked his rearview mirror. *Shit, shit, shit.* He'd hoped to avoid the whole Aerin Kelly thing for as long as possible.

The car was silent, so Maddox decided to give Seneca a mini tour as they drove. "That turnoff leads to a park where a couple of people saw a Sasquatch. You ever go on a Sasquatch hunt? People are crazy about them around here. It leads to some sick parties."

No response. He pulled onto a long boulevard bordered by a huge complex called the Dexby Recreational Center. "Here's where I practice with Catherine."

A long pause. Seneca fiddled with the flap on her purse. "Who's Catherine?" she finally said, as if he'd forced the question out of her.

"My running coach."

Seneca gave him a strange look. "You need someone to *show* you how to run?"

He shrugged. "Catherine got me to drop six seconds off my 800. That's insane. It's how I got the scholarship to Oregon." He glanced at Seneca, assuming she'd find this impressive, too, but her gaze was out the window.

They passed Windemere-Carruthers Prep School, where Aerin Kelly and a bunch of kids Maddox knew attended—he went to Dexby Public. Windemere had a pristine green lawn, and its main building was an eighteenth-century brick compound that gleamed in the sunlight. Next was the Dexby police station, a modern marvel of stone and glass. Then came the flagship Scoops of Dexby with its ice-cream-cone-shaped sign whirling by the road. Seneca blinked solemnly at every landmark that passed. Maddox racked his brain for a joke he could tell, but the only good jokes he knew were dirty.

The houses morphed into block-long monstrosities he knew well. Years ago, Maddox used to sit in the backseat of his mother's car, imagining the insides of these places. The fortresslike one on the corner contained a room full of action figures. The stone-and-brick twenty-bedroom estate on the hill had an indoor pool with a waterslide. But that was ancient history.

Seneca turned to him. "What was this place like after Helena vanished?"

He widened his eyes. "Insane. News vans clogged every street. They camped here, overran the town. They interviewed everybody. Really got in your face about stuff."

The Kellys' house was at the end of a cul-de-sac, a classical structure of stone and archways with an expansive backyard against thick, lush woods. It all was so familiar Maddox could have drawn it from memory. He turned off the engine and sat back. Well, they were here. He just had to spit it out.

He cleared his throat and looked at Seneca. "So listen. Aerin Kelly . . . knows me."

Seneca rolled her eyes. "Did you *date* her?"

Maddox was momentarily disarmed. "N-no. About ten years ago, my mom worked for her family." He shrugged nonchalantly. "She was sort of a nanny."

Now Seneca was the one who seemed off-kilter. "For how long?"

"Oh, three years or so." He tried to keep his tone light and easy. "I was too young to stay by myself, and I wasn't into after-school sports yet, so sometimes I tagged along." He coughed into his fist. "My dad . . . left . . . when I was four. I don't know if I mentioned that. It's no biggie. And now Mom's remarried. She doesn't work anymore."

Seneca's mouth wobbled. "Did you not tell me before because you were embarrassed?"

"What?" Maddox waved his hand quickly. "Nah. I probably just forgot." He hoped she couldn't tell he was lying.

Seneca's eyes darted back and forth. "Well, okay," she said after a beat. "Did you hang out with Helena at all?"

Maddox flicked the lanyard attached to his keys. "Not really. She was nice, though, when she was around. One of those people you didn't want to see hurt, you know? I guess that's why I've always been interested in the case. She didn't deserve what she got."

Seneca blinked, seemingly taking all this in. Her fingers curled on the door handle, but then she turned back and looked him over in a way that Maddox couldn't quite figure out—was she checking him out, or was she trying to read his mind? Finally, she blurted, "I don't mean to stereotype, but do your friends know you're into . . . *crime solving*?"

Maddox blinked hard. "My friends from school?"

She shrugged. "Yeah. Your track buddies. Those guys in the parking lot."

He considered his friends. They looked at him and saw what Seneca must be seeing now: jock, ladies' man, whatever. It was like his friends had completely wiped from their minds who he used to be, and he didn't bother reminding them. Why bring up the past?

Then Seneca shrugged. "Forget I asked. You sure you're ready for this?"

He squared his shoulders. "You bet."

They approached the front door. The same painted sign read, *Welcome, Friends*. When he pressed the doorbell, the familiar melody gave him a nostalgic twist in his stomach.

Footsteps sounded. There was fumbling with a chain latch, and

then the door swung open. The huge foyer, full of wood beams and folk
art and Shaker furniture, was unchanged from when Maddox had last
seen it. Maddox only recognized Aerin, however, by her blue eyes. She
was tall, with bright white-blond hair, overly made-up eyes, and very
pink lips. She was wearing a shrunken pink T-shirt, shorts that exposed
an expanse of thin thigh, and a cross between sandals and boots.

Maddox tried not to grin like a fool, but it was tough. In the past
few years, he'd seen Aerin Kelly from afar—at track meets, at big parties, at the Dexby Fourth of July parade . . . but not up close. The rumors
were true, though: The bratty little girl he'd known had become smoking hot.

Aerin Kelly eyed them suspiciously. "Can I help you?"

"We're from an online crime-solving coalition," Seneca said.

"We're here to help," Maddox said at the same time.

Seneca flashed her eyes at Maddox, and Maddox gave her a look
right back. He turned to Aerin and started over. "We read your post
on Case Not Closed. About your sister."

Aerin's face went pale. *"Huh?"*

Maddox frowned. "Did you not write that post?"

Aerin pushed a piece of hair behind her ear. "I wrote it, but . . ."
Her throat caught as she swallowed. "Tell me this is a joke. You guys
are, like, *my* age."

Seneca straightened. "The site has been successful at cracking cold
cases nationwide."

Aerin ran a hand over her forehead. "It was bad enough when I
thought the people posting on that freaky site were forty-year-old los-
ers still living with their parents who wanted to play Scooby-Doo. Is
this a joke to you? Something you think will look good on a college
application?"

Seneca blinked fast. "No! It's—"

"Do you get off on those morgue videos?" Aerin's nostrils flared. "You realize it's illegal to have those up there. Those are real people, you know. With real families."

Maddox shrugged. "The faces are blacked out. And they can be useful, especially if someone who's looking at them knows about exit wounds or injuries. Some of the posters are doctors, ex-cops, and—"

"Do the other posters know you guys are just kids?" Aerin interrupted. "What if I logged on to your site and told everyone you aren't even out of high school?"

"Actually, I *am* out of high school," Seneca said. "So go right ahead. My screen name's TheMighty."

Aerin glowered at her. Then her gaze swung to Maddox, recognition finally flickering in her eyes. "I've seen you around. What is this, some kind of prank so you can brag to your meathead friends?"

Maddox burst out laughing. "Actually, Aerin, it's Maddy Wright. Remember?"

Aerin looked like he'd just smacked her across the face. A long beat passed. "My *nanny's* son?" She touched the doorknob. "Now I really need you to leave."

"But—" Seneca protested.

"*Go.*"

Aerin went to close the door, but Maddox shot out his arm and grabbed it. "Wait." He fumbled for the pen he'd brought. He tore a piece off a random receipt from his pocket and scribbled his phone number and address, tossing it at her. "Here's my number. Call anytime." He raised his eyebrows and, as a last-ditch effort, shot her the smile that usually worked on girls.

That made Aerin frown even deeper. She slammed the door in their faces.

The wreath on the front door jumped at the impact. "Well," Seneca said tightly, making a military-style turn back toward the car. "That was delightful."

Maddox's skin felt itchy. He climbed in the driver's seat and turned the key in the ignition. This was why he hadn't wanted to come here: He worried this would happen. Aerin had treated him just like she always had when he was her nanny's awkward, nerdy kid. Even though he'd transformed. Even though she'd *acknowledged* he'd transformed, that they had friends in common now. He'd hoped, unrealistically, that her attitude toward him would have adjusted accordingly. He hated to be reminded of that time in his life.

"I told you we shouldn't have come," he said. "Aerin's a bitch. Always has been."

"She didn't seem like a bitch." Seneca climbed in her side. "She just seemed upset."

"Well, we shouldn't have gone in with guns blazing. Saying we were from a *coalition*."

"So I should have let you do all the talking, then?" Seneca asked tightly.

"Maybe we should have had a softer approach. Said we understand where she's coming from."

Seneca flinched. "What's *that* supposed to mean?"

Maddox closed his mouth. He really had no idea.

"Why would I know where she's coming from?" Seneca persisted. There were red splotches on her cheeks. "I'm not from here. I don't know her. Why would you say that?"

"Dude. I was just saying some words." *Chill out,* he thought but didn't say. He didn't have to know that much about girls to know that telling a girl to calm down would only make her angrier.

Seneca pressed her lips together. "Maybe this isn't a good idea."

Maddox turned his head sharply. "Huh?"

"Maybe I should go home."

"Wait, *what*? Just because Aerin isn't into it doesn't mean—"

"If you don't want to take me to the train station, I'll find a cab."

Maddox felt his stomach drop. Jesus. She was serious. "How about if we—"

"No, I really just want to go."

Maddox stared at her, but she wouldn't look back at him. He'd never had something go so bombastically awry. Before Seneca had come, he'd relished the idea of having a buddy who was actually into the stuff he was into. But he was wrong about everything. The Seneca he'd known online was warm and funny—nothing like the weird, distant girl in the seat beside him. He didn't know her at all.

What was he doing, anyway, chatting with freaks on that website? He wasn't a freak anymore. He was cool now—and he didn't need any more friends, much less psycho ones like Seneca. Yet somehow, he knew that if he said all that out loud, it wouldn't sound as good as it did in his head.

"You're the boss," he said quietly, shifting into drive. "The station it is."

FIVE

AS EVENING FELL, Aerin sat on the couch in her upstairs library, a time capsule to 2012. A *Newsweek* on the rack recapped Obama's reelection. The DVD player wasn't a Blu-ray. There was a thin line of dust on top of every *Encyclopaedia Britannica*, relics themselves. Since her sister's disappearance and her dad's move to the city, her mom worked hard to keep the huge house pristine—*she* wasn't falling to pieces, no, sir!—but this room was her little secret.

Downstairs, Aerin could hear her mother, in a rare appearance at home, opening a bottle of wine. Her best friend, Marissa Ingram, cheered when the cork popped. "Boy, do *I* need a glass," she said.

Aerin crept out of the library, shut the door, and peered over the railing. Marissa's husband, Harris, was puttering around the great room, checking out Aerin's mother's coffee-table books. Aerin's mom and Marissa sat at the huge farmhouse table, toasting with their wineglasses. Marissa, who had jet-black hair cut to her chin, probably weighed ninety pounds soaking wet. As always, she had on her enormous diamond ring—big enough that it would surely put out someone's eye if she punched them with it. As the women sipped their wine, Marissa gossiped about how her son, Heath, had gone on a date with a new girl. "Is she nice?" Aerin's mom asked.

"You think we've actually met her?" Mr. Ingram—everyone called him Skip—scoffed.

"But the way Heath describes her, she seems kind of . . . oh, I don't know." Marissa sighed. *"Regular."*

Aerin resisted the urge to snort. That was Ingram-speak for *lower-class*. Then again, no one would be good enough for Heath. Even *Heath* wasn't good enough for Heath. Through the years, Marissa had glossed over that Heath had (a) been suspended from Windemere-Carruthers for painting graffiti on the wall of the science lab, which his family had donated, (b) dropped out of Columbia and disappeared to Colorado to be a ski bum, and (c) moved back into the family estate three years later, not getting a job but instead participating in various protests around town, including one against killing the deer to control overpopulation. Marissa probably didn't like the tribal tattoos on Heath's biceps, either. Aerin had seen them at the Ingrams' last pool party.

The wood floor creaked. "Honey, I think we'd better get going," came Skip's gravelly voice that held just a hint of a Boston accent. "We have that thing at seven."

Marissa stood. "I almost forgot, darling."

Aerin kicked the railing with her boot, leaving a scuff. The smoochy way the Ingrams talked to one another was nauseating.

After some kisses, Mr. and Mrs. Ingram sauntered out the front door. Then the only sound in the house was the low drone of the classical station on the stereo. Aerin peered downstairs once more. Her buttery-blond-haired mother, who still looked good in the skinny silk pants she had on, sat at the table, gnawing on the stem of her tortoise-shell glasses. If Aerin had to fill in a thought bubble above her mother's head, she'd have no idea what to write.

Mrs. Kelly noticed her above and jumped. "When did you come in?"

"I've been home for hours," Aerin called down.

Her mother's brow furrowed. "Sitting in the dark?"

She walked to the sink and rinsed out the wineglasses. When she turned and saw Aerin still standing above her, hands in the pockets of her short skirt, she cocked her head. "Is there something I can help you with?"

Aerin's mouth dropped open. Years ago, she and her mom had been close—even Helena had been jealous of their bond. Aerin loved to help her mom make homemade ice cream in the basement. On Fridays, Aerin's mom brought her to her gym, where they'd do a mother-daughter spin class and get massages. They had a special handshake if Aerin was scared: a thumb to the palm followed by a thumb to the back of her hand. Her mom would follow up with three quick squeezes that meant *I've got you.* She bet her mom didn't remember that handshake now.

"I was arrested yesterday," she blurted out. "At Tori's."

Mrs. Kelly's hands fell to her waist. "W-what?"

Aerin couldn't believe it. Her mom was so out of touch, she didn't even have an inkling that Tori's party had been raided. "Forget it." Hunching her shoulders, she spun around toward her bedroom. "I made it up."

Mrs. Kelly sped up the stairs and caught her sleeve. "What's with you?"

Aerin wrenched away. "Do you even remember what anniversary yesterday was, or am I the only one who still remembers Helena exists?"

Mrs. Kelly flinched at Helena's name. Her lashes lowered. "Of course I remembered."

"Could have fooled me."

Aerin closed her bedroom door behind her. She stood in the middle of the room and waited. After a moment, she heard a sigh and footsteps heading in the opposite direction. Typical.

Aerin wheeled around and surveyed her room. If an anthropologist peeked in here, he'd think she was a normal, happy teenage girl. Pictures of Aerin and her friends were her screen saver. Yellow-and-red Windemere pom-poms from the last spirit day were pinned to the wall. A huge hippo Blake Stanfield had won for her at the Dexby Firemen's Carnival last year was propped on her pillow. Yep, a scientist would have to do serious forensic work to find out the truth. Like test her pillow for salt content from the tears she still shed when she knew no one was listening, or look through her browser history to find the Helena memorial websites she still visited, or note that a QuickTime window was open on her laptop showing the Christmas video of Helena from six years ago that Aerin watched nightly.

Did Aerin still dwell on her sister more than anyone else because she'd been there that last day? She'd reviewed that snowy afternoon with Helena a thousand times. Why the hell had she gone inside to get that stupid purse? What had happened to Helena in that infinitesimal span of time Aerin hadn't been keeping her safe? In the interviews she'd given to so many news networks, some reporters asked if she felt responsible for her sister's disappearance. Maybe it was just to elicit tears, or maybe it was what they really believed. Maybe *everyone* believed that. If Aerin had just stayed with her sister, Helena wouldn't be dead. It was as good a theory as any.

Whether or not it was true, she'd always felt like it was her job to find out what had happened to Helena, especially now that the cops had lost interest. So she reached out to an online community, and who showed up? Kids *her* age. Talk about an insult! She hated their eager student council faces. She hated that the girl had called them a *coalition*. And she hated that one of them was her nanny's kid. That dude looked about as far from the old Maddy Wright as you could get. And what, did Maddy Wright think she owed him something, just because he'd hung out at her house as a child?

She wondered where the two of them were now. Looking at old reports, pressing on without her? Aerin grabbed her phone and pulled up Case Not Closed again. Her topic was still almost at the top, and there was a new comment. It was by TheMighty—that was the girl, right? *Traveled to Dexby to check things out. This case is ice-cold. Heading home on the 7 PM train.*

Heading *home*?

"Jesus," Aerin whispered. She looked at her watch, then rummaged in her pocket for that slip of paper Maddy had thrown at her earlier. She'd only picked it up because she didn't want her mom to find it and ask why Maddy Wright's number was on the floor.

She looked at her phone again, then placed a hand over her eyes. She hated what she was about to do.

SIX

MADDOX HAD DROPPED Seneca off at the train station only fifteen minutes before, but her phone had rung about fifty times since then. Now, as she stood at the ticket machine, buying a fare home, his name flashed on the caller ID again. *Maddy,* said the screen. She hit IGNORE.

The whole situation had soured. Everything Maddox said and did in the car had been heartbreakingly different from the person she'd expected, girl *or* guy. She kept hoping his facade would break but it didn't, and that made her feel so disconnected from him that she had no idea how to even conduct a conversation.

And there were all those Dexby landmarks—she'd dreamed of those places years ago, and seeing them for real brought her own memories back in a gushing torrent. And sure, Aerin Kelly *seemed* put together—perfectly styled, perfectly made-up—but there was a halo of haunted, tortured sadness around her. Seneca knew the look. She had that halo, too.

And what was with that comment Maddox had made about Seneca

knowing where Aerin was coming from? Why would he say that? Did he *know*?

Seneca wanted to be strong and keep the investigation going. Maybe if Maddox had been the person she'd built up in her mind, she could have. Or maybe if Aerin had been more receptive. But as it stood, she felt shaky and unsure, and all sorts of warning bells were telling her to bolt.

The moon was rising, creating long stripes across the platform. When Seneca looked around, she realized the platform was eerily empty. Footsteps echoed in a stairwell, and she heard whispers. *"There she is,"* someone said.

Her hair rose on the back of her neck. All of a sudden, a figure bounded up the stairwell, straight for her. Seneca shielded her body. "Leave me alone!"

"Whoa!" a voice cried. "Chill!"

The figure stepped into the overhead light. It was Aerin Kelly.

Maddox stood next to her. And next to him was a guy in oversized clothes and ugly gold sneakers. Seneca knew him, but for a moment, she couldn't place from where. *The train,* she realized with a start. It was the creeper who'd been staring at her this afternoon.

"What's going on?" She looked back and forth at them.

Aerin sank into one hip. "I changed my mind. Hopefully I don't regret this." She thrust a thumb at Maddox. "So I called your friend here. And he brought *his* friend. And here we are."

Seneca gaped at Gold Shoes. Maddox had never mentioned a friend. "Who are you?"

"This is BMoney60, from the boards," Maddox explained. "He wants to help, too. I was going to tell you, but..." He trailed off and shrugged.

Seneca knew who BMoney was: the guy who made the one-line guesses about suspects on the website who often turned out to be dead-on. Actually, he'd been the one who'd introduced Seneca and Maddy, saying they both had similar theories about a case in Alabama and should talk. She looked this guy up and down, from his crooked hat to his filthy hoodie to his hideous rapper sneakers. He reeked of Axe body spray. "You can't be BMoney."

"Well, my real name's Brett Grady," the guy admitted, his voice softer and more sonorous than she would have imagined. "I go to Wesleyan and live in Greenwich. Maddy and I met at a Case Not Closed meetup last fall. You're TheMighty, right? You go to Maryland? You and I chatted about that New Mexico case, the one where the boy was killed. You said whoever the killer was might be like that lunatic in *Mr. Mercedes*, a messed-up guy without a conscience. I'm a big reader, too."

Okay, so most of that was intelligible English. "I saw you on the train earlier today," Seneca said. "You stared at me like a lunatic."

Maddox snickered and nudged him. "Way to be sketchy, bro."

"Sorry." Gold Shoes—BMoney—*Brett*—looked repentant. "I wasn't actually sure it was you. I thought *maybe*, but . . . well, I didn't mean to stare. It won't happen again." His eyes twinkled, and he held up his hand in a salute. "I was going to catch up with you guys earlier, but I had a hunch about something and wanted to do some research first."

"Brett has a really interesting angle about Helena," Maddox said. "I think it's worth all of us talking about . . . though maybe not here."

"Maddy thinks we're being watched." Brett rolled his eyes good-naturedly.

Maddox shrugged. "A Corvette was riding my ass on the way here. Maybe a tail."

Aerin snorted. "Do you think we're in a Fast and Furious movie?"

"We could head over there, talk it out in private," Brett said, jutting a thumb over his shoulder at a restaurant next to the Restful Inn. "It's not bad—I've got a room at that hotel and went there for my afternoon caffeine fix."

"Actually, I was just leaving," Seneca said stiffly, holding up the ticket she'd purchased.

Aerin looked annoyed. "Are you guys in or out? I'm not going to work with you if you're just going to start flaking on me."

The wind gusted again. Seneca was intrigued, and, yes, she did want to talk to Aerin about the case details. But was it enough?

The train rushed into the station, wheels rattling. Maddox looked at her long and hard. "Stay, please? We need you," he said.

Seneca turned away. She pictured getting on the train and going back home. She'd be wondering nonstop what these guys were up to. Or if Aerin really *didn't* work with them without her, she'd feel so guilty.

The train doors slid open, and passengers disembarked. The conductors stepped onto the platform and helped people maneuver their baggage onto the car. Seneca peeked at Aerin. There was a hopeful, holding-her-breath look on her face, the sad halo around her temporarily gone. The drive Seneca had felt back in the dorm room flickered once again.

She straightened and picked up her suitcase. "Okay, I'll stay for a *little* while. Let's go."

FIVE MINUTES LATER, they were all crowding into the diner next to the Restful Inn. It was one of those old-fashioned establishments built inside a stainless-steel trailer, the booths made of orange vinyl, the menu on placards above the counter, a jukebox spouting out oldies. A few people sat on stools, hands cupped around thick coffee mugs. The waitress, a woman with bags under her eyes and a shelflike uniboob, gave them a twitchy smile as they walked in. A creepy feeling nudged at Seneca, but she was probably still shaken from the ambush at the station.

"Okay." Aerin sat down and looked at all of them. "Tell me your big theories."

Brett gazed back and forth around the diner, took a sip of water, and cleared his throat somewhat dramatically. "Did you know Helena wrote her yearbook dedication in skip code?"

Aerin frowned. "What's that?"

"Kids at my old high school whose parents monitored their Twitter accounts used them all the time—they posted something that looked totally tame, but if you knew how to read it, it meant something else. Usually the codes were about who was banging who, or if someone had pills, or if there was a rager happening in the woods that night, you know."

Seneca snickered. "You know this because *you've* been to a lot of ragers in the woods?"

"I wish," Brett said. "I was a loser in high school. None of you would have spoken to me, especially not you."

He gave Aerin what was clearly supposed to be a charming look. She scoffed. "How do you know I'm popular?"

"Oh, girl, you look it." Brett grinned. "I bet everyone wants to go out with you."

"You too?" Aerin asked challengingly—but maybe also flirtatiously. She was suddenly a very different girl than the one Seneca had met on her doorstep.

Brett waved his hand. "No way, man. I know when I'm out of my league."

"Anyway," Seneca said impatiently.

"Anyway," Brett said. "I think Helena's dedi contained a skip code, too." He passed a xeroxed copy of the same Windemere-Carruthers yearbook page Seneca had seen online. There was Helena's dedication: *I'll miss Becky-bee, love is strong, you stay cool forever Kaylee, XOXO my ladies, LOL Samurai swordplay late nite.*

"I went down to the public library this afternoon—they have school yearbooks on file. I wanted to see the physical copy to make sure that the online image we were looking at hadn't gotten messed up when it was scanned." Brett pointed to each word. "So this looks like a shout-out to some friends, inside jokes, whatever, right? But if you skip and only read every third word, it says something totally different."

Seneca squinted and sounded it out. *"I'll . . . love . . . you . . . forever . . . my . . . Samurai . . . nite."* She looked up and made a face. "Okay . . ."

"I'm thinking she meant Samurai Knight, with a *K*, just couldn't make it fit."

"Do you think Kevin is her Samurai Knight?" Seneca thought about Kevin Larssen, Helena's boyfriend. She used to keep a printout of him on her desk at home with her other Helena Kelly materials. He had pale skin and wavy light hair. But that was probably too literal an interpretation.

Aerin didn't look convinced. "This one time, we all watched *Saw*. He hid his eyes through the whole thing. That doesn't seem samurai-like to me."

"Girl, I hid at that movie, too," Brett said sheepishly. He struck Seneca as someone who had no filter, who cheerfully blurted out whatever was on his mind no matter how foolish it made him look. She'd always been amazed by people like that, as she did the exact opposite, choosing each word and gesture with careful consideration.

Brett pulled up Kevin's Facebook, which Seneca knew well. She'd trolled it regularly, scrolling back for Helena references, though most of Kevin's posts were about a government club he was part of, Connecticut Youth.

Today, Kevin's page was all politics; in his main picture, he stood on a podium giving a speech to the Connecticut Board of Education. There was another picture of him shaking hands with Joe Biden. "He's running for state senate, so he tried to delete his posts from high school," Brett said. "But there are ways to retrieve that sort of stuff if you know your way around a computer. And if you *do* get into his old page—"

"—you'll see he talked to Helena on Facebook," Seneca interrupted, suddenly remembering. "Helena called him nicknames. Mr. Man, Hottie, but never Samurai Knight."

Brett raised an eyebrow. "You hacked it, too. I knew I was dealing with a smarty."

Seneca pressed her lips together. Perhaps it was better to let the group believe that than tell the truth—that maybe she'd been a little *too* obsessed back in the day. "Anyway," she rushed on, "you're thinking Helena's referring to someone else in the skip code? A Japanese guy, maybe?"

Maddox laced his hands behind his head, revealing a strip of bare skin above his jeans. Seneca looked away. "Or maybe it's some random joke between the two of them." He cleared his throat. "Your sister seemed to be big on inside jokes."

Aerin's head snapped up. "How would *you* know?"

He sat back in the booth. "We talked, sometimes. She was cool."

Aerin's eyes blazed. "Actually, how do we know *you* didn't do something to my sister?"

Seneca widened her eyes. *Whoa.*

Maddox's relaxed expression vanished. "Excuse me?" Apparently he didn't *always* keep his cool.

"You had access to my house. And you probably had a thing for my sister—what, did she talk to you, like, once? Oh, you're cool now, but back then you weren't. Back then, you—"

"Aerin," Brett broke in, "I really don't think Maddy would hurt anyone."

"Yeah, I don't know . . ." Seneca said. She doubted Maddox could conceal his killer instincts so expertly. And why would Helena's killer want to solve her murder?

"I have an alibi," Maddox said darkly. "I was with my mom. She dragged me to the city that day to look at wedding dresses." By his expression, he was clearly wounded.

"Okay, okay," Aerin said sullenly. "Everyone stop staring at me like that, all right? I had to *ask*." She looked at Brett. "So Helena might have had a secret boyfriend, is that what you're trying to say? How are we supposed to find out who that is?"

Brett drummed on the plaid place mat. "Did your sister . . . have Japanese friends? Was she interested in anything Japanese? Is there *some* sort of link?"

Aerin rolled her jaw. "Three Japanese people probably live in Dexby, total, and they run the sushi bar. And guess what—my sister *hated* sushi, so you're barking up the wrong tree."

She stood like she was going to leave. Seneca caught her arm. "Well, I have a question for *you*." Aerin stopped. "I'm wondering why it took you five minutes to get a purse."

Aerin looked blank. "Excuse me?"

"In your interviews about your last day with Helena, you said you went inside to get a purse for the snowman and came back out five minutes later. Five minutes is *long*, Aerin. Your interviews also say you were grateful to hang out with Helena; you hadn't connected in a long time. If you were so eager to spend time with your sister, why would you waste time away from her?"

Aerin sat down again, grabbed a napkin from the dispenser, and started to rip it into pieces. "I don't see why that matters."

Seneca crossed her arms over her chest. "I think it does. What were you doing?"

Aerin squeezed her eyes closed. The only sounds were the clinking of cutlery. "I snooped through Helena's room, okay? She sent me in there. I just wanted to see what it looked like."

Seneca nodded, satisfied. "Did you find anything interesting?"

Aerin shook her head. "No . . ." Her gaze shot to the side. Seneca could tell she was thinking about something, but she decided to hold off before asking.

"Did anything else come up that day you might want to discuss?" Maddox asked.

Aerin thought for a while. "There was another thing. I told Helena I missed her, and she said, 'We'll talk more, but some of it will have to be under wraps.'"

Maddox looked intrigued. "Like she wanted you to keep things secret?"

"I don't know. And besides, she never told me anything again." A pained look crossed Aerin's face. Then she stood. "It's late. Let's regroup tomorrow." She slung her purse over her shoulder, went a few paces, and then stopped in her tracks and spun around. "Wait. Origami is Japanese, isn't it?"

"Yes," Seneca said, cocking her head. "Why?"

"There was a paper crane in her room, when I went in there. It was . . . weird."

Seneca *knew* Aerin had been thinking about something. "Did the cops see it?"

"I took it before they searched her room. I felt like I needed to protect it somehow."

"Do you still have it?" Maddox asked.

Aerin's eyes darted back and forth. "Yeah."

"Will you bring it to us?" Seneca asked.

Aerin blinked. Her bottom lip trembled. "Yeah," she whispered. "Okay."

"Great." Seneca brushed her hands together. "Well, listen. We'll talk everything over here, and then we'll meet again in the morning. You name the spot."

Aerin thought for a moment. "Le Dexby Patisserie," she said. "Nine. I'll see you then."

She backed out the door. Everyone else remained where they were. Finally, Maddox stood up, too, and stretched. "Paper cranes?" he asked. "You really think it's something?"

Seneca shrugged. "It's what she wanted to hear. And you never know." She picked up her suitcase. "See you guys later. Nice to meet you, Brett."

She walked toward the door. Maddox leapt up and followed. Half-way down the ramp to the parking lot, he called, "Where are you going?"

Seneca pointed to the Restful Inn. "I'm getting a room here."

Maddox studied the hotel's facade. Seneca hoped he wasn't going to comment on the fact that several of the overhead bulbs had burned out and that the shrubs looked very untended. Then he shifted his weight. "I didn't do anything to Helena, you know."

"I know. I don't think Aerin really meant that."

He nodded, seeming relieved by her answer. "You still can stay with me if you want."

Seneca shrugged. "I'm okay here." Maddox's house would probably be more comfortable than the hotel, but she didn't really want to hang around and watch him play *Madden NFL*. Besides, she needed to be completely alone so she could go through everything they'd learned that day without distraction.

Her brain hiccupped, and she recalled an e-mail he'd sent about his favorite books. *One Hundred Years of Solitude* by Márquez. *Underworld* by DeLillo. *The Lion, the Witch, and the Wardrobe*. They were some of her favorites, too. Had he really read them?

Then she had another thought. "Anyway, now you won't have to put *Austin & Ally* on mute."

At the same time, Maddox blurted, "At least tomorrow morning I can gargle."

They stopped and exchanged a glance. Seneca smiled. During one of their chats, Maddox told her that to fall asleep, he needed to watch Disney Channel. She'd told him gargling was one of the worst noises ever. She couldn't believe he remembered that. Strangely, he was smiling at her as if he couldn't believe *she* remembered.

She realized she'd been staring at Maddox for way too long. This fresh Dexby air was messing with her brain.

"See you tomorrow," she said primly. And then, giving him a wave, she turned on her heel and sauntered into the hotel.

SEVEN

A FEW HOURS later, Seneca was watching the news on the barely working TV. It was a story about a party in Dexby that had gotten busted; apparently tons of the kids had been arrested for underage drinking and drug possession. As she turned over, the remote dropped onto the carpet, which had a trippy, swirly pattern and looked like it hadn't been vacuumed since 1972.

Then she heard a knock on her door. She frowned. Who could that be?

There were more pounds, each one more insistent. Finally, she stomped to the door and peered through the peephole, but the thing was so clouded over she couldn't see much more than the outline of a figure in the dark. "Hello?" she whispered.

She heard shifting in the hallway. Then a thin, high voice hissed, *"Go home."*

Seneca recoiled. Maybe this place *was* really haunted? Or maybe this was her recurring nightmare, finally becoming a reality. There was a dark figure in those dreams, too. Hands reaching out for her, grabbing her, dragging her to a dark, damp place . . .

"Go *home*," the voice said again, louder this time, high and grating. Seneca's doorknob started to rattle.

"Go away!" she screamed, backing hard into the sideboard. "I'm calling the police!"

But as she dove for the hotel phone, she tripped over the carpet and accidentally wrenched the cord out of the wall. As she ripped apart her purse, scrambling to find her cell, she realized that she could barely breathe. She looked around, confused and anxious. Smoke was suddenly filling the room. And on her next inhale, her lungs burned.

Heart hammering, she finally noticed her phone, which had fallen under the bed. She crawled toward it as more smoke billowed toward her, growing blacker. Somewhere in the distance, a fire alarm screeched. "Help!" she cried weakly. Her hand finally closed over her phone; she held it to her face, swiping at the screen, trying to dial for help. Her fingers shook, and she kept pressing the pound button instead of nine for 9-1-1.

Through the crackle of the fire, she heard the same insistent, angry banging from before. The thin door gave, cracking on the hinges, and a hooded figure shot inside. Seneca screamed. She fought as the figure scooped her up. "Hey, it's okay," a familiar voice said. Seneca stared at the face under the hood. It was Brett.

He pushed through an emergency exit and into the parking lot. Outside, the air was deliciously clean but frigid. Brett set her down, and Seneca coughed and coughed. The sky was purplish-pink overhead. She rubbed her eyes, and oxygen rushed back into her lungs.

"How did you know where to find me?" she asked.

Brett gestured toward the hotel. "Maddy told me you were staying here. I took a room here, too, remember?"

"Was that you whispering to me through the door? Telling me to go home?"

Brett gave her a crazy look. "No . . ."

A fire truck roared up, its sirens blazing. As the firefighters hopped out of the truck, Seneca stared through the open door into the hall. Her door was the only one with smoke pouring out of it.

Brett was looking at her door, too. "You don't think this could be . . . intentional?"

Seneca flinched. "Because we're looking into Helena?"

"Yeah. Maybe. I mean, you said someone was whispering for you to go home . . . and then there's a fire in your room, specifically. Think that's a coincidence?"

Seneca watched as the firefighter's shadowy figure moved in her room. Then she looked at Brett. "You dragged me out. Did *you* see someone?"

"No, but they could have run away before I got there."

A chill ran up her spine. "Don't be silly," she said, infusing her voice with a confidence that she didn't feel. "It's late, and I was tired. I must have fallen asleep and had a nightmare. I get them all the time."

"You do?"

"Uh-huh," Seneca said stiffly, wondering if she'd revealed too much. And then she shot him a tight smile as if to say, *Subject closed.*

EIGHT

AT 7:00 A.M., Maddox's mom, Betsy, pulled into a parking space at the Dexby Recreational Center, which featured an Olympic-size ten-lane swimming pool, an ice rink, state-of-the-art weight facilities, and indoor and outdoor tracks. Normally, Maddox drove himself to practice, but his mom's car was getting serviced this week, and she needed the Jeep to go to yoga.

She ruffled Maddox's hair. "How's practice been going?"

"Good," Maddox said, noticing Catherine sitting on the bleachers by the starting line, dressed in a pink sleeveless shirt and a short white running skirt.

"You working on 800s? The Oregon coach wants you at sub 1:50."

Maddox resisted the urge to groan, instead focusing on the *University of Oregon* lettering on his mother's sweatshirt. She'd purchased it on the school's online bookshop after Maddox had received his scholarship letter. She was psyched, that was all. A free ride to the best track-and-field school in the country was a huge deal.

Maddox's mom had always been supportive of whatever he was

into, even when that had been eBay toy auctions and video game con-
ventions. He'd always been pretty close with her, but he knew she'd
get weird about him nosing around the Kellys' affairs. After Helena
went missing, he asked his mom if *she'd* noticed anything weird about
her. She'd rubbed her chin and said, "Helena's like that optical illusion
where one way, you see an old lady, and the other way, you see a young
girl. More than she first appears."

He made a mental note to tell that to the group today.

"Tell Catherine I said hello." Mrs. Wright leaned over to peck his
cheek. Maddox squirmed and jumped out of the car.

"Hey, mama's boy," Catherine said with a smirk as Maddox
approached.

Maddox smiled confidently. "What can I say? My mom's a kisser."

"I thought we'd do mile sprints today," Catherine said. "We need
to get you under four minutes if you're going to be competitive. You
up for it?"

"Absolutely." Maddox grabbed his foot for a quad stretch and faced
the rec center. In the distance, he could see Waterdam Street, where Le
Dexby Patisserie was. He was meeting the group there in two hours.
It was an easy walk from here.

Catherine started around the track for a warm-up. Maddox jogged
behind her, watching the ends of her skirt lift in the breeze and show off
her upper thighs. She glanced over her shoulder and winked at him, but
Maddox pretended not to notice. He knew how to play hard to get, too.

This was his sixteenth private coaching session with Catherine.
He'd always been decent at running. As he got older—but before he got
cool—it was like he *needed* to run. It made him feel like a guy. Powerful.
Strong. Important. Then, in ninth grade, he grew six inches. Got his
braces off. His mom remarried, so he was able to afford better clothes.

His first year in cross-country, his times were amazing, and just like that, he was invited to sit at the popular table. Maddy, the loser who scraped together cash to go to *Antiques Roadshow* in Farmington, who farted when he drank regular milk, and who collected Pokémon way longer than it was socially acceptable, had changed. He got rid of his Pokémon cards immediately. Forgot that kid entirely. Well, almost— except when no one else was around, when he binge-watched *Doctor Who* and posted on Case Not Closed.

Every year, his running had improved. He made it to states, nationals. People talked scholarships. It was clear that the track coaches at public school weren't equipped to coach a runner at an elite level, so his stepdad suggested he look for a private coach.

Of course Maddox was going to pick Catherine. Not only was she an amazing runner, but he already knew her coaching style: She'd been an assistant for his school team his freshman year, a freshman herself at UConn. Maddox had such strong memories of that first year of track: the guys trash-talking each other in the locker room, him beating out seniors for coveted relay spots, and beautiful Catherine, with her long chocolate-brown hair, heart-shaped face, sapphire-blue eyes, and perfect boobs, cheering from the sidelines. Every guy on the team talked about how they wanted to do her. Maddox had never been ballsy enough to tell his teammates, but sometimes, in practice, he swore he saw Catherine gazing at him like she was into him. No doubt he'd been imagining it—as if she'd have been interested in a dorky freshman!— but he developed a raging, bona fide crush on her anyway. He spent hours imagining what it would be like to be her boyfriend, what kind of sexy underwear she probably wore, what she might say if he ever worked up the courage to ask her out.

Much to everyone's disappointment, Catherine only coached for one year, but Maddox never forgot her. He kept up with her race times, followed her Instagram, even reached out to her when he won the 800 in the state meet. As the years passed and he got more experience with girls, he'd wondered if his intuition about her had actually been right. Maybe she *did* see something in him—besides just his blazing times. And since they'd started training together? Well, let's just say she still gave him those special looks.

Maddox had told Madison, his stepsister, that he swore Catherine had the hots for him—and that he was into her, too. Madison had looked totally grossed out. "The most beautiful girl at school is dying to go out with you, Maddox," she'd scolded. "*That's* who you should date, not some skeevy older woman who's into high school guys."

Come to think of it, he wasn't sure why he ever bothered confiding in Madison about girl stuff.

"Okay," Catherine said, stopping after an easy mile and pulling a stopwatch out of her pocket. "Four repeats. Remember your form. Don't go out too fast. You ready?"

"I was born ready," Maddox said, crouching down.

He took off, flying around the track, his arms pumping and legs churning. Four laps later, as he crossed the line, Catherine called out, "4:02:23. I think you weren't giving it your all."

Maddox leaned over his thighs. 4:02 was his third-best time *ever*. He wasn't even sure he could eke out another mile. But after minimal rest, she was ordering him back to the starting line again. "Dig deep," Catherine told him, looking him square in the eyes. "You can do this. We've worked really hard. Think of your drills. Think of your posture. Think of your stride."

She took his hands and squeezed them hard, her fingers lingering among his for a beat too long before pulling away. "Think 'Iron Man,'" she said emphatically, referring to how, one day when she asked him what his go-to prerace songs were, he admitted he had a thing for classic Ozzy Osbourne. She said she did, too, and they'd spent the next half hour talking about their favorite Black Sabbath riffs.

"Go!" Catherine yelled, and Maddox shot off the line. This time, instead of keeping his mind empty, he let it wander. He flashed on Aerin calling him yesterday, saying she'd changed her mind about his help. When they'd met in the train station parking lot, Aerin had stared.

"So, Maddy Wright," she'd said. "What happened to your glasses?" "Contacts," Maddox had answered, relishing the appreciative look she gave him when she thought he wasn't looking. "You got tall," she'd added. "Six two," Maddox said proudly. "And you have a stepsister now," Aerin said. "Madison. I know her." "Actually, I think we have a lot of friends in common," Maddox had said, and then rattled off a bunch of names of guys and girls she knew. He hadn't meant to be a brat—but he was sick of the tone she used when she talked to him. Like he was still a total nerd. They were more alike than she thought.

He screamed through his first lap. On the second, he thought about Seneca and how she'd decided to stay after all. Why had she wanted to leave, anyway? Her decision had seemed so abrupt. Well, it was good she was staying—she was smart. They had a better chance of finding something out with her around.

And then he thought about Brett—he liked having another guy on the team. He'd met him at the Case Not Closed event last September near a weekend track camp on the Rutgers campus. Maddox and the other campers were allowed to leave if they told the counselors where they were going, but he hadn't known how to explain Case Not Closed, so he ended up sneaking out. He'd met Brett the moment he'd walked into the meetup at Olive Garden, and they'd sat together the whole night, analyzing cell phone records for a murder case in Texas. After the rest of the group left, he and Brett watched a Giants game at the bar, Brett whistling at Maddox's impressive fake ID. Brett had driven him back to Rutgers in his 7-series Beemer. Maddox couldn't say quite why, but he'd told Brett his stepdad had the same car, even though he really drove a Subaru.

They'd kept in touch since then, and when Maddox told Brett he was going to respond to Aerin Kelly's call for help, Brett had asked if he could join in, too. He'd meant to tell Seneca as soon as she'd arrived, but they'd gotten off on such a bad note that he hadn't felt he could spring anything else on her.

The end of the last lap was coming up. Arms pumping, Maddox lunged across the finish line. Catherine's head was down, studying the watch. His heart sank. It was a 4:04, 4:05 at least.

But when she looked up, there was an excited smile on her face. "3:58:42."

Maddox's jaw dropped. "Crushed it!"

Catherine leapt toward him and hugged tight. "That's close to the *record*, Maddy!"

"I wouldn't have been able to do it without you," Maddox cried breathlessly, squeezing her arms. Their gazes met, and they fell silent. Maddox smiled. Catherine smiled back. *Fuck it,* he thought. He leaned in and touched his lips to hers.

Catherine jerked back. "Maddy, no, wait."

Maddox stepped away. "Oops." He smacked his forehead with his open palm. "Lost my mind there for a sec."

Catherine's cheeks were pink. "It's okay, really! I mean, it's not that I don't find you cute. I *do*. I've thought about us . . . you know." She lowered her eyes. "But I'm your coach."

"Hey, you don't have to explain it to me," Maddox said, inwardly dying of embarrassment. "I was just excited about my time and got carried away. Good thing you weren't my school coach. Kissing Mr. Masters would be *nasty*." He chuckled, hoping his agony wasn't obvious.

"Well, good," Catherine said, though he'd swear she sounded a little let down. "How about we walk a lap?"

But then Maddox's cell phone, attached to a band on his arm, let out a loud *beep*. Maddox pulled it out of the sleeve and looked at the screen. *New text from Seneca.*

My room caught fire last night, Seneca had written. *I'm with Brett now. Might need to take you up on that guest room offer.*

Maddox's mouth dropped open. "Holy shit."

"Everything all right?" Catherine peeked at his phone. "Who's Seneca?"

"I need to go," Maddox said faintly, walking backward toward the bleachers.

Catherine's face fell. "But we have two more mile repeats to get through."

"We'll add them to tomorrow's practice." Maddox pulled on his track pants, shoved his phone into his gym bag, and started across the lawn. "Same time?"

"Maddy," Catherine called after him in a firm voice. He turned back. She looked deeply weirded out, and the pink splotches were still on her cheeks. "You aren't leaving because of what just happened, are you?"

"No way," he said reassuringly. As if she was the one who needed comforting. "We're totally cool." And then he waved and sauntered as slowly as he could away from her. It was only after he was out of her sight line that he started to jog, and then run, and then sprint, hoping that the movement of his arms and legs might erase, at least temporarily, the unrestrained humiliation coursing through his bloodstream like a fever.

It didn't work.

NINE

BRETT GRADY LOOKED at the faux-aged wooden sign over his head. *Le Dexby Patisserie,* it read, with an arrow pointing to an old schoolhouse door. He smirked at the pretentious name, then turned to Seneca, who was next to him. "How come every cool old farmhouse or stable is now a gourmet coffee shop, dog spa, or boutique that sells five-hundred-dollar jeans that only fit girls who don't have butts?"

Seneca gave him a blank look that Brett chalked up to her still being in shock. He adjusted his ball cap, pushed inside, and held the door for Seneca. There were chipped Limoges plates hanging on the walls and chicken folk art sculptures next to the counter. The hull of a boat was hanging from the ceiling. The air smelled like freshly baked bread. Three pretty women in cashmere sweaters and glittering diamond earrings chatted at a front table. "Oops," Brett said to the prettiest one, a tall brunette, chivalrously bending down and picking up her cloth napkin. The woman looked him up and down, then made a little face and lowered her eyes. Brett sighed inwardly. Oh well. She wasn't his type anyway.

Aerin was sitting at the back table, but Maddy was still missing.

Brett waved and headed toward her, feeling psyched. He'd never joined a group solve—usually, he worked cases alone. He wanted to make a good impression on the girls, win them over. These kids were smart. They were going to figure Helena out. He had a good feeling.

"Morning," Brett said as he took a seat across from Aerin. Seneca sat next to her. Brett assessed the girls side by side. Seneca had bunched her wet hair into a ponytail, and she was wearing a wrinkled plaid dress from the luggage she'd been able to retrieve from her room after the fire had been put out. Aerin, on the other hand, had on a pink sheath that looked brand-new. Her hair was blow-dried, and her makeup was perfectly applied.

Brett pointed to her dress. "Hey, is that Diane von Furstenberg?"

Aerin's mouth dropped open. "How do *you* know Diane von Furstenberg?"

Brett smiled mysteriously. "I'm a man of many talents."

Aerin grinned. "Clearly."

Brett felt a warm sensation in his stomach. He hadn't flirted with anyone in a long time, and he wasn't good at it—he could never tell if a girl was serious or just having a laugh. "I know the fashion industry a little," he admitted. "If you ever need a shopping companion, I've also been told I'm a good stylist."

Seneca snorted. "Are you going to watch her change through the dressing room curtain?"

"Of course not!" Brett had determined that Seneca seemed to trust no one. Even this morning, when he'd taken her to his new hotel, the Dexby Water's Edge, so she could shower, she'd been so paranoid he was going to post pictures of her changing on Instagram. "Did you tell Aerin about the fire?" he asked her, deciding to change the subject.

Aerin rolled her eyes. "The Restful Inn is a death trap."

Brett laced his fingers together. "Seneca thinks it was set intentionally."

Seneca scoffed. "No I don't!"

Brett glanced at Aerin. "She heard someone whispering 'go home' through the door, right before the fire started."

Aerin's eyes widened. "Someone's after us?"

"No," Seneca said firmly. "I must have imagined it. Besides, look." She tapped her phone and showed them a news report. *Fire Shuts Down Dexby's Restful Inn.* "The police aren't saying arson."

"Yeah, but they aren't *not* saying arson, either. They haven't even investigated it yet," Brett argued. It wasn't *that* crazy that someone might be after them, was it? Then again, that would mean someone knew they were poking into Helena's disappearance. He looked around at the smug Dexby patrons around him. Maybe someone here knew more than they were letting on.

A waitress in a floral shift appeared and asked him if he wanted coffee. After he ordered, Seneca pointed to the red leather satchel on Aerin's lap. "Do you have the crane?"

"Shouldn't we wait for Maddy?" Brett asked, but the girls ignored him.

Aerin reached into the bag and pulled out the red bird. It was made out of bright, shiny paper that shimmered as it caught the light. As Aerin turned it over, Brett pointed at something written in black pen on its hexagonal-shaped base. "What's that?"

Seneca squinted. *"Hi,"* she read.

Aerin pulled it close. "I can't believe I never noticed that."

"Do you think your sister made this?" Brett asked.

Aerin, who'd ordered her coffee iced, picked out a single cube from her glass and popped it in her mouth. "I never saw her make origami. Not once."

Seneca turned the crane in her hands. "We could have it dusted for fingerprints, maybe."

Brett placed his mug on the table. "No cops. They just ruin things."

"*Okaaay*," Seneca drawled, inspecting him. Brett just shrugged. He wasn't getting into his reasons right now. "How about Becky Reed?" he said, naming Helena's best friend—he'd read about her in old interviews. "Maybe she'd know who gave it to her."

Aerin fiddled with her straw. "Eh."

"My money's on Kevin Larssen," Seneca stated.

Aerin tapped the crane's head. "This just doesn't scream Kevin to me."

"No, I don't think he give her the crane. I meant as a suspect. I was thinking about it last night. *If* Helena had a secret boyfriend, a Samurai Knight, wouldn't the *real* boyfriend be pissed?"

Aerin wrinkled her nose. "Kevin had an alibi. He was at a conference that weekend."

"For student government, right?" Seneca asked. "Connecticut Youth?"

"Yeah. He lived for that club—he got to work with a senator for the summer. I heard about it nonstop whenever he came to dinner at my house—my dad lived vicariously through him. Kevin was like the son he never had."

A wistful expression crossed Aerin's face. Brett drummed on his knees. In many ways, these kids knew this world much better than he did. He didn't know much about Mr. Kelly except that he was as high-powered Wall Street as they came.

Seneca stirred her coffee. "Connecticut Youth is a tight-knit group, right?"

"Yeah, they're okay," Aerin said. "They take themselves so seriously, though. Like they're in a secret society."

Seneca nodded. "Did you know that Kevin was supposed to give some sort of peer leadership speech at that conference, but apparently he didn't show?"

"Where'd you see that?" Brett asked.

"It was in an article right after Helena vanished. The cops didn't follow up on it."

"They suck." Aerin leaned on her elbows. "So maybe Kevin wasn't there?"

"There isn't a picture of him at the conference. There are photos of all the other members."

Aerin twisted her mouth. "But they all said they saw him."

"Yeah, well, it's their word against ours," Seneca said tightly.

Aerin sighed, then stood. "To be continued." She strode off to the ladies' room.

Seneca watched her go until the door shut. It reminded Brett of people who stared at the numbers in elevators so they wouldn't have to make small talk. He caught Seneca's eye and smiled, but Seneca just looked down distrustfully.

"What are you studying at school?" Brett asked, fully aware it was a lame question.

Seneca shrugged, fiddling with the laminated menu. "Core stuff, mostly."

"You pick a major?"

"Nope. Not yet."

"You should, you know. The sooner you do, the cooler classes you get to take."

She gave him an irritated look. "I already have an advisor on my ass, thanks very much."

Brett fiddled with the coffee stirrer. He thought of what he knew about Seneca. He'd been wondering all morning if he should share it. Taking a breath, he decided yes. Keeping it to himself felt insincere. Maybe if she knew that he understood why she was here, it would help? "Um, the reason I know fashion?" His voice cracked. "It's 'cause of my grandma. Maybe you heard of her. Vera Grady? From Greenwich?"

Seneca's eyebrows shot up. "Your grandma is that fashion heiress who was *murdered*?"

Brett nodded, ducking his head.

Seneca blinked hard. "Whoa."

Brett thought of what she must have seen on the news: rich, older woman found hacked with an ax in her backyard. It was the house-keeper, Esmerelda, who'd found her. "She and I were close. I miss her so much."

"Jesus," Seneca whispered, clutching the initial necklace she never seemed to be without.

"I tried to figure out what happened to her by myself," Brett confided in a low voice. "I couldn't make heads or tails of who would do that to her, but apparently I grilled a witness the police were talking to, and they got really pissed at me and demanded I stay out of their way. They said they were going to arrest me for obstructing justice."

Seneca frowned. "That's bullshit."

"I know that *now*." Brett felt his shoulders heave. "It's why I'm not really into using the cops. It's why I'm on the boards. To see if there are any theories about her. And to help other people." His voice broke. "At least I can do *that*."

For the first time, Seneca seemed to really look at him. "I'm sorry, Brett."

"Thanks. I wanted to tell you first." His heart pounded. "I know it happened to you, too."

Seneca flinched. Her pupils got very small. "Huh?"

"I googled you," Brett said, wishing that didn't sound so intrusive. "I was looking up everyone who was helping out with the case. And . . . your mom was killed. Collette Frazier."

Blood drained from Seneca's face.

He slid forward a little. "I'm here if you want to talk. I've been through it. I know how hard it is. And, I mean, I'd love to have someone to talk about it with, too." He tapped his fingers nervously on the table. "Maybe *all* of us could talk about it. You, me, Aerin . . ."

Seneca shot up, shoving the chair back so hard it made a piercing scraping sound. Her eyes were wide. Her mouth made a small, pinched O.

"We don't have to include Aerin if you don't want to," Brett whispered hurriedly. "I totally get it if you don't want anyone else to know."

But then her gaze cut to the left, and a small, torturous sound escaped from her lips. Brett turned his head, too. Aerin had come back from the bathroom and stood at her chair. Maddox had also appeared. Both had stupefied expressions on their faces, as if they'd heard every word.

Shit.

TEN

AERIN WATCHED AS Seneca's spoon slipped from her fingers to the table. Before anyone could say a word, she whipped around and fled the café. Aerin started after her, then glanced over her shoulder at Brett. "Next time you've got a secret about someone, ask first if she wants you to spill it."

Brett looked like he was going to start bawling. "I didn't know you were standing there!"

Aerin believed him—when she'd come back from the bathroom, Brett was leaning toward Seneca across the table, totally oblivious to the world. "She obviously didn't want to talk about it, Dr. Phil," she grumbled. Really, what did Brett expect? That they'd all form a band together, Wounded Kids Who Knew Murdered People? They'd sing uplifting songs and hold hands? *Yeah right.* She didn't blame Seneca for bolting.

And Jesus. Aerin recalled the Vera Grady story—she couldn't imagine how Brett got through that. But Seneca's mom's story was even worse. From what Aerin remembered, it happened shortly before

Helena disappeared, though it hadn't been covered as extensively. The poor woman, a young mother with striking ice-blond hair and a stunning smile, had been found two days later, her body dumped under a pier. Aerin had also heard that the coroner had Seneca, who must have been fourteen at the time, ID the corpse. How was that even legal?

She pushed through the front door of the café. Outside, the sky was gray, and the temperature had dropped. Seneca stood at the edge of the parking lot, her arms wrapped tightly around her torso. When she saw Aerin coming, she pretended to be fascinated by a speed limit sign. "I don't want to talk."

"Fine with me," Aerin said. "You don't have to talk about it ever again. *I* don't want to know. I mean, maybe you haven't noticed, but I'm not super into bonding."

It wasn't true—Aerin would love to know how Seneca got through each day—but she struck Aerin as someone who compartmentalized parts of her life, freaking out when her neatly packed boxes overflowed into adjacent neatly packed boxes.

"I can't *believe* Brett. . . ." Seneca's voice cracked. "This was why I was leaving yesterday. I might not be useful on this case."

Aerin rolled her eyes. "I get it. You have baggage. But just because people know doesn't change anything—you had the baggage an hour ago, too, and you were going to work on the case, right?"

Seneca didn't answer. Aerin blew air out of her cheeks. "Would it help if I told you that you're the smartest one here? Way smarter than those idiot boys? Without you, we definitely won't figure it out. So don't bail."

Ugh. After saying all that, she almost wanted to take a shower. She hated groveling. It made her feel way dirtier than making out with random guys.

Seneca hiked her leather bag higher on her shoulder. "Okay," she said in a stoic, they're-my-feelings-and-no-one-else-can-touch-them voice that Aerin could definitely identify with. "But we're done talking about it. Got it?"

"Deal," Aerin said. "And if I catch anyone *else* talking to you about it, I'll deck them."

Seneca almost smiled, and Aerin's insides warmed. Even though she'd just said she wasn't into bonding, she had a feeling that she and Seneca just kind of had.

Aerin walked her over to an outdoor table and sat down. It was awfully cold to be outside, but she doubted Seneca wanted to go back and face the boys just yet. "Your thoughts about Kevin are interesting. Do you think his buddies were covering for him and lying about his alibi?"

Seneca settled down next to her. The wind whipped her curly hair into her face. "There's no proof Kevin was actually at the conference—only what his friends said. Who's to say they didn't all get together and concoct a story?"

Aerin picked at a splinter of wood on the bench. Could Kevin's buddies have all covered for him doing something awful? She'd kissed one of those guys recently, she realized—Tim Anderson, at a pool party last summer. It gave her a deep and sickening sense of betrayal that he could have looked into her eyes, touched her lips, told her she was *beautiful,* all the while withholding a cruel but critical detail about her sister.

Seneca pulled out her phone. She tapped on a cloud icon, then passed it to Aerin. A story from five years ago was on the screen; it was about the Connecticut Youth conference, completely unrelated to Helena's disappearance. There was a picture of the group from Windemere-Carruthers—yep, a *couple* of guys she'd kissed, Aerin noted, and then one nerdy-looking girl named Pearl Stanwyck who'd probably spent the conference either having sex with everyone or wandering around alone. Kevin stood at the center, a smug smile on his face. Next to him, his arm slung around Kevin's shoulders, was James Gorman, the Connecticut senator the group worked with in the summers.

"Kevin's smile looks sneaky," Aerin said faintly. She hated looking at her sister's boyfriend in a new light, too. He'd sobbed at the memorial service they'd had for Helena. She remembered how he'd volunteered with Helena at a hospice care. "We mostly just hold their hands," Kevin had explained sadly during a family dinner. Helena had touched his shoulder, admiration in her eyes, and for a moment, Aerin had gotten why she liked him.

Her stomach swooped. Talking about Helena was messing with her mind. She had moments of thinking Helena was actually back, a filmy apparition by her side. Aerin even found herself lapsing into routines from when Helena was alive, like crying "boop!" when toast popped, which Helena loved saying. Early this morning at home, toast in hand, she'd even turned around, anticipating Helena's laughter.

Seneca clicked over to the Windemere-Carruthers virtual yearbook and flipped through the pages. Besides more pictures of Kevin and the Connecticut Youth political group, there were also a lot of Kevin candids. Standing on the basketball court. Giving a speech in the auditorium. Leading a group of kids down a hallway. Hugging an overweight woman identified as Mrs. G, the school's librarian.

Seneca sat back. "He strikes me as the kind of guy who'd help an old lady cross the street, but who'd also want credit for the good deed."

"Totally," Aerin agreed.

"What do *you* remember about him?"

Aerin sat back. "He seemed . . . okay. Kind of stiff, almost like his joints needed oil. I had a nickname for him—Puppet. Like a marionette. Helena didn't find it funny." Her throat caught, remembering how Helena's face had crumpled when she told her. "When did you get so mean?" she'd snapped.

"I wasn't kidding when I said he and my dad were tight," she went on. "When Kevin came over, he and my dad talked nonstop. Helena barely paid attention to them. And, I mean, she started dressing so differently, at the start of that summer. Like a hippie. Kevin would make fun of her outfits. I always wondered why she didn't go for this guy from our school named Raj Juniper. He was tall and sexy and made his own shoes out of recycled tires."

"Maybe she dated Kevin to please your dad."

Aerin hugged her chest—her skin was getting goose bumps from the cold. "My parents fought a lot. Maybe bringing in Kevin was her way of keeping Dad happy."

"Your dad's not around now, is he?"

She shrugged. "He's in New York City. It's not like it's far."

"But he's not *around* around. Like, you don't see him much."

Aerin felt a prickle of annoyance. When had the conversation turned left into Touchy-Feelyville? "It's partly my fault. I hate New York, so I don't go very often. It's so dirty."

Seneca glanced at her, then flipped to Kevin's senior page. Her eyes widened. *"Look."*

Aerin leaned over and looked where Seneca was pointing: his dedication, italic letters under his picture. It was in the form of a poem.

You'll thrive, pilgrim
don't get a big head
what a pterodactyl laugh!

You, sweeter than honey, deserve it all,
loving H as a gas.

Aerin snorted. "He should stick to politics."

"I know. But look: Count every four words, starting with *you'll*."

Aerin cocked her head. "Another skip code?" she asked uncertainly.
She started to count. When she finished, she gasped.

You'll get what you deserve, H.

ELEVEN

A FEW HOURS later, Seneca and Maddox pulled up to Maddox's house, a huge blue Colonial with three dormers, window boxes, a big front porch with two yellow rocking chairs, and a white wood fence. "It's so . . . Connecticut," Seneca drolled. She couldn't believe she could even make a joke right now, but then, masking what she was feeling wasn't really anything new for her.

She pulled her suitcase from the back of the Jeep and grabbed the bouquet of daisies she'd bought at the flower shop near Le Dexby Patisserie for Mr. and Mrs. Wright as thanks for letting her stay. Maddox led her up the front path, through a foyer with parquet floors and a console table holding family photos, into a large, homey kitchen done up in yellows and reds. She put the flowers in water, and then they headed up a Berber-carpeted staircase to a door. Maddox nudged it open with his shoulder. "Here's your room."

Inside was a long couch, a polka-dotted rug, cool, splashy art on the walls, and a small kitchen with a breakfast bar. Maddox strode through the space. "You got a little kitchen, and the TV has cable." He opened a door to the back. "Bathroom. Fresh towels." Seneca peeked her head in and saw a fish-print curtain. "And here's the bedroom." He walked through another door to reveal a queen-sized bed with a striped comforter.

"Thanks, this is great," Seneca said. "I'm kind of tired. I think I'm going to lie down."

Maddox nodded, but he didn't move. Seneca's arms twitched. It was weird standing here in a bedroom with him. She felt even more naked than she had at the café, having her whole past laid out on the table like a meal for everyone to enjoy. She moved to unzip her suitcase just as Maddox turned for the doorway, and they collided, Seneca ramming straight into his side.

"Oops," she said through gritted teeth. She stepped away and so did Maddox, but not before his eyes met hers. A smile twitched on his lips. Her cheeks burned. His abs had felt so firm under his T-shirt—just thinking that made her feel embarrassed and disoriented. It still bothered her that yesterday at this time, she was still expecting a very different Maddy. A person who didn't have washboard abs. A person whose abs she wouldn't have noticed.

Then Maddox crouched down and swiftly pulled something out of the bag he'd brought upstairs. "I almost forgot. Here."

He handed her a bottle of Red Stripe beer. It was still frosty with condensation. Seneca frowned at it. "I'm not really in the mood to party right now."

He shook his head. "It's just in case you change your mind. I snagged it out of the fridge on the way up." He moved a step closer. "After the kind of day you had, I thought it might . . . help. And I remember you said it was your favorite." He shrugged and turned for the door. "Bottle opener's in the drawer by the fridge. I'm going for a run." And then he was gone.

Seneca stared at the closed door, and then at the beer in her hands. Maddox's gesture was oddly touching, and actually just the thing she needed right now. Not a long talk, as so many others offered once they found out about her mom. Not a hug. Not a card or a shoulder pat. Well, good for Maddox for figuring it out. So why did it make her even more annoyed with him?

She found the bottle opener, popped off the cap, and surveyed the room. On the fridge was a bumper sticker that read HIGH SCHOOL IS SO LAST YEAR. Clearly Maddox had put it there for her benefit, which gave her a guilty pang. On the shelf in the corner were mystery paperbacks— she'd read all of them already—and a copy of *14,000 Things to Be Happy About*. Feeling an angry pang, she turned it over so the cover faced the wall. Hopefully Maddox hadn't put *that* there for her. After her mom was murdered, their elderly next-door neighbor, who Seneca always called Bertie with all the Airedales, had given her that same book. No offense, Bertie, but reading about the delight of garden gnomes didn't always do the trick.

She felt her throat clench. *You are not going to cry.* But Brett had put a crack in her armor. All she could think about now was her mom. The one thing she tried so hard to forget.

Taking a big swig of beer, she thought of that numbing day when her mom, Collette, went missing, those frantic calls to the police, her father stuck in Vermont because of snowstorms. After they found her car at that Target parking lot and her body by that pier, the news outlets spent a few days on her strange murder, but then moved on to Helena's case. Seneca's family didn't get to go on *Nancy Grace* like the Kellys did. Their story didn't make the *New York Times*. No one cared about the grieving black dad or the biracial daughter, even if her mom had been pretty and white. Instead, Helena and her perfect Connecticut family had swallowed up the spotlight, pushing her mom's case to the bottom of a long list of unsolved crimes.

Meanwhile, Seneca no longer had a mother. Her voice no longer woke Seneca up every day. Her face never appeared in the kitchen when Seneca arrived home from school. Seneca never even got to say good-bye. The last memory she had of her mother was of an unrecognizable face in a cold, sterile, hellish room.

The grief had been too powerful to battle against, like a strong riptide sweeping her out to sea, surmounting everything else—eating, breathing, sleeping. For weeks, she'd huddled on her bed clutching her mother's *P* necklace, the same one she still wore today. It stood for *Pinky*, Seneca's mom's nickname, earned because she was so petite and fine-boned. For more than a month, Seneca didn't leave that bed. Didn't *move*, really, except to use the bathroom. She heard worried whispers outside the door. Her father brought in a priest, a social worker, a therapist named Dr. Ying. He flew in Seneca's favorite aunt, Terri, but even she couldn't break her shell. Half-comatose, she heard the term *psychiatric unit* being kicked around. She heard *post-traumatic stress disorder*. Bright lights were shined in her eyes. Gentle questions were aimed at her hourly. But she'd felt like she'd sunk about seven layers into herself. She was unable to tunnel out.

Until one day, when she just sort of came out of it. Maybe the medication they'd been giving her had finally started to work. Maybe her body and mind had decided to dig to the surface and fight. She started to go to school again. Declared herself fine. There were some hiccups— she once lashed out at a guy in the cafeteria because she thought he was snickering behind her back, and she once got aggressively impassioned during an English discussion about Hamlet deciding whether or not to murder his stepfather/uncle. But she got through high school. Got into college. She was *dealing*.

Well, sort of.

There was a *thud*. Seneca's phone fell from her lap to the floor. When she picked it up, the screen flashed to the last texts that had come in, including one from her dad. *How's Annie?*

Seneca drank more beer, feeling listless. She longed to tell her dad the truth . . . about everything. About how the pain of missing her mother had never left. How it was a hot, gnawing ache in her chest, and it was just growing worse. But she couldn't do that to him. Lately, she'd thought about calling the therapist he'd found for her, but Dr. Ying would probably make her do random art therapy drawings or coo in an empathetic voice that she understood what Seneca was going through. How the hell could she? How could anyone?

Okay, except Brett. And Aerin. But it seemed contrived to confide in them, like she'd really just come to Dexby to form a support group. She was afraid, too—afraid that if she started talking about her mom, she might never stop.

The doorknob started to rattle. Seneca's head shot up. The rattling persisted. Seneca stood, thinking about that dark figure looming at the hotel door. *Could* someone be onto them?

The door swung open. Seneca's whole body tensed. Then an Asian girl with long, dark hair, wearing an ultra-short candy-pink terry-cloth dress, white tights, and boots breezed in. Seneca breathed out. It was Madison, Maddox's stepsister. She'd recognize her anywhere.

"Excuse me?" Seneca called, peeking over the couch.

Madison wheeled around and yelped. "What the—" She came closer. "Oh! Are you Seneca? Maddy's friend?"

She had a cheery, high-pitched voice and exaggerated makeup. Her perfume smelled like peaches. *Pixy Stix,* Seneca thought immediately, playing her and Maddox's game.

She shot over to Seneca and grabbed her hands. "I'm Madison! I thought you were coming last night! You're just visiting my bro for a little bit? Are you going to stay for the Easter Bunny party? You guys met on the Internet, didn't you? What site? Personally, I want to try Tinder, but I heard the guys on there are pigs." She made a high-pitched *eeee.* "If you ever need time away from my brother, come by my room—I can give you a mani-pedi. I even have an LED light for gels. And look at those cuticle beds! You need help. Do you mind if I smoke up?"

"W-what?" Talking to Madison was like trying to keep hold of a hummingbird.

Madison whipped out a pink-and-purple glass pipe. "Don't tell my brother, cool? He knows, but he's always lecturing me." She rolled her eyes. "He runs, like, three times a day. One day, at dinner, he said he ran a whole *marathon* on the track. That's like a hundred miles."

"I think it's twenty-six." Madison gave her a blank look. "Didn't he get a scholarship, though? Maybe he needs to run that much," Seneca added.

Madison conked herself on the side of the head. "I am such a bad hostess! Guests first."

Seneca stared at the outstretched pipe, then held up her beer. "I'm fine."

Madison shrugged, fished out a Zippo that was embellished in what looked like Swarovski crystals, and lit up. Seneca tried to reconcile this girl with the one she was "friends" with on Facebook.

Then Madison leaned closer. "So you're not here for a hookup, are you?"

Seneca burst out laughing. "No way."

"Right." Madison nodded sagely. "I didn't think so."

Seneca made an effort not to let her smile slip. Madison seemed awfully dismissive of the possibility. Had Maddox made some sort of comment that they weren't compatible? Was she just not his type? Well, *obviously*. And yet—what, wasn't she good enough for Mr. Track and Field?

"So why *are* you here?" Madison rushed on.

Seneca blinked. She felt like she'd just walked into a cave full of vipers; any sudden move would set them rattling. "Track," she said. "We're track friends."

"Then why aren't you running with him right now?"

"I . . ."

Then Madison's phone beeped. She checked it and shrieked. "Is that a penis?"

She thrust her phone in Seneca's face. Seneca glanced at the image on the screen. It was a guy's lower half in a very sheer bathing suit. "Ew."

"Not ew. That's the captain of the lacrosse team." Madison jumped up. "I have to send a picture back." She peered into a round mirror embossed with seashells and fluffed her hair.

Seneca stared at her. "Please don't say you're going to get naked."

"Uh, *no*." Madison wrinkled her nose. "But I'll show some cleavage." She smoothed down her dress. "This is all wrong. Want to help me pick out something else?"

"That's not really my specialty."

"Boo," Madison simpered. She scooped up her pipe and whipped open the door to the stairs. But then she turned back and gave Seneca a sly look. "It's Helena Kelly, isn't it?"

"W-what?"

"That's why you're here. He's looking into her again."

Again? Seneca fumbled for an excuse, but she knew that her expression gave her away, because Madison scurried back into the room. "Let me help."

"Help?"

"I knew Helena, too." Madison edged closer, her hair smelling like weed. "Before my mom died, she was in hospice care, and Helena was a volunteer. She stopped at 7-Eleven to get my mom Naked Juice because it was the only thing she could get down. She didn't have to do that."

"I'm sorry about your mom," Seneca said automatically. "But I don't think it's a good idea. This could get dangerous."

Madison snorted. "I can take danger."

"Actually, it's not going to be dangerous at all—more like boring," Seneca said, reversing her story, trying to shake Madison. "We're probably going to quit soon. We've gotten nowhere."

Madison glanced at Seneca's cell phone, which was faceup on the table. Seneca's text to her dad was gone; the thing had switched to Google seemingly on its own. In the search box were the words *Kevin Larssen, campaign schedule,* plain as day. Seneca tried to hide the screen, but the damage was already done.

"You think it's that Kevin guy?" Madison squeaked. "He was a hospice volunteer, too. I didn't really know him, but he didn't seem like a raging, murdering crazy-man."

"We just want to talk to him," Seneca said quickly, feeling self-conscious. "Certain things don't make sense about his alibi."

"So call up his campaign office. It's right in town."

Seneca scoffed. "If he's guilty, he'll never talk. We have to catch him off guard."

Madison's smile widened. "You're in luck, then. I know somewhere where he'll be off guard for sure. The Dexby Country Club, tomorrow. It's his engagement party."

"How do you know *that*?"

Madison cozied up to Seneca and linked an elbow through hers. "Because I've got an invitation."

TWELVE

THE NEXT AFTERNOON, Maddox stood in a bedroom full of faux-fur throws, pink leopard curtains, Katy Perry posters, and Hello Kitty everything. His bare feet sank into a Pepto-colored shag rug, and he stared into the closet, which was stuffed with dresses, tops, shoes, and bags. Seneca, Aerin, and Brett stood behind him. And standing in front of him, grinning maniacally, was his stepsister, Madison. It was her closet; this was her room.

"All right, ladies." Madison gestured to the open closet doors. "For a party at the Dexby Country Club, I'll direct your attention to the Marc Jacobs section in 3-A."

Aerin tittered. "Your closet is organized like a parking lot?"

The two of them started talking about hem length, fabrics, and designers—well, he assumed it was designers, though he didn't really know. Seneca hung back, looking like a fish out of water, but then Madison held a dress up to her thin frame and pulled her in. Maddox laid his head against the wall and pretended to snore. This sort of bullshit put him to sleep.

Last night, there had been a knock at his door. He'd hoped that it was Seneca—maybe she wanted to talk about her mom. He couldn't stop thinking about her. He'd looked up her mom's story and read a few of Seneca's interviews. He'd lingered on a CBS News link, too, staring at a picture of Seneca from five years before. Her little face was so innocent and scared.

How had she concealed that so well? How did she function? It also explained why she'd freaked at his maybe-we-should-have-said-we-knew-where-she-was-coming-from comment. Seneca *did* know where Aerin was coming from.

Instead, it had been his sister at the door. "Meet the new member of your team!" Madison had crowed, raising her arms over her head. "We're so going to catch Helena Kelly's killer."

Maddox had been blindsided. "Did Aerin tell you?" Aerin *had* mentioned knowing Madison. "Nope, Seneca did," Madison answered. That was even weirder. Why hadn't Seneca played better D? "You people need me," Madison insisted. "You want to talk to Kevin Larssen, and I have an invite to his engagement party. It's a win-win."

Maddox and his stepsister were cool. When their families merged, she'd never been bitchy or manipulative, like stepsisters were on TV. And when Maddox became popular, Madison practically lost her mind with joy, saying they needed to throw him a Maddox Is an Alpha Dog party, which he'd immediately shot down. But that was the thing: Madison had a way of making everything into a fun free-for-all, a goofy, frothy party full of pink Silly String and pillow fights and pot—super hot when Maddox wanted to spy on girls at a sleepover, but kind of inappropriate when solving a murder. Aerin had said it herself: This was her life. Not a game.

Still, Madison had promised she'd take it very seriously. Maddox didn't know what else to do but let her help.

His gaze fell to his sister's Hello Kitty clock on the bedside table. It was 2:03. He was supposed to be running with Catherine, but he'd bailed. It had nothing to do with the kiss, though. Well, almost nothing. Seriously—he'd barely even thought about it. It was more that they had to get ready for tonight.

Brett reached into the mass of clothes and plucked out an iridescent gold dress with a tie up the back. He handed it to Aerin. "This would look great on you."

Aerin gave him a circumspect look and studied the label. When she held it up to her body, the color immediately brightened up her pale skin.

"Gorge," Madison said appreciatively.

"Yeah, I kind of can't believe it." Aerin glanced at Brett and grinned.

Maddox rolled his eyes. "Dude, Brett, you are *such* a girl."

Brett just shrugged. "What can I say? I'm a natural-born stylist."

"Well, I should *hope* so, considering who your grandmother was," Aerin pointed out.

Maddox nodded, reflecting on Brett's true identity as well. The Grady dynasty was legendary . . . but what a nasty thing to have gone through. In some ways, Maddox felt a little naive to be around three people who'd experienced such heinous losses, like they were wise in ways he wasn't. Then again, was it like he *wanted* to be wise to murder? Hell no.

"Pick one for me," Seneca urged Brett, pointing to the closet.

Brett chose a dress made of red satin and handed it to Seneca. As

Seneca gazed at herself in the mirror, Maddox felt a rise of impatience and cleared his throat. "Can we put a pin in the fashion show? How are Brett and I getting into this party?"

Brett looked up from the shoes and snapped his fingers. "*I* know how we can get in. Maddox, my man, you and I are going to be cater waiters."

Aerin wrinkled her nose. "You mean you're going to pass around drinks?"

"Yep. My family used to have catered parties all the time. You circulate with trays, butter people up, hang out. Rich people totally don't notice the waitstaff. Kevin might say something in front of one of us. Or we could get him drunk and then start asking questions."

Madison shrugged. "Sounds fun." Brett shot her a wink and an I-like-your-style point.

"I agree," Seneca said. "But how are you going to get a catering job there so quickly?"

"We'll just take someone's place," Brett said.

"How are we going to do that?" Maddox asked.

Brett pulled a bottle of Patrón tequila from his bag. Madison lunged for it. "Me want!"

Brett slipped the bottle back into his bag. "This is for the caterers. We give them the bottle, say we'll take their job but they'll still get the check, and we're golden."

Maddox sat down on the Hello Kitty quilt on Madison's bed. It sounded like a crazy idea, but it wasn't like they had anything else. "I'm game."

Brett slapped Maddox's hand. Madison gave him a high five. And out of the corner of his eye, Maddox noticed Seneca smiling. But when he turned, she averted her eyes and pressed her mouth into a line, like he'd just caught her doing something naughty.

Well, well. It seemed like Seneca was starting to warm up to the team, finally . . . even if she didn't want to admit it.

THIRTEEN

A FEW HOURS later, Brett stood in the men's locker room at the Dexby Country Club, which smelled of shoe leather and old-guy aftershave. He zipped up the pair of tuxedo pants he'd borrowed from the caterer and winced. The pants were too short and so tight they looked like, well, tights.

Then he looked at Maddox and groaned. The suit *he* got fit him perfectly. "How is it that you look like James Bond and I'm in a tux made for a toddler?"

Maddox glanced at him and burst out laughing. "I got lucky, I guess." He twisted in the mirror, admiring himself.

Brett knew he should just take comfort in the fact that his plan had worked. He'd ridden over here with Maddox while the girls got ready. At the country club, they'd found a bunch of caterers standing outside the kitchen entrance, smoking. Two dudes named Jeffery and Tim had accepted the Patrón bottle eagerly, handing over their tuxes and heading off on a golf cart, singing a hokey song in Spanish Brett remembered from Señorita Florez's class in ninth grade.

Maddox's phone pinged, and Brett glanced at the message. *We're here,* Seneca had texted.

The locker room exited into a long hall that was flanked on either side by plaques bearing the names of the winners of the Dexby Country Club Golf Invitational dating back to 1903. Outside were sweeping views of the golf course, the pool, and the tennis courts.

"Why's this party on a Tuesday, anyway?" Brett asked as he hobbled, penguinlike, down the hall. It was kind of hard to breathe in these pants.

"Because this weekend is the Easter Bunny party," Maddox answered. "It's a huge deal on the Morgenthau estate. You don't dare schedule anything else the same weekend."

Brett raised an eyebrow. "You going?"

Maddox shrugged. "Maybe. I don't know."

"Why not? I bet there will be some hot girls there. . . ."

Maddox didn't answer, but Brett could sense some internal squirming. "You having girl trouble?"

Maddox waved his hand. "You kidding?"

Brett grinned. "Have to fend 'em off with a stick, huh?" Then he spied the girls at the end of the hall. "Whoa," he breathed.

Madison looked like a confection in her hot-pink dress and banana-yellow heels. And Seneca's hair was up, showing off her big eyes, pointed chin, and high cheekbones. Without all her layers and denim and flannel, her legs looked longer, her arms sculptural. But Aerin . . . *whoa.* She was in the gold dress Brett had chosen, and her hair was swept up, revealing her long, slender neck.

Brett tried not to stare. He already thought Aerin was gorgeous, of course, but today, all dressed up, she seemed . . . older. More interesting.

Crazy sexy. The kind of girl you didn't just flirt with but seriously pursued. He plucked a rose from a vase and handed it to her wordlessly.

Aerin twirled it between her fingers. "Well, well. I feel like I'm in *The Bachelor*."

Seneca was giving Brett a strange look. "What's with your pants?"

Madison giggled, too. "They look like leggings."

"I know, I know, I look like a freak," Brett groaned, irritated. His wardrobe malfunction was a buzzkill. "Can we just go up now?"

The group tromped up a back staircase that emptied into a dining room. Brett pulled up the rear, trying to come to grips with his sudden rush of emotion for Aerin. *Keep your head on straight,* he told himself. This had happened before—he fell head over heels, got his feelings hurt. He needed to backpedal. Take a breath.

At the top of the stairs was a huge foyer crammed with people. Everyone was dressed in cocktail dresses or lavish gowns; the flashing white smiles and glitter of diamonds were blinding. In the middle of the group was a face made familiar from hours of staring at the news reports. Kevin Larssen was taller than Brett had expected from his pics online, his weak jaw belied by calculating ice-blue eyes. In the span of four seconds, he swiftly kissed an older, stately woman's cheek, pumped the hand of a silver-haired guy with a potbelly, and gave a younger woman an enormous hug. And still his eyes scanned the room hungrily.

Seneca strode up to a table and selected three glasses of champagne, handing one each to Aerin and Madison. "Where's Macie Green?" she whispered, referring to Kevin's fiancée. Madison had filled them in on Macie this afternoon: She was a soft-contact-lens heiress from Dexby, graduated top of her class at her boarding school and at Middlebury, showed champion Irish wolfhounds on the weekends, blah, blah, blah.

"There." Brett pointed to a tall, willowy blonde who'd approached Kevin's side. Macie had a long face and small ears, and she smiled without teeth. Her silver dress seemed tailored to perfection, and her huge diamond engagement ring sparkled in the lights. Her body was turned away from Kevin's, and she was talking animatedly to an older lady in enormous pearls.

Brett felt Seneca watching Macie, too. The party was so loud, suddenly, and he shifted until he was next to the girls. "Hey," he whispered. Seneca looked up. "I'm sorry. I shouldn't have googled you. And I definitely shouldn't have brought up what happened. I didn't mean for—"

"I know," Seneca cut him off, but her eyes were forgiving. "It's okay." Brett felt like she meant it. He looked at her searchingly, wishing he could say more, wishing he could just undo that moment entirely, but then someone poked his shoulder. *"Buddy."*

A woman with broad shoulders, frizzy hair, and a unibrow glared at him. A brass name tag on her tuxedo jacket said, *Sandy.* "I'm not paying you to stand around ogling the guests, *Jeff,*" she hissed. "Get your tray and start circulating."

Brett gazed at Sandy, rapidly assessing. She looked like a tired, overworked older lady who probably needed a good foot rub and a compliment. He gave her a salute. "You got it. Did anyone ever tell you that you look like Anjelica Huston? A younger version, of course."

Sandy's frown cracked just a teensy bit. "I have to admit I don't mind her—and I *hate* most celebrities." She seemed to think for a moment, then leaned his way conspiratorially. "Tell Doris I said to give you martinis. They're much easier to unload than canapés."

The kitchen was filled with busy prep cooks and sous chefs and hazy with steam. Brett sauntered in and gathered his martini tray. Maddox was behind him as they swirled into the ballroom again. A few girls checked Maddox out with interest. He gave them friendly but slightly standoffish smiles.

Brett skirted around a massive table filled with raw shrimp and oysters, passing a group of women who were talking about getting Botox in their vaginas—*wha-what?* Then he spied Kevin in a back room, leaning up against a mahogany bar. A bunch of guys were around him; Brett recognized quite a few from the Connecticut Youth group photos he'd seen online. Heart quickening, he sauntered up to them, careful not to spill any of the martinis.

Kevin was busy talking. "They're thinking I'll have a good shot at state senate, so we'll see. I've got really great people working on the campaign, and—"

"Martini?" Brett interrupted.

Kevin shrugged and took one. "Yeah, sure." He shot Brett a tight smile and took a tiny sip. Then he put the drink on the bar.

Brett cleared his throat. "You should drink that while it's still cold," he said smoothly. "The chill brings out the flavor in the vodka."

Kevin took another obligatory swig, then switched to telling a story about a camping trip he and the others had taken early senior year. Brett listened for a mention of Helena's name, but it sounded like it had been a guys-only thing. Even as Kevin talked, his gaze was still scanning the room like he was looking for someone.

The attitude was infectious; Brett swiveled around the room, too, searching for Aerin. She had broken away from Madison and Seneca and was standing next to a petite dark-haired girl holding a drink. The girl whispered something and pointed at a guy near the shrimp bar, and Aerin rolled her eyes. Brett followed their gaze, trying to figure out who the guy was. He seemed like a completely average high school dude, with a jutting chin and a prominent Adam's apple. Brett could totally take him.

He picked up his tray again and presented martinis to a blonde who was definitely underage, an old woman dripping in diamonds and using a walker, and a beefy dude he swore was wearing a Super Bowl ring. He found Maddox across the room, swarmed with people wanting drinks. "Take a load off," Brett advised him after they were gone, gesturing to an empty table for him to place his tray.

Maddox set his tray down and blew air through his cheeks. Brett leaned against the wall and assessed the crowd. "This is like a who's who of Dexby, huh?"

"Yep," Maddox said. "You know anyone?" Brett looked at him blankly. "Some of these people probably live in Greenwich," Maddox added.

Brett shook his head. "I've been out of that scene for a while. But I wish I knew *her*." He pointed at Macie Green. "I love me some icy blondes."

They watched as Macie coolly selected a prosciutto-wrapped melon slice from a roving tray and glided into Kevin's room. Kevin, who was making a good dent in that martini, nodded at Macie and murmured something in her ear, his brow furrowed. Macie abruptly turned and retreated. There was a sheepish look on her face, as though he'd told her she'd forgotten to shave her armpits. Brett's insides soured. When it came to how to treat women, some guys just didn't get it.

Maddox pointed out a tall man walking past. "Isn't that James Gorman? The senator the Connecticut Youth kids worked for? Guess he and Kevin kept in touch."

Brett squinted. "Well, he's running for office. Maybe Gorman's supporting him."

When Brett checked Kevin's martini glass again, it was empty. "Another round?" Brett asked, sweeping up to him.

Kevin nodded and took one willingly. "Good advice about drinking it cold." He inspected Brett, hopefully not noticing the high-water pants. "You look familiar. Do you work Sundays?"

"Nope." Brett felt a nervous tingle but pressed it deep. "I'm here just for tonight."

Kevin slung his arm around Brett's shoulder. "Have one with me."

Brett demurred. "I'm on the clock, man."

Kevin pretended to seal his lips. "I won't tell."

Brett waited the obligatory few seconds. "Well, you twisted my arm." He selected a glass. "So I hear congratulations are in order."

Kevin grabbed his martini glass and took a long swig. "Thanks. I'm excited." He sounded anything but.

Maddox strolled up just then, widening his eyes at the drink in Brett's hand. Brett clapped his shoulder. "This is my buddy. Mind if he has a martini as well?"

"Why not?" Kevin said expansively, throwing open his arms.

Brett plucked a drink from the tray. Maddox seemed a little unsure at first, but after a few swigs, he relaxed. *Attaboy,* Brett thought.

"I also heard you're running for office?" Brett placed his chin in his hand as though he was truly interested.

Kevin launched into a description of his position as state senator and the platforms he stood for. Brett nodded like he was listening, but he'd zoned out. After Kevin finished, Brett stood back. "Wait, *I* know where I know you from. You dated that girl in high school, right? The one who vanished? What was her name?"

Maddox was giving him another look, but Brett ignored him.

Kevin placed his drink on the bar, his face clouding. "Uh, Helena Kelly."

"Right, right." Brett shook his head solemnly. "Man. What was that like?"

Kevin studied a portrait of a pudgy man behind the bar. The band in the other room started to play "New York, New York." "You a reporter or something?" he finally asked.

"No!" Brett held up his hands. "Shit—forget I asked. I'm being nosy."

There was a long pause. When Kevin picked up his drink again, the liquid sloshed out the sides and onto his sleeve. "She was a sweet girl."

Brett gave him an incredulous look. *Sweet girl?* That was like something his grandmother might say. "Were you guys close?"

"Yeah." There was a hitch in Kevin's voice. "But . . ." He trailed off.

"What?"

Kevin waved his hand sloppily. "We weren't that serious. It was a high school thing."

"Love can be real in high school," Maddox piped up.

Kevin stirred his drink thoughtfully. A smile played across his face. "I guess it's just that there were a few things in my relationship with Helena that *weren't* real," he murmured.

Brett felt an excited flare inside him and cocked his head. "How do you mean?"

Kevin looked up and blinked as if he'd come out of a trance. For a split second, a dangerous look cut through the booze, transforming his features completely. Brett held his breath. Kevin tapped him on the shoulder. "I'm sure other people want drinks, don't you think?"

And with a smile that could only be described as chilling, he turned his back on them.

FOURTEEN

AERIN HAD BEEN to fabulous parties in her day, and this one was pretty much like the others, with its floor-to-ceiling Swiss chocolate waterfall, nine-piece swing band, and the usual suspects name-dropping, posing for the roving photographer, and trying very, very hard to act as perfect as possible. James Gorman, the Connecticut state senator, was here, which was an added touch of class. He had an Abraham Lincoln chin, a George W. Bush smile, and a Bill Clinton swagger. She could so picture his face on a coin.

She stood in a corner with Amanda Bettsworth, a friend who'd been at Tori's party but had escaped the cops. Amanda, who was swilling a vodka tonic she'd told her mother twice was just ginger ale, nudged Aerin. "O'Neill's checking you out by the shellfish yacht."

Aerin peeked from behind her drink. Sure enough, Brian O'Neill, a wild-haired, dark-eyed kid in a crisp white shirt and striped tie, was peering at her from behind a mizzenmast made entirely of Dungeness crab legs. Aerin had shown him her bra in the locker room in ninth grade, and he'd never gotten over it. For months after that, Brian had sent her love letters via text, her phone pinging ten times in a row for him to fit in all the characters.

Sometimes Aerin regretted being so forward and willing.

Amanda nudged her. "Who are those kids you came with? I recognize Madison. That's her stepbrother, right? Isn't he practically an Olympian? Are they your friends?"

"I guess," Aerin answered, not knowing what *else* to call them. But maybe *friends* wasn't that bad of a label. She'd warmed to Seneca, and she'd always found Madison bigger than the sum of her I-love-Hello-Kitty parts. Brett wore his heart on his sleeve, but she was kind of tempted to take him to Sparrow, Dexby's best boutique, and see what he picked out for her. She even appreciated that Maddy had grown out of his awkward, dorky phase into someone vaguely hot and interesting. And practically an Olympian? Impressive rumor, even if it was exaggerated.

So yeah, they were friends. And if she thought about it, the Case Not Closed group knew more about her, *cared* more about what really mattered to her, than anyone else here. People she'd known her whole life.

She felt a tap on her shoulder and winced, fearing it might be yet another blast from her hookup past. Marissa Ingram beamed at her. "Aerin! What a lovely surprise!"

Marissa wore a green silk dress and a choker with jewels so huge and bulbous it was a wonder her scrawny neck didn't snap under its weight. Skip stood by her side, swirling a brownish drink. His bow tie was cinched too tightly, making him look choked, but he managed to give Aerin a warm smile after a beat. And then Heath appeared behind them, dressed in a well-fitting black suit and a gray tie. "Aerin, hey!" He pecked her on the cheek. "Long time no see!"

"Hi," Aerin answered awkwardly. It was especially weird seeing Heath—he, Aerin, and Helena used to be tight. She wanted to ask him what was with the stuffy outfit—he used to show up to formal country club events in dirty khakis and loafers with holes. She'd respected that.

Marissa scanned the crowd. "Is your mother here?"

"She, um…" All at once, Aerin couldn't take the overpowering scent of beef at the carving station. "I have to go," she mumbled, and darted away, giving Amanda a half wave, too. It wasn't that she didn't like the Ingrams. Being here, fake-hobnobbing, just wasn't her style.

She stepped out onto an empty terrace. Down the hill was a very familiar white gazebo that was a favorite for Dexby hookups. It was known as the Pube Cube, for reasons Aerin was all too familiar with.

There was a whisper behind her. Hair on her neck rose; it felt like someone was watching. But when she turned, it was only Macie Green whisking by in a cloud of Coco Chanel. A cell phone was pressed to her ear, and her voice was gummy, like she had been crying. "You wouldn't believe who's here. I'm going to kill him." Aerin strained to hear the rest, but the wind shifted, carrying her conversation elsewhere.

This was the weirdest engagement party ever.

"Aerin?"

A familiar guy with close-cropped hair and prominent cheekbones stood by the doors. It was Thomas Grove, Aerin realized. The cop from Tori's yard… and the Easter Bunny party.

"Hey." Thomas walked over to her. "I was wondering if you were coming to this. All of Dexby is here, huh?"

Aerin blinked at his calm blue eyes and well-proportioned face. He was way cuter when not arresting people on her friend's lawn. Not as gangly. Not as pale. She also didn't remember him standing almost six inches taller than she was—and she was five foot eight. "Are you here as a guest?" she asked.

"Nah, I've got a side job as a valet. You wouldn't believe the tips these people give." He winked, kind of adorably. "You look really nice, by the way."

Aerin stared down at her dress and blushed. Everyone kept saying how *great* she looked. As if she usually looked like shit. Assholes.

"Wanna go back in?" Thomas asked. "I'm on a break. We could hit the buffet. The shrimp is awesome."

She winced. "Actually, I'm in hiding. These people make me break out in hives."

Thomas raised an eyebrow. "In that case, I have somewhere even better you could hide."

"Oh yeah? Where?"

"It's a surprise. I promise you'll like it, though."

Aerin hesitated. Last winter, an instructor at the local ski mountain had given Aerin that very same line when convincing her to check out his cabin. The surprise was—surprise!—his penis. He'd stripped off his long underwear the moment they'd gotten inside. Total skeev.

Then again, she had a feeling Thomas Grove couldn't be skeevy if he tried.

"CHECK IT OUT," Thomas whispered, unlocking a low-slung red Ferrari 458 Spider—Aerin only knew the name because Thomas had just reverently whispered it about six times. The car was parked at the very back of the country club lot; the only other vehicle around was the groundskeeper's golf cart. The owner, Mr. Levine, liked it parked far away, Thomas explained, so he knew the car wouldn't get dinged.

Thomas slid into the tan leather driver's seat and gripped the steering wheel, making revving sounds like a three-year-old. Aerin snickered. "Since when do cops go on joyrides?"

"I'm not." Thomas shook the keys. "But there's no rule against us sitting in it. I can tell Mr. Levine we're just making sure it doesn't get hurt." He patted the passenger seat. "C'mon."

Aerin liked how Thomas was okay with bending the rules. She walked to the other side of the vehicle and maneuvered into the passenger seat, which had an image of a rearing stallion stitched into the top. Even the seat belt was race car–like, a five-point harness that held every part of her in.

"This thing's got 549 horsepower," Thomas said, awestruck. "It goes from zero to sixty in like three seconds. I'd kill to have one."

Aerin chuckled. "I think you're in the wrong line of work to afford this, Officer."

He sighed. "I know. But there's always the lottery. Or marrying rich."

"True." Aerin was afraid to touch anything in the car; it was all way too leathery and pristine. Her father had never had a ride this nice.

They fell into a silence and stared at the golf course. The sun sank over the green hills, and a lone cart wound down the path. Aerin peeked at Thomas, but he seemed totally comfortable with not talking. It was nice, for a change.

After a while, she cleared her throat. "I'm kind of crashing this thing."

Thomas ran his finger along the stitching on the steering wheel. "Funny you came at all, considering rich people give you a rash."

"Hives."

"Right."

Aerin sighed. "I'm looking into my sister's death, actually." She eyed him, contemplating explaining the dead-end case, but that was probably asinine. Everyone in Dexby already knew.

Thomas looked intrigued. "Have you found out anything?"

"I'm suspicious about Kevin Larssen. His alibi for the weekend Helena disappeared is a little thin. There are no pictures from the event, but a report says he didn't show up for a speech he was supposed to give."

A hard-to-read look crossed Thomas's face. "Huh."

Aerin straightened her spine. "'Huh' what?"

Thomas stared into the middle distance. With the sun shining on the angles of his face, he was suddenly and alarmingly handsome, his eyes big and extra blue. He had an almost buzz cut, which accentuated his small ears and a tiny scar on his forehead. Aerin could easily bend over and kiss him. She pictured it for a second, her heart beating fast. It would feel a lot better than talking about Helena, actually dealing.

But before she got up the nerve, Thomas cleared his throat. "I'm just thinking of something I read in Helena's file about him." He looked sheepish. "After I saw you a couple days ago, I looked through it."

"What did it say?"

Thomas smiled apologetically. "I can't tell you."

"Can you at least tell me if he's guilty?"

He didn't meet her gaze. "I don't know."

"What do you mean you don't know?"

"I'm sorry. I shouldn't have even brought it up."

He shrugged, and it hit her: Thomas, as a cop, had access to a lot of stuff. What else was in that confidential case file?

Thomas turned to her. "Want to go out with me sometime?"

Aerin stared at him. "What?"

His eyes twinkled. "I'm sure I could find a good place that serves Cream of Wheat."

"Ha-ha." Aerin couldn't believe he remembered that. She pointed to the controls, deciding to change the subject. "Start this up. Just for a minute."

Thomas reared back. "No way!"

"Come on," Aerin teased. "You could always tell Mr. Levine we were just making sure it was still in working order."

Thomas pulled his bottom lip into his mouth. "What if someone sees?"

"If you were really worried about that, we wouldn't be sitting in here, would we?"

Thomas fingered the start button for the ignition but didn't press it. "Pussy," Aerin said, leaning across him. Her shoulder pressed against his chest. She could smell his sweet, fruity shampoo—she was almost positive it was Herbal Essences. She pressed his finger down over the button, and the car roared to life so enthusiastically that they both jumped. All sorts of lights came on. Alerts marched across a center screen. The radio had been up loud, and a Led Zeppelin song blared through the speakers.

Thomas pressed the gas. The car growled. He pressed it again, and the RPM needle jumped. They exchanged a naughty smile. *Put it in reverse,* Aerin mouthed over the loud music.

Thomas's hand inched toward the gearshift when something caught his eye out of the rearview. With a start, he stabbed at the ignition button, shutting the car down. Aerin swiveled around. A police car was driving slowly down the main road that paralleled the country club.

"Get down," Thomas whispered, pressing her lower in the seats.

Aerin did as she was told, his hand hot on her shoulder, hardly daring to move until the car was a good distance away. Then she burst out laughing.

"And I was just starting to respect you as an officer of the law," she whispered.

They pushed open the doors and awkwardly climbed out. Just before Thomas took off across the parking lot, he gave Aerin one last look. "I'm serious about that date."

Aerin shrugged. "Maybe when you get one of these bad boys," she said, patting the car's hood. Then she sauntered off, shaking her hips exaggeratedly. She hoped Thomas was watching.

Just as Aerin stepped back into the foyer, Brett and Maddox went skidding past. Brett stopped short and flagged her over. "We were *looking* for you!" he cried. "Have you seen Kevin?"

"Uh, no." Aerin gestured outside. "But I *did* see his fiancée crying."

Maddox pulled Aerin down an auxiliary hall. "We almost got Kevin to admit something, but then he got squirrelly. When we went back to the room he was hanging out in, he was gone."

Seneca and Madison caught up with them, too. The guys filled them in on Kevin's strange comment about things in his relationship with Helena not being real. "What do you think that means?" Madison asked.

"I don't know," Maddox said. "Maybe he was talking about love, like his love for her was real, but her love for him wasn't. That could indicate she was seeing someone else."

By now they were at the end of the hall. They peeked into a smaller bar area—a bunch of guys were gathered around a hockey play-off game—and then another dining room, and then a huge room with a piano and a harp. No Kevin. More rooms swept by: One had a lot of hunting trophies, another had a billiards table, another was filled with hardcover books and reading chairs. The hall was dim at this end—one of the grand overhead chandeliers was missing a few bulbs. Aerin squinted uneasily at the glow of the exit sign at the end of the hallway. "Let's go back to the dining room," she suggested.

But then, as she whirled around, she slammed into someone tall and solid. "Oof," she said, backing up. When she looked into the man's eyes, her nerves snapped under her skin.

Kevin. Here he was.

FIFTEEN

MADDOX'S HEART POUNDED hard. Kevin Larssen stood over them, the only light on his face the spooky red glow from the exit sign. As his vision adjusted, he realized that there was a door on one side of the hall marked *Men's*.

As if on cue, the door swung open again. Everyone stood back to let a second man pass. Maddox recognized Senator Gorman by his salt-and-pepper hair and flag pin. The senator glanced up and saw them, giving the group a bland, diplomatic smile. Maddox caught a whiff of strong cologne as he passed. It was an old-school smell, something he'd never wear.

Kevin was about to go, too, but then peered at the group. His eyes widened at Aerin, and he gave her a look like he didn't understand why she was there, but then he just nodded and started down the hall. "Wait," Aerin blurted. "Was Helena cheating on you?"

Kevin stopped. "Helena . . . your sister?"

"Do you know anyone *else* named Helena?"

Kevin offered her another tepid, possibly dangerous smile. His controlled composure was making Maddox feel edgy. He could be one of those people who seemed perfectly calm but then randomly snapped.

"You told my friends that elements of your relationship with Helena weren't real," Aerin said. "What did you mean?"

Kevin stared at Brett and Maddox accusingly, like they'd betrayed him. "Nothing. Nothing at all. I'm going back to my party now."

He started past the rest of the group, this time brushing against Seneca's shoulders kind of hard. She wheeled back a little, lifting a hand to massage the spot where he'd hit her. Maddox was about to chase Kevin down, call him out for being an asshole, but then Seneca got this look of discovery on her face. *What?* Maddox mouthed to her, but she just shot him a sneaky smile.

"Kevin," she called out after him. Kevin turned back, giving her a cautious look, and Seneca stepped up to him and leaned in close to sniff his collar, her nose almost touching his bare neck.

Kevin backed away. "What are you *doing*?"

Seneca stepped back. "That's an interesting cologne you're wearing. What's it called?"

Kevin looked at her like she was crazy. "I don't remember."

"Don't remember, or don't know?"

His jaw tensed. Maddox felt uneasy. Maybe they should leave this guy alone.

"It's Bay Rhum," Seneca filled in. She chuckled. "You really don't know the name of the cologne you put on tonight?"

Kevin jutted his chin into the air. "Macie picked it out for me."

"I think Macie would have better taste," Seneca said. "My dad wears Bay Rhum, too, and the sales clerk in the store where he bought it said that it's for older guys—no one under forty would be caught dead with it on."

Kevin stared at her. "I wear old-man cologne. Who cares?"

Maddox watched her, wondering where she was going with this. "You know what's interesting? Senator Gorman was wearing the same cologne just now—I smelled it on him when he left the bathroom. It's very distinct. Such a coincidence that you *both* have it on . . ."

Kevin's eyes flashed. "What are you implying?"

Seneca blinked innocently. "I'm not implying anything."

Maddox stared at Seneca, connecting the dots. Suddenly, he got it. He looked at the others, who seemed surprised, too. Kevin and the senator . . . *together?*

Kevin balled up his fist. "I didn't invite you people. I'll call security."

"Oh, we'll leave," Seneca said smoothly. "But before we do, we'll tell everyone. I'm not sure the senator would appreciate people knowing what he was up to with his old protégé. I'm *really* sure he wouldn't want his wife to find out."

"And, for that matter, *your* almost wife," Maddox said.

Kevin looked furious. A peal of laughter sounded from the dining room. Kevin shut his eyes. "I'm at my engagement party. My whole family is here. My ninety-year-old, ultra-conservative grandfather is here." He stumbled over the word *conservative*. "I just need to get through this, okay?"

Need to get through this? That seemed like a strange way to phrase something that should be joyful. Then again, maybe Kevin didn't want to marry Macie. He wanted someone else, someone he couldn't have.

Maddox thought of Kevin's Facebook page again. All those enthusiastic links to Connecticut Youth events. All those pictures of him standing next to Senator Gorman. Never with Kevin on one end, Gorman on the other—always side by side.

He pointed at Kevin. "Your whole *relationship* with Helena wasn't real. You didn't love Helena like that. That's what you meant."

Aerin stared at him. "What are you talking about?"

Seneca was nodding along. "Aerin, that thing you told me yesterday about how you called Kevin a puppet and Helena got angry? Kevin *was* a puppet. You hit the nail on the head."

"I did?" Aerin still seemed confused.

Maddox glanced at Seneca, knowing where she was going. They were on the same wavelength, like they'd been so many times while solving cases online. He touched Aerin's arm. "Helena was Kevin's beard."

Aerin's eyes narrowed. It took her a moment to digest the news. She glanced at Kevin's face, and he didn't deny it. "But that doesn't make any sense. My sister could have gone out with anyone. Why would she choose a boyfriend who wasn't even into her?"

Everyone turned to Kevin. A quick whiff of steak wafted from down the hall. A glass broke, and someone laughed. Kevin tried to slip away, but Aerin grabbed his arm. *"Tell us,"* she said through her teeth.

Kevin wrenched his arm away. "God, *fine*. She might have been seeing someone. Someone she didn't want anyone to know about."

Maddox's heart stopped. "Who?"

Kevin sniffed. "I don't know *that*."

"But you knew there was someone else?" Aerin's voice was shaky. "How could you keep that to yourself?"

Suddenly, she lunged for Kevin. Maddox caught her and pulled her back. "Hey," he said warningly.

Kevin glowered at them. "All I knew was that the guy was older. Into art, museums. I think he lived in New York."

"New York *City*?" Maddox felt bad as he heard Aerin's voice crack.

To her, this was more than just a fascinating development in an un-solved case.

Kevin nodded. "We went once, in the fall. She disappeared for a while. Said she was going to an art gallery, but I had a feeling what she was really up to."

Brett tapped his bottom lip. "You might not have been attracted to her that way, dude, but still, letting your girlfriend run off with some *random*? What, you were totally chill with him wining and dining her in his Upper West pad? Taking her for romantic carriage rides in the park? Didn't you care that she was making you look like a fool?"

"I don't know," Kevin sputtered. "Maybe?"

"Why didn't you tell anyone about this? Like the police?" Aerin cried.

"I didn't think it mattered." Kevin's voice registered higher and higher.

Didn't think it *mattered*? That seemed so weak to Maddox. Maybe he was hiding something.

"Why did you not show up for your speech at the leadership con-ference the weekend Helena went missing?" Seneca asked.

Kevin narrowed his eyes. "Are you trying to say *I'm* a suspect? I have an alibi. I was already cleared."

"News flash," Brett said. "We don't trust you or your friends."

"Well, the cops do," Kevin said, puffing out his chest.

Maddox stepped forward. "What about that angry message you wrote for Helena in the yearbook? We figured out the code. It said—"

"You'll get what you deserve, H?" Kevin offered quickly. "That code was friendly. She'd done me a huge favor by keeping my secret. I meant that karma was going to bring her good things in return."

"Why is your secret so horrible?" Seneca said. "So you're gay. It's not that big a deal."

Kevin looked away. His expression was tortured, like his secret was bigger than just that. Maddox put the last pieces together. "It was the senator, wasn't it? Even back then. *That's* why you couldn't tell anyone."

Kevin gritted his teeth and stared into the middle distance.

"Whoa," Brett whispered.

Madison placed her hands on her hips. "And that's why you didn't tell the cops, because you were worried about yourself? That's pretty selfish, dude."

"You have me all figured out," Kevin muttered.

"Did Helena know about the senator?" Aerin asked.

Kevin shrugged. "We didn't exchange details. We were just there for each other so people didn't ask questions."

"Did anyone else know you guys weren't for real?" Seneca piped up.

"No one." When Kevin glanced at Aerin, his expression was bleak. "I'm sorry."

With that, he turned on his heel and walked solemnly back to the party, his back straight, his hands limp at his sides. He seemed so much less dangerous than he had a few minutes ago, as though revealing his secret had stolen his power. Maddox felt bad for the guy.

Once Kevin rounded the corner, Maddox pointed at Seneca. "You read his mind."

"I just smelled him," Seneca said offhandedly, though she had a pleased smile on her face.

Maddox turned to Aerin. She was leaning against the wall limply, like she'd been hit over the head with a golf club. "Are you okay?"

Aerin shakily took out a compact and started to reapply her lipstick.

"I don't know." She glanced at Maddox, then Seneca. "That was amazing. I didn't think you guys had it in you."

Maddox beamed. "If Kevin *is* telling the truth, maybe Helena really had a boyfriend from New York."

"Some guy she must have met *before* she started dating Kevin, because otherwise she wouldn't have needed to recruit him to cover for her," Brett said. "Guys, we should go to the city. It makes sense."

"Let's not get ahead of ourselves," Seneca said. "Aerin, when did Kevin and Helena get together?"

Aerin squinted. "July, I think."

"Did your sister ever go to New York that summer?"

There was a dazed look on Aerin's face. "She did a summer program at NYU, also in July. Maybe she met the guy then?"

"See?" Brett urged. "All signs point to New York. It's easy to get there on the train."

Kevin might have left in a daze, but everyone figured he'd probably call security within minutes. They found an exit door that led straight to the packed parking lot. Brett looked around for the two caterers who'd taken their Patrón, but they weren't back. In fact, the parking lot was eerily empty.

"Screw it," he said, tearing off his jacket. "Let's just leave the tuxes on the curb." He unbuttoned the shirt, revealing tight, sculpted abs. Then he proceeded to strip off his tiny pants, too, letting out a sigh of relief. He stood in the parking lot in a pair of black Under Armour boxer-briefs.

Madison whistled. Maddox gawked. He might be an elite runner, but he'd never be that jacked. "Holy Magic Mike," Aerin murmured appreciatively.

Brett struck a jokey male-stripper pose, then bunched the clothes from the back of Maddox's Jeep under his arm. "Can someone run me back to my hotel?" he asked nonchalantly.

"I'll drop you after Madison," Aerin offered. She was still eyeing him up and down. Brett made a move to get into the front seat of her car, and Aerin giggled. "You going to put your clothes on first?"

"Oh, yeah." Brett quickly pulled on his shirt, stretching all his taut stomach and chest muscles as he lifted his arms over his head. *Show-off,* Maddox thought good-naturedly.

Madison slid into the backseat. "I need to smoke, eat some Cheez-Its, and go to bed."

"I can't believe you people are ready for bed," Seneca said. "I'm way too wired."

"Me too." Maddox looked at her. "Wanna stay out?"

Seneca turned to him with a look of surprise. "Um. Yeah. Okay."

Aerin started the engine and cranked Katy Perry's "Firework." Soon enough, the parking lot was silent again, the only sound the buzzing crickets. Maddox grabbed his jeans, ducked behind one of the cars, and stepped out of his tux pants, too.

"Lucky," Seneca said dourly. "You get to change, while I'm still stuck in this." She twisted uncomfortably in her tight dress, making the skirt twirl.

"Yeah, but you look good," Maddox said idly, before he remembered it was Seneca—she probably wouldn't appreciate him treating her like one of the airheaded girls at school, always fishing for compliments.

Seneca's head shot up. "You mean the *dress* looks good."

Maddox blinked, not sure how to respond to that—was he really supposed to agree that it was the dress that was pretty and not Seneca herself? But before he could dig the hole any deeper, he heard a loud crack behind him. He grabbed Seneca's arm and whipped around, scanning the line of cars. He heard a fluttering sound, and then a whisper. The shadows rippled. The moon drifted behind a cloud.

"What is it?" Seneca hissed, her eyes wide.

"I don't know." Maddox felt a sudden prickly sensation, like he was being watched. He glanced sidelong at her. "I keep thinking about the fire. And that voice you heard through the door. I guess it's just freaking me out."

Seneca was about to speak, but suddenly, there was a *whoosh*. Something gigantic dove for his head. He ducked and yelped. When he looked up, two huge, majestic, outstretched wings flapped skyward.

The owl settled on one of the peaks on the roof and glared at them, its round yellow eyes glowing. Maddox and Seneca clutched each other, neither of them breathing. Then Maddox laughed weakly, slowly untangling himself from Seneca. Unsure where to look, he kept his attention focused on the owl.

After a calm, thoughtful blink, the owl lifted off the roof and swooped away.

SIXTEEN

FOR A FEW blocks, Seneca and Maddox walked in tense silence. Seneca could tell the owl had shaken up Maddox. What was pathetic was that it had kind of freaked her out, too.

"There's no one watching us," she assured herself as much as him. "That's nuts."

"But maybe we're on the right track. Maybe Helena's secret boyfriend is trying to silence us."

"If Helena did have a secret boyfriend, who's to say he wasn't a nice guy?" Not that she believed that. Still, she couldn't possibly believe that someone was spying on them, even trying to hurt them.

The country club was nestled in a neighborhood where every property was at least seven thousand square feet of mansion and sat on ten acres of pristinely landscaped lawn. Horses whinnied at a fence a few yards away. An import sports car rumbled at a stop sign ahead of them, its rear lights winking. Finally, Maddox gestured down an embankment at a large parking lot that led to a long line of 4-H barns. It seemed to have popped up out of nowhere. "Check it out."

He was pointing at a carnival in the parking lot. Seneca must have been really lost in her thoughts, because she heard the loud, jarring calliope music and smelled the lardy, sugary funnel cake all at once, as though jolting out of a dream. A Ferris wheel with spokes that looked as spindly and breakable as Popsicle sticks whirled. A rocket ship ride, neon lights blinking, shot screaming kids into the air. There were yelps from spinning teacups. In the distance, a large structure called the Time Machine twinkled. *See the Future!* read a neon sign on the top.

A pathway opened in Seneca's brain, and she glanced at Maddox. "It's the Dexby Firemen's Carnival, isn't it?"

Maddox cocked his head. "You're like a Dexby-pedia."

Seneca shrugged. "I just do my homework." Truthfully, Helena used to post about this on Facebook. "It's definitely a breath of fresh air after that country club. All that opulence and pageantry freaks me out."

Maddox gestured toward the midway. "Go, then. Be with the common folk."

Seneca started down the embankment, careful not to slip in Madison's uncomfortable heels. She was serious about hating what she was wearing—she felt constricted in the shoes and stiff dress. Still, she tried to forget about it and let the soul music from the merry-go-round wash over her. On the right were a bunch of hokey but fun games like Guess Your Weight, Ring Toss, and Balloon Pop. People smiled in Seneca's direction, probably amused at how overdressed she was, and she smiled back, embracing it.

"What a night," she sighed. Part of her wanted to grab Maddox's arm and rehash the situation, saying, "Can you believe Kevin *cracked*?" or "Do you think they were making out in the *bathroom*?" But then, she didn't want to seem overly excited. She should act like she interrogated people all the time! And she still wasn't exactly sure where she and Maddox stood. She'd appreciated the Red Stripe he brought for her at his house. It was also satisfying that they'd both come to the same conclusion about Kevin at the same time. So were they friends again? Co–crime solvers?

As they passed a big booth full of cheesy-message T-shirts, Maddox blurted, "Dude, that was crazy back there. I never thought Kevin was going to spill his guts!"

Seneca grinned. Guess he'd been thinking the same thing. "I feel bad for him. It must be terrible having to hide such a big truth about yourself." As soon as the words tumbled from her mouth, she caught herself. Hadn't she been doing the same thing by omitting the truth about her mom? She glanced at Maddox, wondering if he'd made that connection, too, but his expression gave nothing away.

"I guess Helena lied, too," Maddox said.

Seneca considered that. All this time, she'd maintained that Helena must have had a secret, but she had actually hoped that she was wrong. Helena had seemed so carefree, so innocent in pictures and videos. If this young girl could be hiding dark secrets, that meant that anyone could be. Even her mom.

Only, she'd known her mom best. Collette often hummed when she was hiding something, and she doodled when a problem was on her mind. That fateful morning, she'd been relaxed and composed, placidly doing Sudoku. There had been no inky, distracted squiggles on her day planner. She'd hummed no nervous tunes. If Seneca were to make her best educated guess, Collette hadn't known she was going off to her death when she pulled into Target. It had just been . . . a *day*.

A scream rose up from one of the rides, and Seneca whipped around, still on edge from the screech owl and the confrontation with Kevin. Maddox had crossed the midway to the cotton candy booth, purchasing big, flossy whorls for both of them. He handed Seneca one. She took a huge bite of it, the sugar dissolving on her tongue. "*Uch*, I can feel the cavities forming," she scoffed.

"And yet you're still eating it." Then he peered into the crowd. "Who here screams cotton candy to you?"

Seneca licked some sticky sugar off her lip. Maddox was referring to the candy game they'd made up, but it felt too intimate now. She didn't answer.

"Come on." Maddox nudged her. "I say her."

He pointed to a blond girl across the midway in tall wedge heels and a white minidress that barely covered her butt. Seneca burst out laughing. She looked a lot like the girl who'd sat across from her on the train, the one who'd been reading *OK!*

Seneca decided to join in after all. "I guess he's the guy version." Seneca pointed at a built, chiseled-faced guy on a bench near a T-shirt stand. He wore tight hipster jeans and complicated high-tops, had a blue streak in his hair, and kept checking a huge iPhone.

Maddox looked surprised. "That's Chase Howard, from my school. His parents have houses in five countries. I would have said he was something complex that a lot of people don't know about. Like Japanese candy that tastes like green tea."

Seneca watched as the kid glanced shiftily in all directions. It was like he was making sure people were checking him out. "I don't see him as a deep soul."

Maddox chuckled. "And here I was going to set you guys up. He seemed like your type."

Seneca flinched. Was it weird to talk about dating? Or was she just thinking that because Maddox was a guy and kind of told her, earlier, that he thought she was pretty? Then again, maybe she shouldn't read too much into that. It was probably just the heels-and-dress thing that he was into.

She jutted her chin in the air. "You don't have a clue who my type is."

"Then enlighten me." The corners of Maddox's mouth pulled into a teasing smile. "I already know it's not someone who likes football."

Seneca felt her cheeks redden. She couldn't believe he remembered that conversation. "Sorry if I want someone to pay attention to me instead of what's on TV," she snapped.

"Yeah, but wasn't that Super Bowl weekend?" Maddox asked.

"So?"

"See, that's what you don't understand about guys." Maddox made a clucking sound with his tongue. "It's the *Super Bowl*. Of course his eyes were going to be glued to the screen. You should be flattered he agreed to even leave the house." He cuffed her shoulder. "It's comforting that a college girl still doesn't get it. But don't worry. Girls are tough to figure out, too."

Seneca wanted to snort. As if Maddox ever had trouble with girls! "I bet I'd have better luck finding your type than you'd have finding mine."

Maddox put his hands on his hips. "Go on. Try."

"Okay, then." Seneca peered through the crowd. A girl with long, straight blond hair, huge brown eyes, a skimpy pink tee, and frayed white denim shorts walked in a line with three other, less pretty girls dressed just like her. "Her. The blonde in the middle."

Maddox sucked in his breath. "Oh. That's Tara."

The name resonated in Seneca's mind. "*Hot-booty* Tara? The runner?"

"You don't have to scream it," he muttered.

"Why?" A smile crept onto Seneca's lips. "*Do* you like her?"

Before he could answer, Tara's head swiveled toward them. She waggled her fingers at Maddox, then hurried over gracefully. She was probably the type of girl who never tripped in heels, Seneca thought with a mixture of disdain and envy. "Maddy!" Tara said when she got close. "I didn't know you were coming tonight."

Maddox shrugged. "Decided at the last minute." He gestured at Seneca. "This is my friend Seneca."

Tara's eyes narrowed at Seneca's dress and heels, but then her gaze snapped back to Maddox. She touched the cotton candy still on his stick. "Did you actually eat this? I thought your body was a temple." She tittered girlishly, edging closer to him. Maddox moved slightly but pointedly away. Only Seneca caught the pained look on his face . . . and the enamored look on Tara's. And that's when she got it: This beautiful girl was crazy about *him*.

She tried to see Maddox as Tara might. He was certainly nice and tall. His green eyes kind of shone in the diffused light of the fair, and his hair was especially wavy from the humidity. The blinking carnival lights showed off the edges of his jaw and cheekbones, and his shoulders were broad, though he wasn't quite as built as Brett. Even the soft gray Giants T-shirt he'd changed into looked sexy suddenly, when before Seneca had just thought it seemed sort of blah and predictable. She blinked furiously, trying to get her old vision of Maddox back, but it was as though Tara's presence had transformed him—now all she could see was Cute Guy.

Tara touched his forearm again, saying something about a 5K race. Maddox pulled away once more. He still had the polite smile, but he kept rubbing his thumb and middle finger together, a tense tic Seneca had noticed before. She found an appropriate pause and edged in closer.

"Uh, Maddox? I think I've smoked too much weed. Can you take me home?"

Maddox gave Seneca a brief, confused look, but then seemed to get it. "Of course." He nodded to the girls. "See you later. Have fun tonight."

"Call me!" Tara cried after them.

Seneca yanked his arm around a series of booths and finally came to a stop behind a cart that sold strudel. Maddox leaned against a trash can and breathed out. "Good save. You're an awesome wingman."

Seneca bit her lip. She felt kind of annoyed being called a wingman, especially after being in the presence of such a pretty girl. "Yeah, well, I was getting sick of your big-man-on-campus act," she muttered.

He crossed his arms over his chest. "You mean you weren't impressed?"

"No," she snapped. "I'm not into big egos."

Seneca knew her tone was snooty and superior, but she hadn't expected the wounded look on Maddox's face. "Right," he said. "I guess for a college girl like you, I'm a total jackass."

Seneca lowered her eyes. She didn't know why she'd said that. She hadn't meant to hurt him. "Actually, I'd have to be *enrolled* in college for you to call me a college girl."

Maddox stared at her in puzzlement. "Wait, what? Did you drop out?"

Seneca studied some ants devouring a watermelon rind. "Not really. But forget it."

Maddox frowned. "Come on, Seneca. You can tell me. You used to tell me everything."

She glanced at him. *Used to.* Yeah, online. When she'd thought he was someone completely different. But suddenly, she did want to tell him. She needed to tell *someone*. And after their encounter with Kevin, she didn't want to pretend she was something she wasn't.

"So you know how I told you I was struggling in school?" She sighed. "I'm kind of . . . *beyond* struggling. Failing everything is more like it. My advisor pulled me aside before spring break and said I should take a little break from school, regroup, and come back next year."

Maddox chewed on his lip. "Shit. Did you tell your family?"

"Hell no. I put my stuff in storage because I didn't want to move home over spring break and tell my dad." She tried to chuckle, like this was all just a silly misunderstanding that could be easily straightened out, but the laugh caught in her throat. "U of M is his alma mater. He was so excited when I got in—especially when I got a scholarship. After everything I've been through . . . it seemed like this huge victory."

Maddox's throat bobbed. He looked like he wanted to ask all kinds of questions, but Seneca was happy he didn't give in to the temptation. "So what do you want to do?"

"I don't know." She fiddled with her necklace. "I went to college because it seemed so healthy and wholesome. It's what he wanted for me. What *everyone* wanted for me." She was the success story, after all. The girl who'd been through so much but had also managed to get a 4.0 GPA, an almost perfect score on her SATs, and a full ride to Maryland's state school. Her hands trembled as she smoothed down her dress. "But college doesn't feel right at all."

Maddox looked bowled over. "Maybe you're at the wrong college?"

Seneca wished it were that easy. She wished there was some ideal place for her where everything just felt . . . *right*. And then she realized: Being here, in Dexby, questioning Kevin—*this* felt right. The hot feeling in her chest that usually never left had subsided tonight, she noticed for the first time. But it wasn't like she could do *this* with her life, be some kind of professional Veronica Mars–style PI or something. Life wasn't a TV show.

When she looked up again, Maddox was staring at her sympathetically, his eyes crinkling at the corners. It looked like he was going to say something nice—maybe something achingly nice. She wasn't sure if she deserved that right now.

A figure emerged at the corner of her eye, and she leapt up, glad for the distraction. "Tara at ten o'clock!" she cried, dragging Maddox to his feet. "And she's coming our way!"

"I'm outta here." Maddox turned and scampered in the other direction. Giggling, Seneca chased after him toward the bounce house. Zigging and zagging, they raced around the Time Machine ride, which featured antiquated drawings of flying cars. Seneca gasped for air as she tried to keep up with him, sprinting by a photo booth that said *Visit Your Past!* where people were dressed up in turn-of-the-century petticoats, wide-brimmed bonnets, and pants with suspenders.

She stopped to catch her breath, suppressing a laugh. She'd just literally run by the future and the past. It was like some benevolent God was trying to teach Seneca a lesson, tell her that she needed to deal with her issues. Well, maybe she would, eventually. But right now, staying in the present was feeling pretty good.

SEVENTEEN

WEDNESDAY MORNING, MADDOX heard breakfast sounds in the kitchen and started down the stairs. Seneca was seated next to Madison at the kitchen table, dressed in a heather-gray T-shirt and pale blue polka-dotted pajama pants. She had her hair pulled up, and the leaping dolphin temporary tattoo she'd gotten at the carnival was still affixed to the back of her neck. In a fit of silliness, they'd picked ironic tattoos for one another. Maddox's was a peeing Calvin from *Calvin and Hobbes* on his biceps.

Madison, who had on pink skinny jeans and a filmy black top that already smelled like weed, was doing her usual ask-fifty-thousand-questions-all-at-the-same-time routine, grilling Seneca about an after-school job and what her favorite bands were. When she asked Seneca if she liked college, Maddox caught her eye and raised his eyebrows.

Seneca pointed at him warningly. *Don't say a word,* she mouthed over Madison's shoulder.

Maddox held up his hands in surrender. "I didn't!" Then he held up the coffee carafe. "Want some more?"

Seneca held out her mug. "Yes, please. You people make it so weak it's practically decaf." She looked discouragingly at the bag of grounds. "*And* it's not fair-trade."

Maddox scoffed. "You think the funnel cake you ate last night was fair-trade?"

"I needed *something* to refuel from burning off a zillion calories running away from *your* girlfriend." Seneca rolled her eyes at Madison.

"Don't listen to her." Maddox snagged a donut from the box on the counter.

Madison remained at the table, smiling sagely. "You know, you two are super cute."

"Why, thank you!" Seneca said.

Maddox rolled his eyes. "She means *us*, Seneca. Together."

Seneca snorted out a laugh. "Please."

But when Maddox and Seneca both looked back at Madison, she was staring at both of them with a dreamy half smile. "You've got it all wrong," Seneca said as she headed for the powder room in the hall. "Maddox likes someone with a hot booty."

"Lies, all lies," Maddox shouted after her.

When the bathroom door shut, Maddox pointed at his stepsister. "Don't try to be Cupid, okay? Things started out weird enough between us. I'm only finally feeling like our friendship is getting back to normal."

Madison blinked innocently. "I didn't say anything."

"I know what you're thinking." Maddox had had fun with Seneca last night. More fun than he'd had in a while. Because they were so different, the whole situation felt . . . safe. Cool. The last thing he needed was for Madison to screw that up. He wasn't sure he'd ever *had* a girl as a friend.

"So then you don't find her cute at *all*?" Madison cried.

Maddox glared at the closed bathroom door. Madison wasn't even trying to be quiet. "Of course she's cute," he whispered. "But she wouldn't be into me anyway. We're too different."

Madison crossed her arms over her chest. "Why'd you tell her you were into your coach?"

Maddox frowned, then realized why Madison had assumed Seneca had been talking about Catherine when she said Maddox liked someone with a hot booty. He started to correct her that it was Tara Sykes he'd run from, but then Seneca emerged from the bathroom, and the conversation didn't feel appropriate.

Catherine. Actually, he had a coaching session in a half hour; he couldn't cancel again. How should he play this? He'd never been in a predicament where a girl had rejected him—and, okay, maybe it *was* sort of bothering him, the incident playing over and over in his mind like a crappy refrain. But whatever—Catherine wouldn't bring it up again. They'd just forget about it, and soon enough they'd be comfortably coach and student again, the universe back on its axis.

He had nothing to worry about.

TWENTY MINUTES LATER, Maddox pulled into the parking lot at the rec center, checked his reflection in the rearview mirror, and got out of the Jeep. It was freezing outside, and he hadn't brought a warmer layer over his tee. The smell of the pines assaulted him, fragrant and strong.

Catherine instantly appeared from behind the bleachers like she'd been lying in wait. "Let's go inside, shall we?" she said in a neutral tone he'd never heard before, gesturing to the entrance to the indoor track. "We need to talk."

Maddox stiffened. *Talk?*

Catherine had a sober look on her face as she walked. All sorts of scenarios wound through Maddox's mind. What if what he did got him in trouble? Maybe Catherine was so weirded out she didn't want to work with him anymore. Would his college future be in jeopardy? Catherine had been hugely influential in convincing the Oregon coach to give him a scholarship—her family had connections at the school, which she'd used to persuade the Oregon coach to review his times and watch a video of his best races.

The indoor track was empty, and their footsteps echoed on the bouncy red floor. Catherine, who also worked as an athletic director here, led him all the way into her office, a small room tucked into the girls' locker area. It was filled with schedules of the summer track team she coached. At the back was a small desk littered with papers, and there were a few medals piled on a dusty shelf. The air smelled musty and astringent, like Ajax.

Catherine perched on her desk and looked at him. "You missed practice yesterday."

Maddox blinked, surprised. "Sorry. I'll make up for it. Run double today."

She waved her hand. "It's fine. I just wanted to make sure you were...okay."

There was a sensitive but possibly patronizing look on her face, but Maddox grinned confidently like he hadn't noticed. "I'm awesome. I missed yesterday because I had plans. I should've explained."

"Kevin Larssen's engagement party, right?"

He raised his eyebrows, surprised. "Yeah. How did you know?"

"Because I belong to that country club, too. My family knows the Larssen family." She smiled. "It was a nice party, huh?"

Maddox rolled his jaw. Had Catherine *been* there? "I didn't see you," he said slowly.

Catherine's smile didn't waver. "I came late. I saw you in the parking lot—I think you were leaving. Did you have fun?"

He shrugged. "Sure."

"Were you there with friends?"

"Uh-huh. And my stepsister."

"And that Seneca girl? The one you were worried about?"

"Yeah . . ."

"Is she the half-black girl? With you in the parking lot? You guys went off together?"

A warm sensation washed over his skin. She'd been watching him? What, was she jealous now?

"She's really pretty." Catherine's smile quirked. "I thought you had a thing for older women, though. Authority figures."

She fluttered her eyelashes. Maddox struggled to shift gears. Had she changed her mind about being with him?

"I was scared when I pushed you away the other day," Catherine said softly, her breath warm on his cheek. "But I can't stop thinking about you. I can't stop thinking that I made the wrong decision and that I let what could be an amazing thing go."

Maddox took stock of her gaze. There wasn't any playfulness there. Her eyes were intense and smoldering. "Um," he said, finally finding his voice. "Okay . . ."

A small, ethical part of him wanted to ask her if she was sure, but he'd dreamed about this for years—how could he pass up the opportunity if she wanted him, too? So he leaned closer. Touched her shoulders. Pulled her toward him, closing the space between them, sliding his hands down her slender back and then just under the hem of her shirt, feeling her arch into him. Finally, he pressed his lips to hers.

He tasted the ChapStick on her lips, felt her shift and moan softly against him. She deepened the kiss quickly. Was he doing this right? He'd never made out with an older girl before. Of course he was doing it fine. She wasn't stopping, was she? Why couldn't he just turn his brain off and enjoy this?

As they broke apart, breathing deeply, Catherine shot him a sexy smile, and he pulled her right back in. He'd been overthinking things for way too long. He needed to break the habit.

Nothing a little practice wouldn't fix.

EIGHTEEN

LATER ON WEDNESDAY, Aerin clonked down all three tiers of her patio and padded several paces into the yard. That was as far as she went, though. Even five years later, Helena's ghost ruled the property. Aerin could almost see her by the deck, rolling an imaginary snowball. Or near the three-tiered bird feeder, telling Aerin Cap'n Crunch was a good puppy name. Aerin envisioned the red leather gloves she'd found at the edge of the woods. Had Mystery Dude ripped them off her and thrown them into the snow? Didn't he know they'd cost three hundred bucks at Bergdorf's?

Buzz.

It was a text from Thomas Grove. *Ferrari Guy says I can borrow his car for the nite. Pick u up at 7?*

Ha, ha, Aerin wrote back. *Good one.*

The phone buzzed again. *Damn, I thought that would work. I guess u would have been pissed when I showed up on the motorcycle, though.*

What kind of bike? Aerin texted.

A Norton. Used to be my grandpa's.

Aerin smiled. She had a weakness for vintage bikes.

Her phone pinged again. A picture popped up. *Just call me Magic Mike,* read the caption, and Brett stood half-naked in front of a mirror, flexing his pecs. He squinted with a look that was clearly supposed to be sexy, but really he just looked kind of constipated. Aerin giggled.

A Jeep rolled into the driveway. Seneca climbed out of the passenger seat, dressed in a black tee, a flouncy denim skirt, and red Converse. The back door opened, and Brett emerged next, then Madison. Maddox was typing on his phone. He didn't look up the whole way to the back gate.

Aerin opened the latch to let them into the yard. Brett caught her eye. "Like my text?"

Aerin lowered her lashes. "Loved it, big boy. Especially your sexy face." She gave him the lightest tap on the butt with the tips of her fingers. He was fun to flirt with. It was so nice that they were on the same page about it, too—bantering back and forth with no pressure of anything more. How refreshing, to hang out with guys who didn't just want to get into her pants.

She walked back up the first level of the patio and settled onto a chaise. Maddox poked a planter overflowing with impatiens. "So how are we going to figure out who this secret Samurai Knight might be?"

"I'm going to call Helena's old friends," Aerin said. "I've already started making a list of everyone she was close with."

"I put in a call to Becky Reed," Seneca said, referencing Helena's old best friend. "But she didn't tell me anything new. Just about that summer program she did in the city."

Aerin remembered Helena going off to the city that July. She'd wanted to meet her during those two weeks, but Helena said she was too busy. Aerin had thought it was because her sister didn't want to be seen in New York City with an eleven-year-old, but maybe she had other reasons. Maybe she'd met someone she didn't want Aerin to know about.

Seneca crossed and uncrossed her legs. "Maybe her secret boyfriend was a precollege kid, like her. In that same program."

"Kevin seemed to think he was someone older," Maddox reminded her.

Aerin squinted. "A guy who taught the course?"

Seneca made a face. "I suppose it's possible. We could look up who was teaching."

Maddox held up his phone. "Here we go." On the screen was the NYU home page for a summer program in film and comparative literature. He clicked on the list of course instructors and frowned. "Well, there are a bunch of men on the roster for this year's program. But how do we know who was teaching six years ago?"

Seneca put her finger to her chin. "Let's call NYU."

"Let's *go* to NYU," Brett urged.

Seneca looked at him. "We can't just go without having someone to look for. As far as I'm concerned, *Kevin's* still a suspect. What if he killed Helena to keep her quiet about him and the senator?"

"I agree," Maddox said. "We can't rule Kevin out until we have proof that he really *was* at that conference. Just because he was keeping a secret for Helena doesn't mean he's innocent."

Aerin pulled her bottom lip into her mouth. In the Ferrari, Thomas had mentioned that he'd read something about Kevin in Helena's file. Was it about him and the senator, or something else?

Seneca looked at Aerin. "Can we look through Helena's room?"

Aerin's stomach knotted. She'd figured this moment would come, but it still felt unwelcome. "I guess . . ."

She opened the sliding glass door and started inside, then stopped short. Her mom stood in the kitchen—Aerin had thought she'd left for Scoops already. Marissa Ingram stood next to her, holding a long, breezy maxi dress up to her scrawny figure. "Skip is going to *love* this."

Aerin tiptoed backward. Her ankle turned, and she banged loudly into the vertical blinds on the sliding door, knocking them together.

"Aerin?" Her mom craned her neck. Then she spied the others, who were jumbled up behind her. "Who've you got there?"

Seneca stepped up and held out her hand to Mrs. Kelly. "Seneca. Aerin's study partner."

Marissa put a hand to her chest. "Studying even over break?"

Madison stepped forward. "And I'm Madison. I think we met, Mrs. Kelly—I love your ice cream."

Brett shook Mrs. Kelly's hand emphatically and said, "This is a beautiful house for two beautiful ladies."

"Um, good to see you again, too," Maddox mumbled, and Mrs. Kelly just stared at him, probably not making the connection. Aerin didn't fill in the blanks. The less her mom knew, the better.

Marissa touched Aerin's elbow. "It was lovely to see you at the party last night."

Aerin grimaced. *Shit.*

Her mother's head swiveled. "What party?"

"Kevin Larssen's engagement," Marissa chirped.

Mrs. Kelly's mouth dropped open. "*You* went to Kevin's engagement?"

Aerin shrugged, pretending to be overly interested in the scented candle on the island.

"It was divine, Elizabeth," Marissa cooed. "The food...the band...very tasteful. You should have come. But you *will* come to the Morgenthaus' Easter party, right?"

Mrs. Kelly was still looking quizzically at Aerin. For a moment, the only sound in the kitchen was the rushing of the water filtration system inside the refrigerator. Aerin braced for a confrontation—and maybe she wanted one. But then her mom turned to Marissa. "Let me show you which annuals the gardener is putting in this year."

"Of course," Marissa said, taking her arm.

Aerin saw that as her cue, and she guided the group upstairs. After a moment, she heard the sliding glass door to the deck open again. She pointed the others to a closed door at the end of the hall. "That's her room."

Brett was first down the hall, but he stepped aside and let Aerin turn the knob. He seemed to understand that no one had been in this room in a long, long time.

The room smelled like dust. Helena's bed was carefully made with the same pink sheets that had been there when she vanished. Her bureau was clear of clutter, which was different than Aerin remembered it—the police had left the place tidier than they'd found it. Aerin's heart squeezed. She'd come into this room one or two other times since Helena vanished. All she could think now was of how the police had swabbed the place for fingerprints and hairs. Forensically, so much of her sister was *still* here—dead skin cells embedded in the mattress, picked-off fingernails ground into the carpet, DNA from her lips adhered to her lip gloss. If only all those atoms could gather together and reconfigure Helena.

She looked over her shoulder at the others in the hall. "Come in."

Everyone stepped inside and started to look around. Aerin walked across the room and ran her fingers along the spines of books on Helena's bookshelf. *Twilight.* *To Kill a Mockingbird.* She picked up *Wreck This Journal* and flipped through it, but Helena hadn't filled out a single page. Next to it was the diary Aerin had poked through the day Helena had taken off, neatly put away. It was one of the first things the police had looked at, hoping for clues, but besides a few pages of copied song lyrics and a list of vintage items Helena wanted to buy (*quilted Chanel purse, Pucci shift, silver belt buckle*), the journal was blank.

"Look," Aerin said, holding up a course catalog for NYU's summer program from six years ago. Everyone gathered around as she flipped to the pictures of the professors. All the guys teaching the film classes looked sort of average.

Brett grabbed his phone. "I'll look up details about these dudes. Maybe one of them has a record. Or maybe we'll see evidence on Facebook that they flirt with college girls."

Aerin nodded, then went back to searching. Seneca poked in the closet. Maddox had Helena's laptop open on the bed—which Aerin wasn't thrilled about, especially because the cops had already gone through it. Brett trolled Facebook, but after a few minutes, he let out a sigh. "Not a single teacher has a Facebook page. What are the odds of that?"

"And you know, the police have already gone through all of this room," Aerin mumbled. "I don't know what we think we're going to find."

She moved to Helena's desk, yanking open the top drawer. There were a few pencils with worn lead, pink rubber erasers, a blue Sharpie. Aerin touched an old punch card for Connecticut Pizza; apparently, Helena needed to eat only two more slices to get one for free. Then she noticed a ticket stub stuck to the inside wall that could have gone

unnoticed. It was for a band called Gel Apocrypha dated the July
before Helena went missing. Aerin squinted at the location of the show:
Houston Street, in New York City. She flipped it over. *Call me,* read
messy scrawl. And then the name *Greg*, a phone number, and then the
words *Love U.*

Aerin must have had a strange look on her face, because Seneca
came over and inspected the ticket. "Do you know that band?" Seneca
asked. Aerin shook her head faintly.

"*I* remember them," Maddox blurted. "This was one of the bands
Helena listened to a lot. She told me to download them. They're very
melancholy."

Aerin raised her eyebrows at him. "Wonder who *Greg* is."

Maddox was on his phone again. "There's someone named Greg
Fine in the band. And, hey, they still play gigs. They live in New York
City—and they did back then, too."

Aerin blinked hard. "Greg Fine. That name sounds familiar. I think
he spoke to the cops."

"Meaning he must have had a *reason* to speak to the cops," Seneca
said thoughtfully. "Like someone had seen him and Helena together
maybe. Perhaps someone knew they were an item?"

"Did he have an alibi?" Maddox asked.

"He must have said enough to elude police suspicion," Seneca said.
She clucked her tongue. "What girl doesn't have fantasies about dating a
rock star? Maybe she met him when she was at the summer program—
Houston isn't far from NYU, is it?"

Brett pursed his lips. "I took *cultured* to mean art galleries, not rock
shows, but I guess you never know."

"We should at least try and reach out to him. See what he's
all about."

"Maybe his number still works." Maddox typed into his phone. He listened for a moment, then raised his eyebrows. "Voice mail. But it's his name in the outgoing message."

Then Brett held up Helena's old white iPhone. "We could see if she called him."

"I guess." Aerin shrugged. "Though the cops already scoured that thing before they finally gave it back. Phone records, texts, everything."

"We might as well look, too." Brett surveyed the room. "Got an old charger?"

"In my room, I think," Aerin said. Actually, it was a good excuse to get everyone out of Helena's space. She was starting to feel claustrophobic in there.

She led the group into her bedroom, retrieved a charger from her desk, and plugged it into the phone. The battery-charge icon appeared, and then, after a long pause, a welcome screen popped on. Helena's wallpaper, a cheerful picture of her and Becky Reed, appeared. An icon up top showed four bars of connectivity.

Aerin's mouth dropped open. "This still has service."

Seneca walked over. "You think your mom forgot to disconnect it?"

"I bet she couldn't make the call to Verizon," Aerin said softly, remembering how Helena's subscription to *Teen Vogue* had arrived at the door a full year after she disappeared.

She clicked on the contacts icon and scrolled through the list. Sure enough, there was someone named Greg in Helena's phone contacts; the number she'd entered matched the number on the ticket. Aerin scrolled through Helena's received and dialed calls, and Greg's number popped up a few times. What had they been talking about?

Bzzzt.

Aerin almost dropped Helena's phone. "Oh my God," she whispered, staring at the new message on the screen. *One new voice mail.*

Maddox crowded behind her. "Did this just come in?"

"I—I don't know," Aerin said shakily.

Maddox grabbed the phone, made a few swiping motions, and then his eyebrows shot up. "The message is from January 27, five and a half years ago. I'm surprised Verizon even saved a message that old." He pressed the screen a few times. "She got a text that day, too. It just says, *Call me.*"

"Is it from Greg Fine?" Seneca asked excitedly.

"Actually, no." Maddox looked confused. "It's from a 917 number she entered as Loren, no last name. Spelled L-O-R-E-N. Wonder if that's a girl or a guy."

"Is *she* in the band?" Seneca asked.

Maddox shook his head. "I didn't see anyone named Loren on Gel Apocrypha's *Wikipedia* page." He looked at Aerin. "Does the name ring any bells?"

Aerin felt stunned. "I've never heard that name in my life."

Maddox pressed the CALL VOICE MAIL prompt, then set the phone to speaker. Everyone gathered around to listen. *Please enter your password,* an automated voice said.

Seneca looked at Aerin. "Any idea what it might be?"

Aerin's mind felt blank. She picked up the phone and typed in Helena's birthday, but that wasn't it. The year she would have graduated? Their address, 1564 Round Hill Lane? Then she thought of those silly numbers on top of the karaoke machine. *Contains 1,045 songs!* With shaking hands, she typed in *1045. You have one new message in your mailbox,* the voice said.

Aerin's heart thudded. Seneca nodded encouragingly. Brett squeezed her shoulder and whispered that it was going to be okay. Taking a deep breath, Aerin pressed 1 to listen.

There was a whooshing noise on the other end. Horn honks. And then an unfamiliar, gravelly male voice blared through, aggressive and insistent: "It's Loren, bitch. We need to talk. I'll be at Kiko, same details as before. You'd better show up."

Click.

NINETEEN

ON THURSDAY MORNING, Seneca and the others rode a Metro-North train toward New York. The sun shone brightly through the dirty windows. The clouds in the blue sky looked plush and fluffy, the kind you could make animal shapes out of. Inside, though, Seneca felt gray and tumultuous, the way she always did when she was wading into the unknown. They'd left Greg Fine a couple of voice mails posing as reporters for a college paper wanting an interview about his band, but he hadn't called back. And Loren? Well, *he* sounded dangerous. Seneca couldn't believe the detectives had missed his message. They should have monitored Helena's phone a little longer. They should have called this guy and interrogated him, asked him what he was so pissed about.

It made her wonder what the detectives had missed in her mom's case.

Her phone buzzed, and she directed her attention to the screen. A Google Alert for a Dexby news report read, *New Investigation Shows Restful Inn Fire Possibly Arson.*

A sick feeling welled through her. She tapped to read the story, but there were no real details—just that the hotel's electrical wiring was solid and the police were shifting gears. Should she tell them about the thin, ragged voice she'd heard outside her door? Had she even *heard* a voice?

To take her mind off worrying, she clicked on the huge bank of old interviews from right after Helena disappeared. Randomly selecting one, she watched as a scene outside Windemere-Carruthers school appeared. "All the students have been in intense questioning since Helena Kelly disappeared," a reporter was saying to the camera. Behind her lurked a brunette girl with sharp eyebrows and full pink lips. Seneca frowned. Even years ago, she'd noticed this girl—she'd been in the background during a few other interviews, too. There was something off-putting about her.

She tapped Aerin, who was sitting next to her. "Who is this?"

Aerin squinted. "Oh. That's Katie. She was in Helena's grade." Her face clouded. "They used to be friends, but . . ."

Seneca cocked her head. "Did something happen?"

"All I remember is that my mom asked if Helena wanted to invite her to her birthday dinner, and Helena was like, *definitely not*. It was right around the time Helena started changing—dressing differently, hiding stuff, you know."

Seneca stared at the screen. She had hit PAUSE at a precise moment where Katie's lips were pursed mischievously. "Should we talk to her?"

Aerin wrinkled her nose. "They weren't friends when she vanished. And anyway, I remember the cops interviewing her. She had an alibi."

Seneca didn't feel convinced. But she let it drop—they had bigger suspects to question.

Then Aerin gestured to Maddox across the aisle. He had his head tilted back, and his eyes were closed. "Can you believe he's sleeping right now? I'm so nervous I can barely breathe."

"Seriously."

Maddox made a blustery sleep snort. Seneca giggled. "Well, at least someone will be well rested when we arrive." Smiling devilishly, she wadded up her ticket stub and tossed it at his head, aiming for his mouth. It bounced off his cheek, and he jolted up with a gasp.

Maddox twisted in his seat and caught her staring. He raised his eyebrows challengingly.

Seneca rolled her eyes, then turned to face the window.

She hoped he hadn't seen her blush.

AFTER A BUMPY cab ride so short they probably could have just walked, the group pulled onto Twenty-Sixth Street in Chelsea. Wind gusted down the street. Tall concrete buildings rose on either side, some with scaffolding papered with band posters and advertisements. The Hudson glittered at the end of the block. A jogging path ran parallel to the river, with people biking and walking. It seemed so peaceful there. Not a place where a murderer spent his days.

Last night, they'd decided to focus on Loren first. The threatening phone message put him at the top of the list. After him, they'd concentrate on tracking down Greg the guitarist. They looked up Loren's phone number on Google, but no results appeared. After listening to Loren's message a dozen times, they'd determined he was saying the word *Kiko*. They'd searched for matches in New York, and there were a dozen listings for businesses called Kiko in the city: a store that sold professional-quality makeup; a no-kill animal shelter;

a place in Chinatown that, as far as they could guess, sold goat meat; a wireless accessory wholesaler. Finally, Brett found an entry for a Kiko Art Gallery in Chelsea. According to its website, the place specialized in Asian art from the twentieth and twenty-first century. *"Asian art,"* Seneca had said, her excitement building. "Like the cranes. Like *Samurai*." And Kevin had said Helena's secret boyfriend was cultured. If Loren was that guy, then maybe Kiko was their rendezvous spot. Maybe they'd fought about something. Maybe Helena had told him she wanted to end their tryst. Maybe he'd traveled to Connecticut and stolen her out of the woods that snowy day.

Halfway down the block, the word *Kiko* was etched translucently into a front window of a building. Inside was a sparse-looking room; a bloblike sculpture in blond wood sat on a pedestal toward the back. An Asian woman leaned coolly against a front desk.

"How are we going to get past her?" Aerin said out of the corner of her mouth.

In their research about Kiko, they'd discovered that the gallery was semiprivate, only open to serious buyers. To pass through the doors, you had to sign a guest book. The hope was that Loren had signed in . . . and perhaps left an address. The problem was getting access to the guest book. They'd kicked around some ideas last night—they were private investigators; they were Loren's personal assistants taking care of his tax documents and wanted to know when he had last visited; they were from an art magazine wanting details on who was interested in the gallery's pieces. Nothing seemed right.

A garbage truck rumbled noisily down the street. Seneca shifted from foot to foot. Brett stared at the Asian girl in the gallery window, then nudged Madison. "You talk to her."

"Why me?" Madison thumbed her chest.

"Don't Asian chicks stick together? You could say something to her in Chinese, maybe. Do some kung fu. We'd be in for sure."

"Brett!" Seneca chided, half-teasing, half-horrified.

Madison looked confused. "I'm *Korean*."

"Oh." Brett looked blank. "Shit, girl. Sorry." Then he snapped his fingers. "I've got it. I know how we're going to get in. I'm an investor. And I'm from LA—no, *Vegas*. I'm ridiculously wealthy and also ridiculously insecure."

Aerin snickered at him. "Where do you come up with this stuff?"

Maddox rubbed his hands together. "And you're one of those guys who only wants to buy art if it's trendy and everyone else is buying it. So you're ready to drop some cash, but you want to see the guest book to make sure other power players are interested. Because if it's a bunch of no-names on that list, you're not biting."

Brett held out his hand for Maddox to slap five. "Dude, I like the way you think."

Aerin started laughing. "You guys are crazy."

"What?" Brett cocked his head. "It's a perfect plan."

"How are you two going to make them believe you're billionaire art collectors?" Seneca snickered. "You're not really *dressed* the part. . . ."

"We could give you a role," Maddox offered.

"Yeah!" Brett brightened. "You could be my business partner, Seneca. And, Aerin"—he turned to her—"you can be my girlfriend."

Aerin pouted. "How about I'm your girlfriend *and* another business partner?"

"Can I be a model slash heiress you picked up along the way?" Madison asked excitedly.

Seneca rolled back her shoulders and crossed the street. "I have another idea."

"Hey!" Brett called after her. "We're not ready yet! We haven't even come up with names!"

Seneca buzzed to be let in, then pushed open the glass door to the gallery. The room was so air-conditioned that she immediately felt the urge to shiver. The only sounds in the space were the woman's fingers as they tapped a keyboard and Seneca's shoes as they clacked on the wood floor. Finally, the woman stopped typing and glared at Seneca. She was younger than Seneca first thought, wearing a complicated-looking black matte top and leather pants over the skinniest legs Seneca had ever seen. There was a copy of *Cosmo* in her bag. Seneca peeked at the computer screen. She had been looking at OkCupid.

"Can I help you?" the receptionist asked, her tone snooty.

"Hi." Seneca tried to ignore her pounding heart. "I'm supposed to meet someone here, and he says he's a buyer with your gallery. Is there any way to confirm anything about him?"

The girl's gaze returned from the keyboard. "I'm sorry. Our client records are private."

Seneca figured she'd say that. She leaned in confidingly. "I met him on this dating site for rich guys, and he bragged that he's got major cash. Like has-his-own-plane cash. I just want to see if he's legit before I go through with it." She smiled warmly and confidingly. "You don't want me to get catfished, do you?"

The girl ran her tongue over her teeth. A clock ticked above them. "I can't promise you anything. What's his name?"

"Loren...something. Spelled L-O-R-E-N. I don't know his last name yet, so I wasn't able to google him."

The assistant let out a truncated laugh. "I can tell you right now we have no clients named Loren, but I *know* a Loren. Loren Jablonski: He *works* here—in security." She shook her head. "He told you all that?"

Seneca's mind was doing flips, but she tried her hardest to stay in character. "Y-yes," she stammered, faking surprise. "He's a security guard? He doesn't have a private plane?"

"I *doubt* it."

Seneca scoffed. "Wow. That is just . . . wow. Thanks for your help." She moved to leave, but then swiveled back around. "I want to call him out—but I am so not showing up for our date this weekend. Is he in tomorrow?"

The girl clicked something on the computer. "He's here tomorrow morning."

"And you won't tell him I'm going to show up?"

The girl gave her a pitying look. "No way."

As Seneca pushed open the door to the street, she gestured at the blob in the middle of the room. "What's that supposed to be, anyway?"

The girl smiled. "It represents the quiet, steely power of the female essence."

Seneca grinned. Damn right.

Everyone was staring at her as she crossed the street. Brett rushed toward her. "What did she tell you? Did you say we were investors?"

"Loren's a security guard, his last name's Jablonski, he'll be in tomorrow morning, and he doesn't know we're coming," Seneca said confidently, sidestepping a rushing taxicab. "You're welcome!"

Madison let out a low, appreciative whistle. Maddox and Aerin exchanged an impressed look. "Like a boss," Brett murmured. *Boom,* Seneca thought triumphantly. Occasionally, it was fun to blow everyone out of the water.

TWENTY

LATER THAT EVENING, Brett sat on an off-white leather chaise in the middle of a giant suite at the Ritz-Carlton on Central Park South. Three girls sat around him, and he was waxing poetic about Vera Grady's fashion empire. The one closest to him, Sadie, pursed her glossy lips. "Did you get to go to her shows in Paris?"

"Yeah, a couple times," Brett answered. "It was incredible."

"Do you know any celebrities?" the girl on the end asked.

"Matt McConaughey and I hung out once at an after-party," Brett said. "And I had lunch with that guy from *Guardians of the Galaxy*."

The girls swooned. When Brett looked up, Aerin appeared through the crowd like a sunbeam breaking through a thundercloud. Brett found an appropriate moment to say good-bye to the girls and pushed through the throng, weaving around land mines of broken glass and a breakdancing competition. Grabbing a newly opened bottle of champagne from the sideboard, he rushed to Aerin's side.

"Drink?" he said, waving the bottle hypnotically under her nose.

Aerin wobbled from foot to foot. Her eyes were shiny, and her cheeks were flushed; Brett wondered how many drinks she'd already had. "Or maybe not," he said quickly.

But Aerin grabbed the bottle anyway, and before Brett could stop her, she put the whole thing to her mouth for a swig. When she was finished, he directed them to a leather couch in the corner. It was next to the booming speakers, but at least it was semiprivate. "You having fun?" he shouted over the music.

"*Duh,*" Aerin slurred. She swatted Brett clumsily. "This is probably pretty normal for you, huh? Hosting spur-of-the-moment parties?"

Brett shrugged modestly. "I guess I've thrown a few." He didn't want to take all the credit, but he'd put together this shindig himself. Once they realized they had a whole evening to kill before they met Loren, he'd gotten on his phone, scored a hotel suite, ordered ten bottles of Moët & Chandon from a local wine store, and called a Midtown chef to cook the sick spread of food that was sitting on a long buffet table by the wall. He'd found kids on the street, in Starbucks, and shopping on Fifth Avenue, and invited anyone who looked cool to party. He'd even changed out of his oversized-everything outfit and into a sleek button-down and skinny jeans. When he'd first walked out of the bathroom, Aerin had whistled.

Which, of course, was exactly the effect he was going for.

"What were you doing with those girls over there?" Aerin asked in a teasing voice.

"Oh, making shit up to impress them," Brett said modestly.

Aerin snorted. "Yeah right." She pointed at the girls who were still gathered on the chaise. "You sure you don't want to go back? It's like your own little Brett Grady fan club."

"They're beautiful, but I'm not into them like *that*," Brett said quickly.

One eyebrow shot up. "And why not?"

If *that* wasn't a leading question, Brett didn't know what was. He grabbed the champagne and poured some down his throat. Liquid courage, right? He'd tried to keep his feelings for Aerin in check, tried to focus on the case, but it was impossible. She kept flirting with him. He'd caught her checking him out when he'd stripped out of the tux at the country club, and he could tell she was impressed by his stylist skills. And yeah, okay, so she'd mistaken the text of him at the mirror for a joke, but she *had* sent him a selfie back later, her body leaning toward the camera, her lips puckered in a pout.

She liked him. She had to. It made sense: They had so much in common. They shared a tragic history. They came from the same world.

He took a breath. "You know this party is for you, right?"

The corners of Aerin's mouth pulled into a crooked smile. "Me . . . and *just* me?"

"You deserve a party. You deserve a *hundred* parties."

A muscle twitched by Aerin's eye, and she looked out at the crowd. "Hope you've got the cash to pay a clean-up crew." It came out like *crean-up clue.*

"I'm good for it." Normally, Brett would try to corral the group—cleaning bills for hotel suites could cost a fortune. But tonight, he didn't care. The destructive chaos was actually kind of romantic, totally adding to the moment.

He turned back to Aerin. "I'm serious, though. I put this together for you. So are you having fun?"

Aerin blinked at him, her cheeks adorably pink. "You already asked that, Brett, but yes, I am. Thank you."

She sounded grateful. Appreciative. Enamored, even? His heart thudded. He went to grab the champagne bottle, and Aerin did, too.

Their hands bumped. Brett didn't pull away, and neither did Aerin. They looked at each other and laughed. Aerin's face was so close to his that he could feel wisps of her blond hair brushing against his cheek. *Do it,* whispered a voice in his mind. *Kiss her.*

"Guys." Seneca plopped down next to them. "Greg Fine is here."

Brett bit down hard on the inside of his cheek, annoyed. *Worst timing ever.*

"Wait, what?" Aerin swiveled her head around the room. "Where? How?"

"Maddox left him another voice mail saying we want to conduct the interview here, tonight, if he's game. And that's him, by the door." She pointed to a skinny dude in tight jeans. He had a rocker mullet, a pierced nose, and several days' worth of stubble. "I recognize him from his band's Myspace."

Aerin started chewing on her thumbnail. "What should we do?"

Seneca fiddled with the jangling bracelets on her wrist. "Well, interview him, obviously. We could play it like the Kevin thing—get him drunk, see if he talks about Helena."

"Looks like Madison's already on it," Aerin murmured, pointing. Madison had sidled up to Greg and was offering him a bottle of Moët. The dude looked uncomfortable and waved her away.

Aerin caught Brett's eye and gave him a conspiratorial wink. He tried to swallow his impatience and turned back to Fine, who was murmuring something to the buddy he'd brought with him, another rocker with a fauxhawk. Moments later, one of the girls who'd stretched out next to Brett proffered him a Solo cup. Once again, Greg shook his head. Brett wasn't a master lip-reader, but even he could decipher what Greg told her: *Sorry. I don't drink.*

Aerin raised her eyebrows, catching it, too. "What rocker doesn't drink?"

Seneca stood up. "I'll sniff around."

She flounced off, *finally*. Brett turned back to Aerin, relaxing. "So where were we?"

She gave him a saucy smile and edged closer. In this lighting, Aerin looked angelic, her hair glowing around her face, her eyes large and doelike. Brett's heart thumped. *Okay,* he told himself. *Here goes nothing.* He shifted so that he was facing her. Reaching out, he touched a lock of her soft hair and curled it around his finger. It was like spun gold. God, blondes made him crazy.

But then he noticed again how glassy her eyes were. How she wavered back and forth a little as she was sitting next to him. How each time she blinked, her eyes stayed closed a moment too long, as if she was struggling to stay awake. It was clear she was ready to kiss him, but would she even *remember* it? Brett wanted their first kiss to be memorable. Something she wanted to do when she was sober, too.

"Actually," he said, backing away from her slightly and gesturing to a pillow on the couch. "Why don't you lie down? Just for a minute?"

Aerin didn't move. She was looking at him with something like love in her eyes, he was sure of it. "You're so sweet." She tipped toward him, arms outstretched. "Sweet Brett," she mumbled, falling right into his arms.

And then she threw up all over his lap.

TWENTY-ONE

MADDOX SAT ON the suite's balcony, staring out at the city. Inside, everyone was dancing and drinking and wrecking the place, but he was out here trying to make sense of his swirling thoughts. Catherine had kissed him. Catherine *wanted* him. He should be psyched about that. So why wasn't he? Why was he just sort of . . . *meh*?

He pulled out his phone and looked at the text she'd sent him a few minutes ago. *Hey, cutie, what's up?* He knew he should text her back. He'd been dying to go out with her for *years*. And yet, whenever he opened a new window, his fingers stiffened and his mind emptied out.

The sliding door squeaked, and Aerin teetered onto the balcony, a panino in her hand. "I threw up," she announced drunkenly. "But now I feel better."

Maddox chuckled. "Good for you." She still seemed pretty wasted to him.

Aerin plunked down, stretching out her long, bare legs. "Guess who Madison and Seneca just spoke to?" She took a bite of the panino. "Greg Fine."

"What?" Maddox stood up halfway. "Is he still here?"

Aerin shook her head. "He said this place held way too much temptation." She stared back into the party. "He's a recovering alcoholic. Said he's done several stints in rehab, starting the same fall Helena vanished." She widened her eyes. "So he *could* have an alibi. The problem is, there's no way we can check it. Rehab records are confidential."

Maddox thought for a moment. "Maybe Dexby PD knows."

"So what are we going to do, sneak into the station and hack their computers?" Maddox grinned, clearly eager to play 007, but Aerin shook her head. She tipped in her chair a bit at the motion, ingredients spilling out of her sandwich. "You've watched too many movies."

"Did he say anything about Helena?" Maddox asked.

Aerin shook her head again. "I don't think Seneca got that far. He bolted after he saw all the booze."

"Did he seem . . . weird to you? Did you get a vibe?"

Aerin thought for a moment. "Not really. But what do I know? I'm so lost at this point, Helena's killer could be here at this party and I wouldn't have any idea."

Maddox waved his hand. "That's ludicrous."

Inside, two kids they'd met in the Apple Store popped the cork of another champagne bottle, which flew across the room and shattered a lamp. Everyone laughed drunkenly. Madison, who was now wearing an enormous stuffed Hello Kitty hat she'd bought at the Sanrio store earlier, tipsily kicked the glass into a messy pile.

Aerin turned back to Maddox and appraised him shrewdly, suddenly seeming far less drunk. "So how's your mom?"

Maddox blinked, startled. "She's well. And, um, doesn't your dad live somewhere around here?" He gestured out at the city.

Aerin's face clouded. "Downtown. Luckily, we're nowhere near."

"You're not going to visit him?"

Aerin scoffed. "You like hanging out with *your* dad?"

Maddox was about to say that his situation was different—he didn't even know where his dad was. But maybe, when it came down to it, broken families were all the same. They sucked.

Then Aerin snickered. "You know what I used to think about you? You reminded me of that guy from *Despicable Me*. Gru. The one who had all the Minions."

Maddox's mouth dropped open. *"Huh?"*

"You were this weird kid, sitting on my couch, always looking so freaking *angry*. I figured you were hatching a master plan."

Maddox reached for his drink only to remember he'd finished it. "I wasn't angry." Was Aerin making this up because she was drunk? The past felt very muddled suddenly.

"I know. I realize that now." Aerin lowered her eyes. "I feel bad that I accused you of having something to do with my sister. I shouldn't have said that."

Maddox nodded, touched. That Aerin had even said that out loud had hurt. "Thanks."

Aerin offered her hand. "So . . . friends?"

"Definitely." Maddox shook. "Glad you no longer think I'm Gru."

"You are definitely *not* Gru anymore." Aerin raised a glass. After swallowing more champagne, she kissed Maddox's cheek, slid the door open again, and danced back into the crowd, hips shaking to the music. Madison saw her and whooped.

Maddox watched the traffic for a while, trying to remember sitting on the Kellys' couch while his mom babysat. What had he been think-ing about back then, before Helena's murder, before he made the track team, before his mother had married his stepdad and their lives had forever changed? When the sliding door opened again, it was Seneca, who he hadn't seen all night. His stomach dipped when he saw her—it was crazy that he was still nervous around her. Probably because he still couldn't reconcile this beautiful girl with his friend from online.

Seneca settled on the arm of a chair across the deck, where she could peek over the guardrail at the city below. "You heard about Greg?"

Maddox nodded. "Aerin told me. Think he was in rehab when Helena disappeared?"

"I don't know." Her brow furrowed as she typed on her phone. "I'm trying to find him on Facebook, but no luck so far. But guess who I *did* find? Loren Jablonski."

"Really? Anything still there from around the time Helena went missing?"

Seneca gritted her teeth, gaze on her phone. "I'm working on it. The page is taking forever to load."

Maddox chuckled. "You know, you don't have to work *all* the time."

Seneca looked up, a coil of hair falling over her eyes. Maddox was sure that if Seneca knew how adorable it made her look, she'd fix it right away.

"Enjoy the view. Have a drink." The words felt lame as soon as they came out of his mouth. What was it that made him off-balance around her all over again? He'd thought they were past this.

"I've already had enough to drink," Seneca laughed, but she tucked her phone in her pocket anyway and grabbed her cup, taking a swig of champagne. "This view *is* pretty sweet," she admitted, gazing out at the skyscrapers and the dark greenery of Central Park.

Maddox meant to look out at the view, too, but found himself staring at the way the city lights illuminated her profile in the dark instead.

"You know what Aerin just called me?" he said abruptly. "Gru, from *Despicable Me.* She said I was like some supervillain when I hung out at her house. Always angry."

Seneca cocked her head, fixing that intense gaze on him. "*Were* you?"

"I don't know." Maddox ran his hand over his hair. "I thought she was the bitchy one, but maybe it was the other way around."

They met each other's eyes and smiled. With the fading light on her profile, with her pink cheeks and dark hair loosened from her ponytail and flying everywhere, Seneca looked more than just adorable, Maddox realized. What was she doing out here, with him? Why wasn't she inside, with all the cool older guys Brett had found to come to this swanky party?

Seneca turned to the view again. "I came here with my mom once, a long time ago," she said after a long pause.

Maddox froze. It was as if a cold draft swept through the terrace. He'd held back from asking her about her mom, giving her the space he'd thought she had wanted—but maybe he'd been wrong. "Tell me about it," he said.

Seneca's eyes flicked back and forth. "She took me for tea at the Plaza, which was pretty boring, but at the end, when the waiter had her sign the receipt, he gave her the most amazing pen to use. She looked at me and said, 'How about we steal this?' She slipped it into her pocket and walked out with it."

Maddox laughed, watching Seneca carefully. "Your mother stole a pen?"

"Almost." Seneca started to giggle. "We were halfway out of there, but then the same waiter—this old guy, probably eighty or so, with these little chicken legs—scuttled after us and said, 'Ma'am?'" She deepened her voice for effect. "'I'd like my pen back, please.'"

"That must have been embarrassing."

"Not really. She just laughed and gave it to him. She didn't care. That's the way she was. Nothing got to her. The world was more fun with her in it."

Her face crumpled. "Hey," he said, standing and moving over to where she was perched, huddled against the guardrail. "It's okay."

Seneca hunched her shoulders. "She's always with me." She sounded choked. Then she held up the *P* necklace. "Especially because of this."

"She gave that to you?"

Seneca laughed sharply. "Uh, *no*. Not exactly."

She stared into her lap. Maddox had no idea what to say, so he stayed silent. "When they found her body, my dad was away at a business conference, and there was bad weather that delayed his trip home. I wanted to see her body—I couldn't believe it was actually her—so I lied to the coroner so I could be the one to identify her. I had a fake ID already. I said I was eighteen."

Maddox stared at her, unable to breathe.

"So anyway, there I was. In the morgue." A muscle in her jaw twitched. "She was wearing this necklace on the, you know, slab. I don't know what came over me, but when the coroner turned his back, I took it off her." She glanced at Maddox as if daring him to judge her. "It might not have been legal. My dad would be shattered if he found out—he just thinks I found it in her jewelry box. He was already really messed up that I'd seen her like that. He tore the coroner and the police who handled it a new one."

"God, Seneca," Maddox whispered. He dared to reach over and touch her hand, which was warm against the coolness of the night air. "I'm really sorry."

"It's fine," Seneca said distantly, but she didn't let go of his hand. Then, abruptly, she turned to him. "Thank you."

"Y-you're welcome." When he looked down at her, Seneca was looking at him differently. Had he said something wrong again? What was the matter with him?

Seneca pulled back. "You're doing that thing again."

He flinched. "What thing?"

"That thing with your fingers, where you rub them together." Seneca pointed to his hand. When he looked down, his middle finger and thumb were indeed touching. He pulled them apart immediately.

"You feeling . . . nervous?" she asked.

"*Me?* I'm never nervous." Maddox tucked the offending hand behind his back.

"It's okay if you are." Seneca's smile wobbled. "The Maddy I knew online got nervous sometimes. I liked that."

He met her gaze again. The horn honks from the street below suddenly sounded muffled. Even the party music inside faded. It felt as if champagne coursed through Maddox's veins, bubbly and warm.

His skin started to prickle with anticipation. "Um," he fumbled, not having the slightest clue what to say.

"Um," Seneca teased, her eyes shining. And then, astonishingly, Seneca grabbed his other hand and pulled him down to her. Their lips touched, softly at first. Maddox lifted a hand to the back of Seneca's neck, his fingertips on fire. The kiss deepened into something hungry and urgent. Seneca pressed into his hands, and he wrapped an arm around her hips, pulling her up until she was crushed hotly against him.

"I can't believe this is happening," Seneca whispered, meeting his gaze for a moment.

"I know," Maddox breathed. Being with Catherine was nothing like this, he realized.

Catherine. He pulled back sharply, almost gasping. "Wait."

Seneca opened her eyes, too. She searched his face. "What?"

Maddox lowered his eyes. "I can't do this. We can't do this."

Seneca's gaze upon him felt laser precise. A small sound escaped her; then her lips tightened. "What is it?" she asked, stepping backward, out of his embrace. "Do you have a girlfriend?"

Maddox could feel a headache starting, a sharp spike drilling into the side of his head. "It's . . . complicated. But—"

Seneca cut him off with a wave of her hand. Her eyes were slits. *"Complicated."* Her voice cracked. She yanked the sliding door open and slipped back inside, closing the door behind her with a violent jerk of her arm.

"Seneca . . ." Maddox went to the door, but she was already lost in the crowd. He slumped back down into a chair and put his head in his hands. *"Shit,"* he said under his breath, and then glared at his phone. He felt a sudden urge to throw it off the balcony.

He sat there for a moment, but soon enough the balcony felt too small, too constricting. He needed to get away from this suite. He needed to clear his mind. Head down, he pushed into the room, barreled past the partiers, and groped for the silver-handled door to the hotel's hall. There was no one in the elevator, and the car made a hollow, screeching sound that echoed in his ears. The lobby, though opulent, was eerily empty, even the front desk unoccupied. Maddox looked warily at the closed gift shop, the dark bar. The clock on the wall said it was past 2:00 a.m. He hadn't realized it was so late.

Out the revolving doors, a line of traffic lights down Fifty-Ninth Street glowed a steady green. Stragglers shuffled along the park's stone walls. A homeless man sat on the sidewalk, shouting and gesticulating, and Maddox sidestepped him. A cab swished past, nearly clipping his side. He jumped out of the way, pulse rushing at his temples.

He turned down Sixth Avenue and hurried past an empty bistro. The subway rocked beneath his feet, its breath hot and stinky through the grate. Had it *always* been that loud?

When a hand covered his eyes, Maddox's first thought was that it was Seneca—she'd come to talk. He tried to wheel around, but a steely arm braced his chest. He caught the scent of leather and—gasoline?

Something cracked his kneecaps, and he let out a strangled wail and dropped blindly to the pavement. He tried to scream again, but the attacker had fallen with him, covering his mouth, rooting around his pockets, striking his back. Something about the person felt slight... but strong. Maddox heard a high voice in his ear: *"Stop, or I'm going to kill you."* Another blow hit his head, and a searing white pain cracked through his skull. Where were the cops? Where were all the people?

Blackness enveloped him. When he opened his eyes again, clouds passed over a half-moon. Streetlights swirled dizzily. Maddox tried to move a finger, then a toe. He tentatively touched his scalp and felt a sticky patch of blood, and when he riffled in his pocket, his phone was still there, but his wallet was gone. How many minutes had passed— one, two, ten?

He sat up and looked around. The street was empty. He was still sitting in front of the empty bistro, the last thing he remembered seeing. He stared inside at a man wiping the bar, stunned that he hadn't seen anything, or done anything. Was this stretch of sidewalk too dark? Did the man just not care?

What had just *happened*?

TWENTY-TWO

AERIN HADN'T FELT this crappy after the rager she'd gone to last year where she and Anderson Keyes did keg stands, or after the time she and Brad Westerfield drank Jäger shots and watched Fourth of July fireworks, or even after that hideous flu she'd come down with last winter, five days in bed plagued by fever dreams of Helena drowning under piles of snow. Why had she drunk so many glasses of champagne? Why had she kept on drinking even after she'd puked? What was wrong with her?

Nevertheless, she managed to get her ass up on Friday morning—the body jets in the shower definitely helped—put on her clothes from the day before, and follow the others down onto Central Park South. It was before 9:00 a.m. They wanted to catch Loren as soon as he got to work.

It was the only bright spot in Aerin's mind. All this might end today. Loren might be the answer. Though Aerin had no solid proof, she just didn't *feel* like Greg Fine was the right fit—he'd acted skittish and insecure last night. She couldn't picture Helena falling head over heels for him—and more than that, she couldn't imagine this guy working up the kind of anger to murder someone. Sure, people were different when they drank—her stoic friend Tori wept for starving people in Africa after one too many shots, for example. Still, Greg seemed even more passive than Kevin.

But hopefully Loren was a whole different story.

Brett stood in line for egg sandwiches, and when he handed Aerin hers, he met her gaze for a moment. "Sure you can keep this down? Don't get me wrong, your puke is really sexy, but this is my last clean shirt."

"I'll make sure to puke on someone else next time, lover boy," Aerin grumbled. She had a vague memory of throwing up all over Brett's lap last night, but he'd been so sweet about it, cleaning them both off in the bathroom, shooing everyone else away, even though Madison kept crashing into the room, saying repeatedly that she had to pee. He'd walked around for the rest of the party without a shirt on, and she sort of remembered doing a shot off his abs later . . . and then passing out on the kitchen floor, only to wake up this morning in a pile of drool. Classy.

Seneca had her arms wound tightly around her body. As a behemoth city bus blustered past, Aerin poked Seneca's side. "You okay?"

Seneca shrugged. "Do *you* feel good this morning?"

Brett bounded back to the hotel doorman and asked him to hail him a cab. As a bright yellow minivan pulled to the curb, Maddox grabbed his arm. "Maybe we shouldn't do this."

"Huh?" Brett frowned.

"Dude, I was mugged last night," Maddox moaned. "I feel like it's a bad omen."

Aerin's stomach turned over. Apparently, while she was asleep, an NYC cop had come to the door with Maddox after talking to him about the person who'd robbed him. It freaked her out that mugging was still even a thing. Wasn't the city supposed to be really safe?

Brett waved him away. "We'll be fine, bro. Promise."

They piled in a minivan cab. Seneca climbed into the backseat. "Madison and Aerin, sit with me." Aerin did as she was asked, but she sensed it wasn't a let's-be-girlfriends request—more like she didn't want to sit with someone in particular. Maddox? Had something happened between them?

"Twenty-Sixth and Eleventh," Brett told the cabdriver. The cab lumbered downtown, getting stuck in Times Square traffic and then maneuvering its way to the river. At Twenty-Sixth, Brett handed over some cash, and everyone got out. To Aerin's sensitive ears, the sounds of construction nearby were almost deafening. She eyed the Kiko Gallery. The lights were off, a metal grate pulled down over the windows and door.

Madison flicked the tassels on her hat. Maddox kept glancing up and down the street. Brett tossed his egg sandwich wrapper into a trash can.

"That's him," Seneca hissed.

Someone had emerged from around the corner. It was a man in his late twenties wearing a dark tee and Ray-Bans. He had longish hair, a round face, a portly body, and pockmarked skin. There were sweat stains under his arms. Even from across the street, Aerin could hear huffing and puffing. He looked like the type of guy who had back hair.

The guy stopped in front of the gallery and pulled out a key. An unlit cigarette hung out of his mouth. Seneca dug her nails into Aerin's arm. "Think he and Helena were going out?"

Aerin wrinkled her nose. There was no way Helena was secretly traveling to the city for this dude.

Seneca seemed to pick up that vibe, too. "Then who was he?" she whispered.

"Only one way to find out." Brett crossed the street, narrowly avoiding an oncoming bike messenger. "You Loren?"

The guy looked up. "Who wants to know?"

The egg in Aerin's stomach curdled. It was the same gravelly voice from Helena's voice mail.

"I'm looking for someone," Brett said. "Her name was Helena Kelly. She disappeared in December five years ago. I think you knew her."

Loren scratched his unshaven chin. "Name means nothing to me."

Seneca exchanged a look with Aerin, then started across the street, too. "Well, she knew you. She had your name in her phone. And January that next year, you left a message on *her* phone. Then she turned up dead."

Loren wrinkled his nose. There was no sign of guilt on his face, but maybe he was a good liar. He lit the cigarette between his lips. "You people cops? You have to tell me if you are."

Brett shook his head. Loren relaxed a little. "What did this message say?" he asked.

Hands shaking, Aerin reached into her pocket for Helena's phone. After punching in her password, she set the phone to speaker and stepped toward the group. Up close, Loren's skin smelled surprisingly like mint. His angry voice blared out again on the message, giving her chills. After the recording was over, Loren glanced up the street, then toward the river to the west. "She was probably one of my clients," he said in a low voice. "I run a delivery service."

"A delivery service for what?" Aerin snapped.

"Depends on what you want. Some people want pills. Some people want pot. Some people want strippers. I'm a one-stop shop."

Aerin's stomach swirled. *Strippers?* "Maybe you left her a message by mistake?"

"Not a message like that." Loren had a seedy grin.

Aerin called up a picture of Helena from her phone. It was from the Thanksgiving just before she vanished. Helena sat at the table, mid turkey bite, her face turned toward the camera, her delicate, graceful features softened by candlelight. "This was her."

Loren made a clucking sound with his tongue as he studied it. "Okay, yeah. She was a client. I delivered to her several times a week."

"Delivered *what*?" Aerin asked, then held up a hand. "Actually, don't answer. I don't want to know."

Madison rubbed her jaw. "If you delivered to her twice a week, that would mean she'd have to have an address in the city, right?"

Loren tossed his cigarette into the gutter. "I don't deliver to street corners."

Seneca looked excited. "Do you remember Helena's address?"

Loren chuckled. The chuckle quickly turned into a hacking cough, which lasted several seconds. He wiped his eyes. "This may come as a surprise, but sometimes I sample my product. My memory's for shit—I can't remember last *week*."

"Well, do you keep a client list?" Seneca asked.

Loren started coughing again. "I'm not a doctor's office, honey."

"You know, I'm not buying this," Brett muttered. "Can't remember an address, no client records, you say you never make personal phone calls, yet here's a *very* personal phone call."

"She probably owed me money. That's the only time I call clients, when they dodge their bills."

Maddox sidled closer to Loren. "Know what I think? You went to wherever Helena was staying and tried to shake her down. But maybe she didn't have the cash. Maybe that made you even angrier. Maybe things got out of hand. . . ."

Loren puffed up his chest. "I could call the cops right now. This is private property."

"But you won't." Brett smiled triumphantly. "Because then they'll find out about *you*. And you wouldn't like that."

There was a brief stare-off. Loren flicked ash. "Are you seriously trying to say *I* did something to this girl?" He started to laugh. "Think about what you just said. Helene, Helena—whatever her name is—she disappeared in December five years ago, right? And we're assuming she was killed around then, too? If you kids had done your research, you'd know I broke both my legs, one of them in four different places that December—I was doing this awesome stunt that kinda went wrong at the end."

He pulled an iPhone out of his pocket, pressed the screen a few times, and showed the group a video. It was dated December 16, five years before. A tubby guy who looked just like Loren did a backflip off a soccer goal. He landed squarely in a large blue vat filled with Gatorade, and then the thing tipped over and rolled down an enormous hill straight to where a high school marching band was practicing in a field. Loren and the barrel knocked over several trumpet players as easy as bowling pins. The cameraman cheered in the background. Loren crawled out of the barrel, screaming in agony.

Madison gawked at him. "Were you on *drugs*?"

"Absolutely." Loren chuckled. "The post went viral. It was all over Facebook—even made the *Today* show! So I ask you, can a dude with a big freaking cast on both of his legs kill a fly—much less a girl?" He rolled his eyes. "You people are total amateurs."

The wind howled in Aerin's ears. Somewhere in the distance, a chorus of horns blew. Loren spun around and opened the gallery door. He walked through it, locked it, and gave them a lingering wave from behind the glass, his eyes mocking.

Brett rushed to the door and knocked with a flat palm. "Wait! Do you know if she had a boyfriend, then? Who was she staying with in New York?" Loren walked to the back of the gallery without answering.

Brett spun around and faced the group. "Damn. How'd we miss that? He said it was all over Facebook!"

Seneca had her hands over her eyes. *"Facebook."*

"Why didn't anyone look to see if he had a page?" Aerin cried.

Maddox pointed at Seneca. "Didn't you find it last night? I thought you were checking it."

Seneca glared at him. "I was going to, but then you were all like, 'You don't have to work all the time! Have a drink!'" She used a dopey, mocking voice, and her eyes bugged wide.

Maddox pressed his hand to his chest. "So now it's *my* fault?"

"Okay, okay, let's calm down." Brett started pacing. "So Loren isn't our guy. But we did get something out of him. Helena had an address here. That's huge!"

"Or else she was just coming to New York City regularly because she couldn't get drugs in Dexby," Maddox said.

"You can get drugs in Dexby, easy," Madison pointed out. "I mean, unless she was on some really crazy shit. . . ."

"She wasn't coming into the city from Dexby." Aerin hated even saying it. "Even if she got pot from him, Loren said he delivered to her twice a week. Meaning she would've been in New York twice a week. I saw her every day that year, except when she did that summer program here. She couldn't have cut school, either—her attendance record was perfect. I know because the freaking office sent her a posthumous award. It's still on her bulletin board with all the rest of her crap because my mom is too sad to take any of it down." She squared her shoulders. "Loren must have been thinking of someone else."

"Or . . ." Seneca cleared her throat. "Maybe Helena didn't die the last day you saw her, in December. Maybe she came here, lived in the city for a while. That's when Loren delivered to her. I mean, maybe he delivered a few times before that December day, too, like when she was at the summer program—otherwise he wouldn't have had her old phone number. But the bulk of his deliveries, the two times a week, maybe they were in late December, early January."

The wind shifted, and the city smelled sharply of garbage. Aerin glared at Seneca. "What are you *talking* about? One minute, Helena was in the yard with me. The next minute, she was gone. Someone *took* her, murdered her." She blinked. "She didn't run *away*."

Seneca didn't look so sure. "That last day you saw her, she sent you back inside to get a purse. Why didn't she go in herself?"

Aerin blinked, confused by the question. "I don't know."

"She could have sent you inside because it gave her time to get away."

Aerin's jaw dropped. "But she didn't take her phone with her. Or any clothes."

"Maybe this New York guy had a stash for her."

There was a rushing sound in Aerin's ears. "Okay, even if it *is* true, why did Helena want to go through the whole charade of building a snowman? Why didn't she just find some other time when none of us were home and go then?"

"Maybe they'd set a time beforehand. Maybe she didn't anticipate you being around."

"Oh, so I was just an annoyance to do away with?"

Seneca pinched the bridge of her nose. "I don't know, Aerin. I didn't know her. Maybe you didn't, either."

Aerin gasped. It felt like Seneca had punched her. Aerin looked at the others. "You guys think she's wrong, right?"

Madison shuffled her feet. Brett shoved his hands in his pockets.

"Right?" Aerin screeched, her throat feeling tight.

"She's not necessarily wrong, but she shouldn't have broken it to you like that," Maddox said.

Seneca turned to him, eyebrows knitted. "Ex*cuse* me?"

"C'mon, Seneca," Maddox said gently. "Have some compassion."

"Agreed," Brett piped up.

Seneca groaned. "Maybe Princess Aerin should just be a little less sensitive. I mean, we're investigating a *murder* case. Did she expect it to be all puppies and rainbows?" Aerin glared at her, opening her mouth for an angry reply.

Maddox cut in. "Hey. Just because you're angry that you spaced out about looking up Loren on Facebook doesn't mean you need to take it out on Aerin."

Seneca looked like she was going to explode. "Why didn't *you* look up his page, Maddox? Why does it always have to be me figuring shit out? Why am I the only one actually *working* here?"

"Hey." Brett's voice cracked. "We're all working."

"Yeah, Seneca," Madison cried.

Seneca pointed at Brett. "Actually? You seem more interested in flirting with Aerin. And Madison? You're cool—I don't know why you're here at all. To get closer to your brother? You shouldn't waste your time."

"Seneca," Aerin said wearily. The anger suddenly drained from her body, until all she could feel was exhaustion. "Be nice."

Seneca turned to her. "Why are *you* defending Maddox? He thinks you're a bitch." Aerin blinked and, shocked at herself, felt tears coming on. She gulped rapidly.

Maddox looked mortified. "No I don't!"

"Oh please," Seneca snapped. "You've said it several times."

Brett crossed his arms over his chest. "Let's take a breath, people. Everyone calm down."

"Shut up, Brett!" Seneca yelled.

Brett's brow furrowed. "Seneca." There was warning in his voice. "I mean it. Calm down."

"What, are you going to make me?" Seneca sneered, placing her hands on her hips.

"You need to chill, Seneca," Maddox ordered. "Take a break."

She whipped around and glared at him. "I'll take a break, all right. Why not? I'm getting nowhere with you. You're all nothing but a distraction for me. I'm better off alone."

She wheeled around and started walking toward the river. Madison started to go after her, but Maddox caught her arm and shook his head. "She won't listen to you right now," he said, sadness in his voice. "Just let her go."

They were silent for a beat. Maddox looked at Aerin. "I really don't think you're a bitch," he blurted out.

Aerin breathed deeply, still fighting back tears. The stress of the weird fight hit her all wrong, filling her with unexpected self-consciousness. It wasn't that she really cared if Maddy Wright thought she was a bitch—or maybe she did. It wasn't that she cared that Seneca had said that thing about her sister or had freaked out on all of them—or maybe she did. All she knew was that she felt even more lost than ever before. "Maybe Seneca's onto something," she said quietly. "Maybe we should be done."

"What?" Brett shot for her. "Aerin, no! We're so close!"

"No, we're not." Aerin's voice cracked. "We haven't gotten anywhere. We know nothing."

Like Seneca, she started walking, though she chose the opposite direction, toward the middle of the city. Thankfully, none of the dwindling group chased after her. She hated how much they knew about her, how her family's dirty laundry and insecurities and imperfections were front and center. She despised the idea of finding out even *more* awful stuff about her sister.

Seneca's revelation rushed back. Aerin hated to think it, but . . . could Seneca be right? Could Helena have *lived* . . . and been *fine* . . . for what, weeks? *Months?* She was here in New York City in late December. Here for Christmas, New Year's. Did she ever think about their parents, about Aerin? Did she watch her search party on the nightly news? Laugh at their parents' frantic pleas for whoever kidnapped her to return her safely? Like it was a *joke*?

It was too hideous to consider.

She marched across the street, passing right by a car with tinted windows. As she peered through the windshield, a blurred face stared back at her, stopping her short. It seemed like the person had been watching her.

Aerin glanced over her shoulder. There wasn't a soul on this block.

Wind gusted around the corner. Metal grates over closed shops rattled. Empty candy wrappers blew into the gutter.

A shadow moved inside the car to open the driver's door. Aerin's heart lurched and she stepped away from the curb and started to run, but her stride was halting and inefficient in her high wedges. She heard footsteps behind her and let out a helpless cry. Her ankle turned, and she stumbled, almost careening to the sidewalk. Scrambling for balance, she hurried around the corner to a busier avenue. People bustled to and fro. A shopkeeper hanging purses on an outside rack gave her a strange look.

You're being ridiculous, she told herself, breathing in and out. *No one is after you. No one cares.*

And sure enough, when she peeked around the corner, the suspicious car had vanished from the parking spot. Maybe it had never been there at all.

TWENTY-THREE

BACK ON THE Metro-North, Seneca sat by herself, her feet on the back of the seat in front of her. Though she'd shown up at the train station separately from the others, they'd somehow all managed to board not only the same train but the same freaking *car*—well, all except for Aerin, but Seneca was pretty sure she'd gotten a taxi home. Typical. Maddox was two rows ahead, and Brett across the aisle from him by the window. Madison was at the back near the bathroom, headphones over her ears. It was like they were strangers. Maybe they were, again.

She stared out the window at the dinky houses whipping past, feeling cranky. It sucked she was going back to Dexby. When she'd gotten to the ticket desk at Grand Central, she'd considered buying a ticket to Annapolis and just leaving her bags behind—but the stupid station only had trains going *north*. Well, whatever. She'd grab her stuff from Maddox's and leave. She couldn't imagine staying with *him* anymore.

She had no reason to be in Dexby anymore, either: At the train station, Brett had mumbled to her that Aerin had called off the investigation. Seneca couldn't believe it. The thing they'd figured out about

Helena living past that day in December cracked the case wide open. They had a whole new timeline now: Helena could have been killed between the time she went missing and Loren's phone call in late January, explaining why she hadn't paid up for her weed or drugs or whatever. Or, she might have lived past that phone call and skipped town again, leaving her debts behind, pulling the same disappearing act twice. The alibis for the weekend she disappeared no longer applied; anyone could be a suspect again. Kevin. Greg Fine. Okay, maybe not Loren and his broken legs, but definitely the mystery boyfriend who lived somewhere in the city.

So why would Aerin want to stop *now*? Wasn't she dying to know the truth? If this was Seneca's mom's case and they'd made a breakthrough this big, Seneca would be full steam ahead, no matter what.

An older woman wobbled past, holding a cup of coffee. She shot Seneca a small, gentle smile, but Seneca couldn't smile back. She was far too upset. Not just about looking like a fool in front of Loren and the group. Not just about being totally off her game and forgetting about Loren's Facebook. About last night, too.

The worst part was that Maddox hadn't even tried to apologize. Last night, she'd waited up for him, but almost an hour passed, and he was still missing from the party. Her fury had just burned hotter and hotter as time went on. *Way to avoid the situation, idiot.* And who was his complication? It probably *was* Tara. They probably hooked up all the time. Why *wouldn't* he want to hook up with her? And Tara probably thought he was a boyfriend, but Maddox just saw her as a booty call. *That's* why he wanted to avoid her at the fair, not because he didn't like her. And like an idiot, she'd helped him!

And okay, okay, then he showed up with the police and said he'd been mugged—which was scary. But somehow her rational brain couldn't conquer her rage. Besides, if he'd been a grown-up about this, if he'd tried to smooth things over with Seneca, he wouldn't have needed to take that walk, and his wallet wouldn't be gone now.

Of course, she never should have kissed him, either. It wasn't like she'd *planned* it. It had sort of just . . . happened. She'd felt close to him after telling that dark secret about her mom. Kissing him had felt so right . . . until it had felt so tragically wrong.

The conductor screeched that they were pulling into Dexby, and Seneca looked up. The other members of the group stood in the aisles, preparing to exit. She felt a pang as she stared at Brett's squared shoulders and Madison's perky ponytail, even the half-disintegrated Calvin tattoo on Maddox's biceps. She took a deep breath. She should apologize, even to him. She'd been angry at her stupid choices and for making herself so vulnerable. She was pissed that she'd spaced out on looking up Loren's history; altogether, it felt like she was slipping in a major way. She so wouldn't have done this if she was on her own. She would have stayed sober, not let her past cloud her thoughts, and definitely not let a guy come between her and finding out the truth. But because she couldn't actually *say* all that, she'd lashed out at the group to hide her insecurities. Maybe if she apologized, if she begged Aerin to reconsider, they could start over again. Right?

Everyone disembarked the train and started into the parking lot. Seneca drifted behind the group, composing her apology in her head. As she passed the first line of vehicles, a voice called out. "Seneca."

She wheeled around and saw a figure, but it was someone so incongruous to Dexby she did a double take. She took in the white Ford Explorer behind him with its familiar dent on the back fender and

Maryland license plate, then peeked again. A sour taste welled in her mouth.

"D-Dad," Seneca said in a wobbly voice. "Hi."

MR. FRAZIER EYED Seneca coldly over his glasses. His mouth was drawn. His shoulders were tensed. Seneca felt huge in the middle of the parking lot. She wished she could melt into a puddle and drip down a manhole.

"How did you find me?" she finally asked, when her dad hadn't spoken.

Mr. Frazier let out a caustic laugh. "It's a funny story." The words came out like little fireballs. Seneca wasn't sure she'd seen him this angry. "You see, it all started this morning, when I got a charge from the U of M library saying you had some fines. I paid them—you're welcome—but then I logged on to your credit card account to make sure you were paying your other bills."

Seneca blinked. "You have access to my card?"

"I *cosigned* for you, Seneca. Of course I have access. I find a charge at an ATM at the Restful Inn in Dexby, Connecticut. And I think, uh-oh, Seneca's card has been stolen. I'd better call her. So I do, *several* times, but you don't answer."

Seneca's stomach sank. She'd been so hungover—and so mad at Maddox—that she'd ignored her phone all morning. Oops.

"So I ring up that number you gave me for Annie," her father went on.

Seneca shut her eyes. *No.*

"It was so strange," Mr. Frazier said, his voice getting more and more high-pitched. "A cleaning woman answered, and she said the Sipowitz family was in Maine for spring break." He was trembling now. "So I just got in the car and drove to Delaware. I didn't know where *else* to go. Halfway there, I remembered Find My iPhone—and thank God I was the one who set up your cloud ID before sending you off to college. It tells me you're in New York City. Then it started to move again, and I figured out where you had to be headed. The little blue dot comes to a stop in—surprise, surprise—Dexby." He arched his back and stared up at the trees. "Suburban Connecticut. Not a bad place to run away to, I guess."

Seneca kept her gaze on the ground. "I didn't run away."

Her father looked like he wanted to punch something. "All kinds of horrible scenarios came to mind, Seneca. I thought someone kidnapped you. I thought you were dead. This brought back a lot of memories, let me tell you. Not good ones."

"I'm sorry," Seneca whispered. "I should have explained, but . . ."

"Seneca, you should tell him the truth."

Madison had stepped next to her. She grabbed Seneca's hand and swung it. Then she turned to Seneca's dad. "Hi there, Mr. Frazier. It's so nice to meet you."

Seneca stared at Madison, confused. Mr. Frazier did, too. "And you are . . . ?"

"Annie." Madison spread out her arms.

Seneca watched as her father took in the Asian girl dressed in all pink wearing a stuffed Hello Kitty on her head. "Annie from Delaware?" he said in disbelief.

"My family's in Maine, but I'm staying with friends here," Madison chirped. "Seneca was worried you wouldn't want her so far away from you. I'm really, *really* sorry. I just missed her so much. I really wanted to see her."

She looped an arm through Seneca's elbow and pulled her tight.

Seneca tried not to gape at her. How did she come up with this so fast? And would it work? Her father had never actually *met* Annie, after all, just heard all about her.

Mr. Frazier's gaze bounced from girl to girl. "*You're* Annie?"

"Uh-huh." Madison smiled.

"Annie *Sipowitz*?"

Madison blinked very fast. "I'm adopted."

Which *was* true, technically, but her pause had been too long—the game was up. Seneca's dad snorted. "Get in the car," he demanded to Seneca, pointing at the Explorer.

"What about my stuff?" Seneca cried. "It's at her house." She pointed at Madison.

Mr. Frazier nudged his chin toward the Explorer again. "She can ship it back. I'll arrange it. I want you in this car right now."

Seneca swallowed hard. For the first time, she peeked at the rest of the group. Brett looked stricken. Madison's eyes were large and solemn. Even Maddox looked conflicted. No one stepped forward to make up another excuse, though. Then again, what *could* they say?

Mr. Frazier slammed into the driver's seat and turned the ignition. Seneca slid in next to him, staring at her hands. They drove past the Restful Inn, which was still closed. Some of the siding was blackened from the fire. *Had* it been arson? Had someone been warning them, or was it just a coincidence?

Her thoughts clicked back to Loren. Whose address was Helena giving for deliveries? A secret boyfriend's? How long had she stayed in the city before someone killed her?

Her father stared straight ahead as he turned onto the parkway. The only movements he made were to switch on his turn signal and take another sip from his coffee. Seneca stared at the cars on the highway. In front of them was a Ford pickup, its bed full of furniture. Beside them was a minivan jammed with kids. Then a slow-moving limo, the words *Just Married* soaped onto the back and side windows.

Buzz.

She looked down at her phone. Brett had texted. *Sorry you had to leave. No hard feelings.* And then: *I know Aerin wants us to be done, but I've been thinking about the word on the paper crane. I feel like it means something.*

Seneca felt a leap of gratitude that he'd reached out. *Like what?* she texted back.

I'm not sure, came Brett's text. *I thought you'd have an idea.*

Seneca moved to write back, but her dad gave her a sharp glare. Anguish cloaked her again. If only she'd just looked up Loren's Facebook last night instead of kissing Maddox. Her head would have been clear this morning; they might have interrogated Loren anyway, but they wouldn't have looked like clueless idiots. She could have convinced Aerin to press forward with the investigation, argued that they were one step ahead the whole time. She would have heard her phone ring and taken her dad's call and smoothed everything over with him, too. He wouldn't have driven up here in a panic, and she'd still be in Dexby, parsing through this new timeline, figuring out the word on the crane, figuring out *everything.*

This was all her fault. Every bit of it.

She gazed miserably out the window again. The *Just Married* limo lumbered along in front of them, the cheerful message on the back irritating her. Beneath *Just Married* was a sloppy drawing of a heart with an arrow through it. Inside were presumably the couple's names: *Kyle Brandon + Hayley Isaacs.* On the side windows was the same heart, but whoever drew the thing couldn't fit their full names inside so just soaped their initials: *K.B. + H.I.*

A light flickered on in Seneca's brain. Then another. She thought of tiny letters elsewhere, then gasped. "Stop the car."

Her father snorted. "Excuse me?"

"Pull over." Seneca's heart was pounding. "*Please.* It's an emergency."

Her father gave her a long look, then rolled the car to the shoulder. "Well?"

"I need to go back."

"You *what*?"

"I need to go back. I need to talk to someone."

"Can't you do that over the phone?"

Seneca felt frantic. "Look, I know I haven't given you many reasons to treat me like an adult lately, but I need you to trust me on this. I'm not doing anything weird. I just need a couple of days. Then, when I get home, I promise we'll talk. About everything."

Mr. Frazier stared at her. "I just drove four and a half hours for you."

"I know. I will explain, I *promise*. But you have to give me a few more days."

He shook his head. "No. No way. Not unless you tell me what you're doing."

She pinched the bridge of her nose. "I just . . . can't."

"Sorry. Then you have to come home."

Seneca's throat closed. "Okay. Fine. One of the people I'm hanging out with up there is Aerin Kelly, okay? The girl whose sister was kidnapped right around when Mom . . ." She trailed off. "We met online. We're friends. Those other kids have been through stuff, too." She glanced at him. "Being with them . . . helps."

Mr. Frazier looked shocked, and Seneca felt a twist of guilt. She'd never played the I'm-still-messed-up-over-Mom get-out-of-jail-free card. It was a great play—and true, even—but she'd always resisted the urge. She knew that if she told the truth, she'd get that obsessive, neurotic, racked-with-worry dad back, the same one who marched in doctor after doctor to see her, the same one who sat outside her bedroom door day after day to make sure she didn't smother herself with her pillow, the same one who called her in high school sometimes six times a day to see if she was coping. She couldn't stand to be that much of a burden. Not again.

But still, it wasn't a lie. Seneca had no intention of bullshitting with Aerin about their murdered family members, but just knowing Aerin had been through it—and Brett, too, though to a lesser degree—gave her steadying comfort. Aerin's life hadn't been easy, either. Aerin struggled. That halo Seneca had recoiled from that first day here now felt reassuringly recognizable—maybe it was *okay* to have the halo. Maybe it was okay to be angry and searching and a hot mess. And Seneca had gleaned all that just by getting to know Aerin a little bit. If she left now, if she went back to her old house and holed up in her old room, she feared she'd slip right back into her old habits. She had to keep trying to solve this case. It was the key, somehow.

More cars swished past. A semitruck blew its horn. Mr. Frazier puffed up his cheeks and slowly blew out a breath. "How do I know you're telling the truth?"

"Call Aerin's mom. I'm staying with that girl, Madison, but I met Mrs. Kelly, too."

"Why didn't you just say *this* is what you were doing instead of lying about Annie?"

Seneca shrugged. "Because I didn't want you to freak out."

He rolled his jaw. "What did you think I was going to do, lock you in the house? Forbid you from speaking to people?"

Seneca stared at the dashboard. *No, Dad, I thought you were going to throw me back into terrible daily therapy sessions,* she thought but didn't say.

"Is there any way you can just continue to talk to this Aerin person on the phone?"

Seneca shrugged. "She and I had a fight. That's why I'd like to go back. To apologize, to make sure everything's okay." She hadn't realized how important it was to her until right then. Maybe her drive to stay hadn't just been about the break in Helena's case. It was about this, too.

Mr. Frazier stared blankly at the steering wheel. Seneca watched as the dashboard clock ticked from 3:34 to 3:35 before he spoke again. "Well, I'd like Mrs. Kelly's number at least."

"Okay."

"And you can have two more days, if that family will have you, but that's it. I want you on a train by eight p.m. on Easter Sunday."

Seneca nodded, thrilled. "*Thank* you."

He didn't look very happy. "If I find out anything weird is going on, I'm coming back."

"Nothing weird is going on, I promise."

He nodded, then met her gaze. His eyes were filled with tears, but his smile was encouraging. "I hope you find what you're looking for."

Seneca lowered her eyes. It occurred to her that she hadn't told him the worst of it, the school part. Summoning strength, she breathed the worry away. She just had to get through this first. Then she'd tell him everything. "I hope so, too," she whispered.

Mr. Frazier still looked torn as he shifted into drive once more, pulled out of the shoulder, and did a U-turn. As they started back,

Seneca caught sight of the limo again, now parked in the rest stop on the other side of the highway. There were those names again in the Valentine heart. *Kyle Brandon. Hayley Isaacs.*

H.I. Hi.

What *else* did that stand for?

TWENTY-FOUR

MADDOX'S HEAD WAS still pounding murderously even after inhaling a one-pound bag of cashews, shooting a Red Bull, and choking down three aspirin. He sat at the kitchen table, staring at the daisies Seneca had bought for his parents. The flowers were still perky and fresh. They'd lasted longer than their friendship.

Ping! It was another text from Catherine. *Had a sexy dream about you last night.*

Maddox put his head down on the table. He didn't want to write Catherine back. Anything he would say would be dishonest. And yet he'd been the one to set the ball rolling by kissing her first. *Be careful what you wish for,* he thought sarcastically.

There was a cough, and Madison appeared in the doorway. Silently, she crossed the room, scraped back a chair, and sat down. Maddox could feel her staring. "What?" he asked impatiently.

"This is all your fault," she said in a low voice.

Maddox pressed his hands over his eyes. "Meaning?"

"Seneca wouldn't have acted like that if you hadn't done something to push her away. And then, when her dad came, you just stood there like a moron and let her go."

Maddox made a face. "What was I supposed to do? Get into a fist-fight with him?"

Madison placed her hands on her hips. "You could have come up with something."

"She threw me under the bus!"

"We both know why. I saw you two on the balcony last night. I saw you push her away. What were you thinking?"

"It's complicated." He winced. He hadn't meant to use the same words as he'd used with Seneca when he'd pulled away from their kiss.

Madison scoffed. "Complicated how?"

"I can't . . ." He trailed off.

He'd wanted to tell Seneca how he felt—and how those feelings had only coalesced when they'd kissed, and how actually he was being the good guy here because he didn't want to two-time anybody—weren't girls supposed to appreciate that? But then there'd been that . . . *incident* on the street. *Stop, or I'll kill you.* In that strange, raspy woman's voice—or had it been a guy, disguising his voice? Or had it just been a mugger, as the police had told him, and he was way overthinking this? They promised they'd call him with a follow-up report if they caught the person, but so far he hadn't heard a word.

Anyway, after all that had happened, he'd felt too scattered to have a heart-to-heart with Seneca. He'd promised himself to do it this morning, but by then, it had been too late. She wouldn't even look at him.

He glanced up. Madison was still glowering at him, waiting for an answer. "Why'd you pull away from her last night?" she demanded.

"Because I'm with someone else, okay?" he admitted. "And I'm trying to be a good guy and not cheat on anybody."

Madison wrinkled her nose. "You don't have a girlfriend."

As if on cue, there was another *ping!* from his phone. *Hello?* Catherine wrote.

Madison glanced at the phone before he could shut off the alert. Her eyes widened. "Oh my God, you're *kidding*. Not her."

Maddox suddenly felt defensive. "Why not her, Madison?"

Madison rolled her eyes. "She's crazy. As in *certifiable*."

"What are you talking about?"

A guilty look crossed Madison's face. She hitched forward in the chair. "I didn't want to say anything before because she's your coach and whatever, but I know some of her sorority sisters from when she was at UConn. They said Catherine's a psycho. Especially when it comes to boyfriends."

Maddox scoffed. "That's not a nice thing to say."

"Why would her sorority sisters lie?"

"Don't girls lie about *everything*?" Maddox retorted weakly, but Madison had already shrugged and started up the stairs. "Get rid of her, Maddox! She's toxic!" she called out. He let out a frustrated groan and waved his arms crazily at her behind her back, then rested his head on the table with a thud.

Just as he was gathering his energy to get up, the doorbell rang. Maddox leapt up, frowning. Maybe it was Seneca. Maybe she'd somehow found a way to convince her dad to bring her back. His heart sped up at the prospect, and he headed toward the door, preparing what he was going to say.

Instead, it was Catherine's face on the other side of the glass. Maddox yanked the door open with a start, looking his coach up and down. "W-wow," he stammered. Catherine was wearing a fitted dark pink dress that grazed the top of her thighs. Her hair was curled, her lips looked shiny, and she smelled like lemons, one of Maddox's favorite scents. Only, there was kind of a strange look in her eye, like she'd pulled an all-nighter and was wired on espresso. She looked kind of pissed, too.

"Hey," Catherine said, fiddling with a lock of hair. "So I was driving by, and I thought I'd stop and see what you're up to." She cleared her throat, then stared at her shoes, the sexiest black heels he'd ever seen. "I haven't heard from you. Were you out somewhere yesterday?"

"Uh . . ." Images of New York flashed through his mind—the party, his conversation with Seneca, their kiss. "I had a family thing," he answered.

"Oh. Well, that makes sense why you couldn't text." She laughed nervously. "I was starting to feel like a desperate loser."

Maddox shut his eyes. He was an asshole. He was totally stringing this beautiful girl along. She didn't deserve it. "Listen," he said soberly. "I think . . . well, I think maybe we made a mistake."

Catherine's eyebrow arched. "Excuse me?"

Her voice was sharp. Maddox felt a swirl in his gut. "What you said the other day was right. You're my coach. I'm your client. I'm afraid that if we start something, my training might suffer." It seemed like a good reason, one that wouldn't hurt her feelings.

A nasty laugh escaped from Catherine's lips. "Since when do you care about your *training*?"

He felt stung. "Since always!"

"Oh, please. This is about that Seneca girl, isn't it?" Her nostrils flared.

"It isn't," Maddox lied, horrified at the turn this had taken. "I swear. I just . . ." He swallowed hard. "I don't . . ."

Catherine crossed her arms over her chest, a very sinister look settling on her face. "Your training won't suffer if we're together, Maddy. I promise. But guess what? If you *do* dump me, it just might." She pointed to her phone in her hand. "I guess you've forgotten that I'm good friends with the coach who gave you your scholarship. I can suggest that he withdraw the offer."

Maddox's mouth dropped open. "You can't do that!"

She smiled sweetly. "Let's not test me, shall we?" She leaned forward and kissed him squarely on the lips. When she pulled back, there was a satisfied, superior smile on her face. "Do we have an understanding?"

Maddox's heart was thudding, and his chest felt tight. He eked out a very, very small nod.

"Perfect," Catherine said, squeezing his hands. Then she spun on her heel, her skirt lifting provocatively. "See you at practice tomorrow!" she called over her shoulder, and sauntered down the lane.

TWENTY-FIVE

FRIDAY EVENING, AERIN poured the rest of the bottle of red wine into her glass, not bothering to mop up the drips that spilled on the carpet. She was standing in the doorway of her sister's bedroom, staring in. There was that perfect attendance award from Helena's junior year on her bulletin board. There were those pictures of her and Kevin on the family's boat. There was the cross-body Coach bag Aerin had bought for Helena for Christmas the year she went missing. For a while, the family had left Helena's gifts under the tree in hopes that she'd return. That March, around the time her dad moved out, the presents were finally moved into Helena's room. By the summer, Aerin had gone in there and ripped all the gifts open, play-acting what she and her sister would have said to each other had it really been Christmas. *Oh, Helena, that eye shadow kit from Sephora is gorgeous! Can I borrow it sometime?* And, *A mini iPad! Lucky!*

Could Helena have been here that Christmas? Could she have opened those gifts herself?

Aerin looked at her phone again and scowled. Aside from Madison, who'd texted to say Seneca's father had unexpectedly shown up and spirited her away, no one else had reached out. She'd expected more from them. Maddox could have reassured her again that he didn't think she was a bitch. Brett could have sent her a parting picture of his torso. And what, had Seneca's dad taken her phone, too? Their split had been so abrupt, like a TV show she'd binge-watched suddenly getting canceled.

The wine had a tinny taste to it. She definitely *did* want to drop the case, though, right? Of course she did. They were getting nowhere. And it was much, much better to keep Helena's past sealed inside a box. Aerin was surprised by how hurt she felt by what she'd learned. All those years of thinking she and Helena were so close. All those years of trusting her sister, admiring her. Even that last day, when Helena had seemed so gentle with Aerin, so sweet and open. But she'd used Aerin as a pawn, sending her inside for a stupid task so she could slip away.

Was Helena really that unhappy to throw her life away and run off with some random guy to New York? She had to have been head over heels in love. Maybe she thought she'd only run away for a little while, then come back. Maybe she'd met with Mr. New York in the woods, as Seneca had suggested, but then he'd turned mean and ruthless and abusive. Helena had naively fallen for a Dr. Jekyll and got Mr. Hyde.

What if it really was all Aerin's fault for leaving her out there alone that day? If she'd balked, if she'd made Helena go get the bag, maybe this wouldn't have happened. And why had Aerin never considered that Helena might have deliberately sent her back inside? Even worse, why didn't the cops? Maybe she should have mentioned snooping in Helena's room in her early interviews. Maybe that could have led to the cops digging more into Helena's secrets, asking around about a secret boyfriend instead of just accepting that she was with Kevin, narrowing it down to someone, and finding Helena before . . . well, before her body turned up in the woods three counties away.

Perfect, another thing for Aerin to feel guilty about.

She tipped the wine to her mouth, but the glass already was empty again. So, okay, maybe she wasn't done with Helena completely. But how could she get to the heart of what happened? There had to be another way to find stuff out. If only she was omniscient and could read everyone's minds. If only she had special access to each suspect's motives and alibis—like if Kevin really had been at that conference, or if Greg Fine really had been in rehab, or if there was someone else she hadn't thought of yet who'd been doing something sketchy.

Then it hit her. There was special access: in the Dexby police station. And she knew someone who worked there.

She messily scrawled on a Post-it that she would be back later just in case her mom cared. Then she typed *Thomas Grove, Dexby, CT* into Google. He was listed. Aerin smiled. It seemed like a sign.

THOMAS LIVED IN a block of apartments on the water next to a restaurant boasting the best lobster rolls in all of Connecticut. The buildings were made to look Victorian, with dormers and turrets and fiddly molding details. Daffodils were starting to bloom in the front gardens, and the siding was painted a cheerful yellow. A bunch of cars were parked in the lot, and Aerin noticed a Norton motorcycle among them. She wondered if it was Thomas's.

Aerin walked up to #4 and rang the bell, wobbling from foot to foot in her kitten heels. She looked down at herself, taking in her tight sweater, tweed mini, and bare legs. Her eyelashes stuck together from all the mascara she'd slathered on, and her lips felt goopy with gloss.

The door flung open. Thomas stood on the other side in a pair of jeans that hung off his hips and a gray T-shirt that read *University of Connecticut Basketball*. His eyes widened. "Oh my God. *Hi*."

Aerin lifted a bottle of wine aloft. "Wanna share this with me? Maybe we could sit in a yacht in the harbor and pretend it's ours."

Thomas's gaze bounced from the bottle to Aerin's face. "Give me one second."

He shut the door softly. Footsteps receded. A minute later, he opened the door again. His hair was combed, and he'd changed into a long-sleeved shirt. His jeans were different, too—a darker wash, no holes in the knees—and he'd traded the yellowing socks Aerin had noticed for a pair of New Balances. Musky cologne wafted off him.

She hid a smile.

Thomas opened the door wider. "Why don't you come in? It's freezing out there."

The apartment was small but very neat—Aerin wondered if he'd quickly tidied, too. The living room was barely big enough for a brown tweed couch. A La-Z-Boy from sometime last century slumped in a corner. A boxy TV sat on a milk crate. Aerin squinted at it. Either she was drunker than she thought, or the baseball game on the screen was in black and white.

"This is . . . nice," she said uncertainly.

"Oh, don't lie." Thomas took the wine bottle into the kitchen. "It's a total dive. But it's cool. I have a view of the water, and it's nice living alone."

Aerin looked around at the rest of the room. There was an oil painting over the couch of a desert sunset. The lamps on either side didn't match and were both ugly in a pleated-lampshade, fake-gold-base kind of way. A scratchy-looking crocheted afghan in browns, yellows, and

oranges hung on the back of the plaid La-Z-Boy, and there were several
Hallmark ceramic figures on the bookshelf. A little boy played baseball,
another carried a knapsack like he was running away, and one more
grinned showing two missing front teeth. It gave Aerin a pang. When
she turned six, Helena had given her a Hallmark figurine of a ballerina.
She'd cherished that little girl, but after Helena went missing, Aerin
had put her away, her innocent smile too difficult to bear.

"Who decorated this place—your grandma?" she called out.

"As a matter of fact, she did. I lived with my grandparents for fifteen years. Grammy helped me move in here. That's her."

Aerin looked at a picture on the wall. Thomas sat with his arm
around an older lady in a muumuu and oversized glasses. She seemed
like the kind of jolly grandma who made her own spaghetti sauce and
fed stray cats and liked to drink beer. Not like Aerin's grandmother,
who barely left her Florida condo and complained about her life constantly to anyone who would listen.

"You lived with your grandparents?" Aerin repeated.

"Yup."

"Where were your parents?"

He uncorked the wine with a pop. "It wasn't safe there. They had
issues. *Have* issues."

Aerin wanted to weigh in that her parents were like that, too,
though she had a feeling her parents were *nothing* like what he was hint-
ing at. "Do you mean drugs?"

"Most definitely." Thomas got out two mismatched wineglasses.

"What kinds?"

"Pretty much anything available."

"Was that . . . hard for you?"

Thomas shrugged. "My grandparents are good people. They went to my soccer games, helped me with my homework, took me to movies they most definitely had no interest in. We went to the Cape every summer. My grandpa was a cop, too. In Norwalk."

His expression was open and unabashed. Aerin was surprised. She'd figured everyone who lived in Dexby—and especially those who went to Windemere-Carruthers—had easy lives. She wondered what that was like to grow up with train wrecks for parents. Thomas seemed to be coping really well.

She blinked. She was here to look for ways to get into the police station, not to bond.

She scanned the room for possibilities. Thomas's coat hung on a hook near the door; its pockets looked full. There was also a bowl in the kitchen that looked like it held odds and ends. But what if he kept things—like keys, or a keycard, or a code—in strange places, like how her parents used to keep petty cash in an unused flowerpot by the garage?

Thomas was staring at her as if he'd just asked her a question. "I'm sorry?" she said.

Thomas fiddled with an empty wineglass. "Maybe you should have something to eat before you drink more. You seem a little unsteady. Toast, maybe. Or a grilled cheese?"

The thought of that was overwhelmingly tempting. When had someone last offered to make her a *grilled cheese*?

"Say yes," Thomas said. "I make the best grilled cheese in this apartment complex."

Aerin couldn't help but laugh. "I'm not sure if that's impressive or not."

Thomas walked over to her, took her hands, and sat her down at the table. He was so close suddenly. She could smell the cologne he'd sprayed on. In any other situation, she would have leaned forward and kissed him hard. It wasn't that she didn't find him cute—in fact, he was much cuter than most of the guys she'd kissed. Sweeter, too. And she already *knew* he was a good kisser. That was probably part of the problem.

Thomas pulled away and sat in the chair opposite her. "So what's going on with Helena? Did you learn anything new?"

"Nah, I decided to drop it." Her voice sounded overly loud.

"Really?" Thomas fiddled with the wine cork. "I was hoping you'd crack it."

Aerin stared out the window. Thomas had a small deck out back with a single lounge chair. "The police were right. It's all just dead ends."

Silence. Aerin waited, hoping Thomas would volunteer something, a secret from those files. It would make this so much easier. Maybe it had been a terrible idea to come here.

She rose from the table, getting another idea. "You know, food might be nice after all."

Thomas bounded to the fridge. "I've got . . . shit. Not much. A hard-boiled egg? Pepperoni? Cottage cheese?"

"Cottage *cheese*?" Aerin stuck her tongue out. "What about Cheetos?"

Thomas peered at her over the fridge door. "Me and Chester Cheetah don't really mix."

"I saw a vending machine on the property. . . ." She fluttered her lashes at him.

Thomas shut the fridge door. "I'll check." He gestured to the couch. "Lie down."

She did as she was told. Thomas placed the afghan over her—it was actually a lot less scratchy than it looked. He pulled it all the way up to her nose, and she giggled, then felt a little sad. He was tucking her in. She had no idea when someone had last been this nurturing.

"I'll be right back, okay?" Thomas said. "Don't move."

The door closed, making the walls of the little place shake. Aerin counted to ten. Then she pushed the afghan aside, sprang up, and stood in the middle of the room, tips of her fingers wiggling. She darted to the coats on his hooks first, reaching into pockets. Nothing. She scampered into the kitchen and opened drawers and cupboards, but all she found were take-out menus, silverware, and random junk. His bathroom, which had a tiny sink and smelled like potpourri, held nothing interesting. His bedroom contained a small bureau by the window. She wasn't sure why she picked a bottom drawer, but inside was an iPad in a black sleeve. She opened it up and inspected the apps. iTunes. Netflix. Notepad. She clicked on Notepad, and a list came up. As her eyes adjusted, she realized what she was looking at. *Chase Bank: XCX1934. Gmail: NorthxNorthwest87.* And so on.

It was a list of passwords.

Aerin scanned the list hungrily. At the bottom was something called *Dexby PD Database.*

Bingo.

There were two passwords for the site, and some sort of keycode ID—too much to commit to memory. Aerin reached for her phone and took a shot of the whole screen. As she stood, she caught sight of her reflection in the mirror over the bureau. Her mascara was smudged. Her lipstick was on her teeth. Her shirt had shifted so that half her bra was showing.

"What are you *doing*?" she whispered to her reflection.

The lock clicked in the front door. Panicked, Aerin shoved the iPad back into the drawer and sprinted back to the couch, leaping under the covers just in time.

Thomas walked into the tiny living room, arms laden with a bunch of small chip bags. "They only had generic Cheetos, and I didn't know if you were a purist about having the real thing, so I also got Doritos, Fritos, a snack mix, and pretzels." He dumped them out on the coffee table, then unveiled a bottle of Cherry Coke. "I thought you might like this, too. It's always my favorite when I've had too much to drink."

Aerin's mind was tumbling. What if Thomas had come in when she was still looking at his iPad? That would have been a disaster. She had to get out of here. She needed to log on to that site *now*.

She sat up and gave him a fragile smile. "I feel worse than I thought. I should go home."

Thomas's face drooped. "You don't want to have the finest vending machine picnic in Dexby?"

"No, I'm really tired." Aerin stood up without looking at him. She could feel Grammy Grove watching from the wall. *I'm sorry, okay?* she yelled silently at the old lady. Now they'd probably never be friends.

Thomas stepped aside to let her get to the door. "I'd drive you, but I've only got the bike, and that might make you feel worse. Let me call you a cab?"

The cab arrived within a few minutes. Thomas packed the snacks in a plastic bag for her and helped her down the stairs. He moved to hand the driver some bills, but Aerin caught his arm. "I've got it. I'm sorry for coming."

"I like that you came over." Thomas patted her shoulder. "Feel better, okay?"

In the cab, Aerin nervously watched the boats bob on the harbor. Once they were off Thomas's street, she typed in the name of the Dexby

PD website on her phone. Fingers trembling, she typed in the passwords from the screenshot in the order Thomas had listed them. Her heart thudded as the little wheel spun. What if she'd input the passwords incorrectly? What if the cops tracked her phone and came to arrest her?

But then a message popped up. *Welcome back, T. Grove.*

Aerin clicked on a button that said *Past cases*, then selected the year when Helena had gone missing. A file folder titled *H. Kelly, Case #23566* popped up.

Swallowing hard, she opened it. There were statements, a missing persons report, and information about Helena's bone decomposition. Aerin saw a folder called *Persons of Interest* and pounced on it. Kevin Larssen's name was first. Inside the folder, the first item to appear were thumbnails of photos Aerin had never seen. She pressed on each to enlarge them, then gasped. The first was a picture of Kevin and Senator Gorman in an embrace. *Connecticut Youth Leadership Conference Center,* read a sign behind them. A date stamp read, December 8— the day Helena had gone missing. Another stamp over the photo said, *Confidential.*

So Gorman *had* been at that conference, and Kevin was with him. Maybe it explained why he'd missed his speech, but also why he was insistent about the alibi. Aerin bet Gorman had paid off the cops to keep the photos quiet. He wouldn't want that information to come out on the news.

There were more photos of Kevin after that weekend, too— heading into school, going to the bookstore, having dinner with Gorman in the city. The cops must have been tailing him obsessively, maybe seeing if he was doing anything suspect. That was reassuring, at least—Aerin doubted he would have been able to sneak away to murder Helena during that time. She'd never wanted Kevin to be the guilty one, not really.

Her gaze scanned the rest of the suspects. Greg Fine was there, too, but inside his file was a report from the Halcyon Heather rehab facility, stating that he'd been an inpatient from November that year all the way until March. So was he out as well?

The cab reached her street and pulled up to her house. "Here we are," the driver said as he turned into the driveway. "Looks like you have a visitor."

Aerin's head snapped up. A figure sat on her front steps, but there was no way it could be her mom. She squinted harder, taking in the longish hair, the drapey dress, the tough-girl booties.

Seneca.

She shoved some bills at the driver and hurried up the walkway, feeling surprisingly elated. Seneca shot to her feet. "I'm so sorry, Aerin."

"It *took* you long enough!" Aerin said at the same time.

The girls stopped and grinned at each other. Then, letting out a little bleat, Seneca hugged Aerin tightly. "I'm a jerk," she muttered into Aerin's shoulder. "I shouldn't have talked to you like that, I shouldn't have said that about Maddox. He doesn't think you're a bitch, I swear."

"I hated how everyone had left so suddenly," Aerin was saying over her. "I don't want to give up on the case—I shouldn't have run away."

Seneca stepped back from their embrace. "You don't want to give up on the case?" she asked. Aerin shook her head. "Well, good. Because I think I figured something out."

Aerin's tongue felt furry with wine. "That's a relief, because all the suspects we thought might be viable aren't looking so hot anymore."

Seneca narrowed her eyes, but Aerin didn't feel like explaining right then. She rolled her hands impatiently, urging Seneca to say what she'd figured out. "That message on the crane," Seneca started. "It's not *hi*—it's initials. H.I. I'm thinking it's either the secret boyfriend, or Helena's name if she were to *marry* the secret boyfriend. And I've been thinking, and I've come up with a name."

Aerin blinked hard. Her brain felt slow and sloppy. She ticked through people in her sister's life—friends, boyfriends, uncles, teachers. She thought of faces at that country club, people who came into Scoops. But there weren't many people whose last name started with *I*. Her eyes widened. She knew someone who had those initials exactly.

A shiver ran down her back. She touched Seneca's arm. "Heath Ingram?"

Seneca nodded. "That's who I thought of, too."

TWENTY-SIX

NOT ONLY HAD Aerin been cool with reopening the case, but she'd also filled Seneca in on her foray into the Dexby PD site. The next day, after a decent night's sleep and a shower, Seneca had FaceTimed with her dad, showing him around Aerin's place and introducing him to Aerin to prove she was okay. Once she was in the clear, the girls set off for the Ingram mansion.

Seneca knew a little about the Ingrams, mostly because they were friends with the Kellys and had pitched in start-up cash for the first Scoops of Dexby store. Years ago, on Facebook, Heath Ingram had been tagged in some of Helena's photos. One was at a Christmas event; he and Helena were both in tartan plaid, making goofy faces. In another, they were sitting on the back of a horse-drawn carriage, huddled in a friendly way. Or maybe *more* than friendly?

"I can't believe Heath still lives with his parents," Aerin whispered now, navigating the country roads with one hand on the wheel. She was wearing a black-and-pink-printed dress that clung to every curve and a pair of nude heels. "He didn't sponge off his family in high school at *all*. He drove an old Subaru. He shopped at consignment stores. When we were little, he made up this play called *Ms. Badger and Ms. Fox Have a Plan*, about how these characters burn down their parents' mansion so that the fire would heat the town. Helena was Ms. Badger, I was Ms. Fox, and Heath was Mummy, who begged us not to burn her hand-bags and shoes. And when we slept over there, Heath said we all had to pretend we lived in a tenement and had to sleep in the same bed."

Seneca gave her a strange look. "You all slept in the same bed?"

Aerin twisted her mouth as if she'd just realized how strange that was. "Maybe that's why Helena kept a relationship with Heath a secret. We were basically raised as siblings."

Seneca widened her eyes. "I heard your mom call him her almost son in an interview once."

Aerin took her eyes off the road for a moment. "What interview was *that*?"

The memory changed shape. "No, actually, it was a YouTube video of your mom making ice cream. Heath and someone else—I can't remember who—were guest stars."

Aerin looked really confused. "I thought my mom took those vid-eos down years ago."

Mrs. Kelly probably had—Seneca had watched them when Helena first vanished. "The timeline fits, too," she rushed on. "Heath attended Columbia the same winter Helena disappeared. That January, Heath dropped out, moved to Colorado, lived at the Ritz in Beaver Creek, and learned to snowboard."

"I thought he was so lucky," Aerin mused. "The Ritz at Beaver Creek is the bomb."

"But I called the Ritz this morning, and there were no lesson records for Heath on file. Maybe he taught himself?"

"He would have definitely needed an instructor. He was a mess on the little slopes around here, even on beginner skis."

"So maybe he *wasn't* snowboarding—or even at the Ritz?" Seneca looked at her phone. "I've called in a favor from MizMaizie, this woman I know on Case Not Closed. She used to work with the Seattle PD, and she'll run ID checks of Heath in Colorado—see if he rented an apartment, got a driver's license, registered to vote. I'll have her run a check on New York, too, as well as some other states. We'll find where he was. And as for this visit, we'll see what he tells us. We'll keep it light and friendly."

Aerin's face clouded. "I'm not feeling particularly friendly right now, if all this is true."

"I know. It goes to show you that you often don't really know a person at all."

She heard the acid in her voice only after she spoke. Aerin cleared her throat. "What happened with Maddy?"

Seneca's cheeks blazed. "He has a sort-of girlfriend he forgot to mention."

Aerin snorted. *"Who?"*

"This girl Tara. She's beautiful."

Aerin rolled her eyes. "His loss."

Seneca pretended to study a red barn whipping past. Maybe Aerin was right. It was a much better way of looking at it than wallowing in misery. She felt ashamed of herself—last night she'd had a *dream* about Maddox. They were on that penthouse deck again, and Maddox had pulled her close and told her that it was over between him and his girlfriend and he chose Seneca. She couldn't believe she was even capable of dreaming something so teenybopper and saccharine. Worse, she hated how elated she'd felt in those hazy moments when she'd just woken up, before reality had set back in.

"Here we are," Aerin said faintly, pulling up to a wrought-iron gate. The place was like a fortress, all stone and slate and iron and grandiose columns. It had double chimneys, ivy crawling up the walls, a greenhouse, and a small vineyard. A gardener was digging in the flower beds in the front. Off to the side was a garage that had space for at least six or seven vehicles.

"When was the last time you were here?" Seneca asked.

Aerin's mouth twisted. "Christmas. They had a big party. But when Helena was alive, we were here practically every weekend."

"Sleeping in his bed," Seneca quipped, then winced.

Aerin put her head in her hands. "I'm so not ready for this."

"I know," Seneca said. "But thanks for doing it today." She'd explained that she only had two more days before she was due home and that they had to put this case on speed-solve.

Aerin sighed and pressed the intercom buzzer. "Yes?" called a tinny, accented voice.

"Hi!" Aerin said brightly. "It's Aerin Kelly. Is Heath home?"

"Uh..." There was a pause. Then the voice said, "Yes, come in."

The gate rolled open. Aerin started up the long driveway. She glanced at Seneca again, looking conflicted. "I think we need to bring the boys back. Not to be sexist or whatever, but in moments like this, it would be nice to have some muscles on our team. And Madison, too—she's just good to have around."

Seneca slumped, but she understood Aerin's logic. "Let's just get through Heath, okay? Then you can call the others."

They parked on the driveway and got out. Aerin led Seneca to the front door, which was opening as they approached. A tall, wavy-haired guy in his early twenties appeared. He was wearing a rumpled gray T-shirt, khakis, and loafers that barely had any soles left. There were three string bracelets on his wrist. He had a winning, I've-been-a-bad-boy smile, made even cuter by two crooked front teeth. Seneca didn't want to stare at him, but it was hard not to.

"Ms. Fox!" Heath said, gliding toward Aerin with arms out-stretched. "How are you?"

"Fine." Aerin touched Seneca's arm. "This is my friend Seneca. We have a question for you—I considered calling, but we were in the area, so I thought we'd just stop by."

"You're always welcome." Heath gave Seneca a once-over, long lashes shading his green eyes. She felt her skin go hot. There was some-thing unapologetically sexy about him. Like the kind of guy you'd make out with at a music festival in the desert.

Heath led them into a huge foyer with marble floors and a double staircase. A vase half the size of Seneca's body stood on a table; phallic lilies protruded from it. By the stairs was a portrait of Marissa Ingram sitting on a divan, her face in profile, her legs outstretched, a long-haired white cat tucked into her side.

They turned and walked through a parlor full of ancient-looking books, leather furniture, Oriental rugs, and fiddly wooden tables bear-ing half-completed jigsaw puzzles. Every painting was of a man on a horse. Finally Heath stopped in a smaller room. It held a grand-looking fireplace, but this one was filled with hardcover books. An egg chair hung by the window. The curtains were paisley silk, and there was a huge saguaro cactus in a pot in the corner.

Aerin looked around. "Didn't this used to be your dad's office?"

"Yeah, but he took a room upstairs. I remodeled." As Heath dropped into a leather sectional, his iPhone rang. "Hey, Mom," he said patiently. "Dad? I don't know where he is. . . ."

Seneca studied the books in the fireplace. *Your Best You. Overcoming Anything. When Life Gives You Lemons, Make Lemonade!* Could Heath's lemons have to do with Helena?

Heath hung up and groaned. "My mom tries and tries and tries, but my dad's so checked out." He leaned back on the couch. "So what's up, Ms. Fox? Can Lupita get you something to drink? Water? Rum punch?" He chuckled slyly. "It's a little early, but she makes a good one."

"We're fine." Aerin moved closer to Seneca. "I told Seneca you went to Columbia, since she's considering transferring there, and she was wondering what you thought of it."

"It's awesome." Heath looked wistful. "I wish I could have stayed longer, but college and me didn't mix at the time. Are you looking for someone to contact? I could probably put in a good word for you with the dean of admissions—he owes my dad a favor."

Seneca widened her eyes. If only she could take him up on that. It would certainly cushion the blow when she had to tell her dad about U of M.

Aerin shifted her weight. "Didn't you give Helena a tour of Columbia?"

A wrinkle formed on Heath's brow. It seemed like mentioning Helena's name made everyone around here bristle. Then again, who wanted to be reminded of such a horrible thing? After Seneca's mom disappeared, no one wanted to say her name, either. "Helena was more of an NYU girl," Heath answered.

"So did you guys tour NYU together?"

Heath shook his head. "I didn't see her in New York. And if she did tour Columbia, she probably went with that Kevin guy." He chuckled. "What did she see in him, anyway?"

Aerin's foot jiggled so wildly Seneca worried it might fall off. "I'm not sure she *was* into Kevin, actually. She didn't mention that to you?"

"No . . ." Heath cocked his head, still smiling.

If he knew something, he was doing a good job of hiding it. Seneca decided to switch tacks. "Where did you transfer to when you left Columbia?"

Heath let out a mix between a laugh and a cough. "You don't know? My mother acts like it was national news that I didn't pick another school."

"What did you do instead?"

"I went to Colorado. Chilled out. Learned to snowboard."

"Oh, that's right," Aerin said. "You lived at the Ritz in Beaver Creek, right?"

"Uh-huh." He furiously rubbed his nose, like he was trying to erase his freckles.

"I've only been to the Ritz for lunch," Seneca piped up. "I can't imagine *staying* there."

"The rooms are pretty sweet," Heath agreed.

"And it's a short shuttle to the slopes, right?" Seneca asked, recalling the research she'd done on the Ritz that morning.

Heath shook his head. "Nope, there's a lift out back. Ski in, ski out."

Seneca jiggled her foot. That was true. "And I'm guessing you met Phinneas?"

Heath blinked. "Phinneas?"

"You totally met him," Seneca egged on. "He's, like, a Ritz fixture."

"Oh, *Phinneas*," Heath said after a beat. "Yeah. Most amazing bartender ever."

The door swung open. Everyone jumped. Mrs. Ingram bustled in. She wore a cream-colored shift with big interlocking Chanel *C*s on the belt. She was pulling her husband behind her, who was frowning at something on his phone. "Heath, I'd really like you to come with us to lunch," Mrs. Ingram was saying, but then she did a double take. "Aerin! Why, *hello*, honey!"

Aerin air-kissed Heath's mother, then hugged Mr. Ingram. "Sorry to drop in on you. We just had a question for Heath about Columbia. My friend is interested in the school."

Mr. Ingram made a sour face. "Heath won't be much help. He never went to class."

Marissa shot him a look, then smiled at Seneca. "Are you from Dexby? Have we met?"

Seneca's gaze swiveled from family member to family member. Marissa's smile was all gums. Mr. Ingram's attention was on his phone again. Heath wasn't looking at his mother. He was looking at Seneca, his focus laser-sharp, his eyes cold. Seneca glanced down at his hand. It was gripping the arm of the chair so hard that blue veins stuck out.

Aerin's gaze was on Heath's hand, too. She jumped to her feet. "Anyway, we don't want to interrupt your lunch."

Marissa scoffed. "Don't be silly. Why don't you both come? We're going to the yacht club."

"Thank you so much, but we're good." Aerin was already at the door. She waggled her fingers at Heath, but he only gave a trace of a smile. A vein throbbed in his neck.

Only when they were safely out the door and in Aerin's car did Seneca let out a breath. "I think Heath's a little confused."

"Why?" Aerin asked, eyes wide.

"Because Phinneas? The Ritz fixture? I did some research on him this morning, too. He's not a bartender, like Heath said." Seneca raised her eyebrows meaningfully. "He's the resort's *dog*."

TWENTY-SEVEN

BRETT SLUMPED ON the leather couch in Maddox's den. The start screen to *Battlefield 4* was on the TV, but neither he nor Maddox had picked up a game controller. The room smelled like feet, Goldfish crackers, and weed—Madison had joined them, too, and was reading a *Vogue* on the chaise.

He hadn't been ready to leave Dexby, so after wandering around town, he'd cabbed it back to Maddox's place. "Can we hang?" he'd asked. He was grateful that Maddox had let him in, because his near hookup with Aerin was eating at him, and he needed a guy's perspective.

"We were *this close*," he was saying to Maddox, describing how Aerin had seemed so into it. "But it just didn't feel right, you know?"

"Wait until she isn't drunk," Madison called from the couch. "So it's real."

"Exactly." Brett sat back and smiled. It was going to happen between them. He knew it.

Maddox's phone dinged. He looked at the screen and made a

strange face. Brett leaned over—his buddy's phone had been dinging like crazy since he'd arrived. A text read, *What are you doing right now?*

He poked Maddox's side. "Who's this Catherine who's so eager to find you?"

"This . . . girl," Maddox said, hesitation in his voice.

Another *ding*. Brett peeked at the screen. *Uh, what's with the silence?* a new text read. *Don't you remember what we talked about?* "Jeez, pushy much?" he murmured.

"I told you Catherine's crazy," Madison said, not looking up from her magazine.

Maddox mumbled something Brett couldn't make out.

"You should call Seneca," Madison singsonged.

Maddox placed his phone facedown on the couch. "What's the point?"

"I'm sure she'd appreciate an apology," Brett said. "Maybe she wants to apologize to you, too. I got an apology text from her already."

Maddox shut his eyes. "I don't know. . . ."

Brett shrugged. "Dial star-67 before you call her. Or use mine." He lobbed his phone across the cushions; it landed next to Maddox's lap. "C'mon. Clear the air."

Sighing, Maddox picked up the phone and scrolled through Brett's contacts. After a moment, he pressed the phone to his ear. "Put it on speaker," Brett instructed.

Maddox shot him a look. "I'm not putting it on speaker!" But he ended up hitting the speaker button anyway. On the third ring, Seneca picked up. "Hey, Brett," her voice blared through the speaker, sounding businesslike. "I was actually just about to call you."

"Actually, it's Maddox," Maddox said into the phone.

There was a pause. "Oh," she said frostily. "Well, I guess you can hear this, too."

"Wait," Maddox said. "I want to talk first." Brett gave him a thumbs-up. "I'm really sorry. About . . . you know. I screwed up bigtime." His voice seemed filled with regret.

Seneca took a while to respond again, but then she sighed. "Okay, Maddox. I'm sorry, too. And actually, we have more work to do on the case."

"You're not in Maryland?" Brett blurted in the background.

Maddox shot him a look. "Hi, Brett," Seneca called out. "I had my dad turn back. Actually, Aerin and I are pulling into Maddox's driveway right now."

An engine purred at the front of the house. Brett, Maddox, and Madison strode to the door just as Aerin and Seneca were stepping out of Aerin's car. Brett was so overjoyed to see them again he gave Seneca a huge hug. "Good to have you back."

"My turn!" Aerin said next. Brett picked her up and swung her around, wishing he could dip her romantically and kiss her right there.

But then Seneca started up the path, all business. "We've ruled out Kevin and Greg."

"How?" Brett said, following them.

"It doesn't matter," Seneca said, shooting Aerin a conspiratorial glance. "But, Brett, your text about the crane got me thinking. What if *Hi* is actually initials—*H.I.?* One person fits: Heath Ingram."

Brett felt proud of himself. "I knew that crane was a clue. But who's Heath Ingram?"

"Kelly family friend," Madison piped up.

Seneca glanced at Maddox. "Do you remember Heath from the Kellys'?"

"Sort of," Maddox said slowly. "He came over with Helena, once. Helena left the room, and he turned to me in the kitchen. And he said . . ." Maddox trailed off.

"Said what?" Seneca urged.

Maddox sighed. "He was like, 'You're into Helena, aren't you? I see the way you look at her. You're spying on her.'"

"*Were* you?" Aerin demanded.

"Dude, *no*," Maddox groaned. "My point is that he seemed paranoid. Like maybe he was making sure I didn't know something."

Seneca sat down at the kitchen table and pulled a laptop out of her bag. "We caught him in a lie this morning." She looked at Aerin. "*Everyone* at the Ritz knows that dog. It's all over TripAdvisor—guests can take Phinneas out for walks, and he hangs out at the front desk—you practically trip over him when you check in. And he was definitely alive five years ago, when Heath was there. If he had really stayed at the Ritz, he would have known about that dog."

"Heath said Phinneas was a bartender," Aerin explained to the group.

"So what *was* he up to?" Brett asked, intrigued.

"We don't know," Aerin murmured.

Seneca started typing on the laptop. "I'm thinking he was back here, in New York, five years ago. Hiding Helena. I have MizMaizie on it."

"From the boards?" Brett whistled. "She's got access to all kinds of databases."

"Guys, wait a minute," Maddox blurted.

Seneca looked up, her brow furrowed. "What?"

Maddox took a breath. "There's something I didn't tell you about when I was mugged." His Adam's apple bobbed. "I remember someone looming over me, saying I needed to stop or I was going to be killed. Okay, it sounds far-fetched . . . but what if it was related to the case? What if they meant stop *digging*?"

Madison went pale. "Wait, what?"

Brett stared at him. "Are you sure they said that?"

Maddox pulled at the collar of his tee. His phone started dinging again, but he ignored it. "It feels pretty real."

"Why didn't you tell the police?" Aerin cried.

Maddox stared at his hands. "Because . . . it sounds nuts."

Seneca twisted her mouth. "It still could have just been a mugger. They could have meant stop squirming, or you'll be killed. Or stop shouting."

Aerin waved her arm. "I agree." Though there was an edge to her voice, like maybe she wasn't so sure.

Brett looked at Maddox. What if Maddox was right, and someone was onto them? But the girls were already studying Seneca's computer. "Huh," Seneca said as she pulled up Heath's page on Facebook, leaning back in her chair and squinting at the screen. "Here's the weekend of December 8, five years ago, when Helena took off. Heath put up a post that he was in Aspen . . . but there's no picture."

Brett leaned over the screen. "If we could get phone records from around that time, we could prove where he really was. My money's here."

Madison looked confused. "But where did Heath and Helena go? Not to his house in Dexby. Not to his Columbia dorm room, either—he dropped out first semester."

"Maybe they got an apartment somewhere in the city," Brett suggested. "Because they had to be in New York, remember? Loren delivered to them."

Snap.

Brett stood up straighter, on alert. "What was that?"

The others frowned and cocked their heads. "I didn't hear any-thing," Madison said.

Another sound, like branches rustling, though it wasn't a windy day. Now Maddox rose and peered out the windows. "Someone's outside."

"I'll check it out," Brett said.

"No, I will," Maddox said, jumping up.

"We both will," Brett said, puffing up his chest.

They moved cautiously through the den toward the sliding glass door. Dusk had fallen, the sky a yellowish-purple. A tire swing way at the back of the property swayed hypnotically.

The air was crisp and held the lingering, wooden odor of a bonfire. Birds chirped loudly, as if in warning. "Hello?" Brett called out as they opened the door. Maddox's phone dinged again, the sound muffled in his pocket.

The air was pointedly quiet, as though someone was trying very hard to stay still. He and Maddox exchanged a nod, then took one step off the patio. Brett walked left. Nothing in the side yard. A coiled water hose. The plastic cover on the grill.

Then he felt a sharp crack on the side of his head. It knocked him sideways, and blood filled his mouth. He dropped to his knees. Some-thing hit him again, this time on the back. He tried to flip over, tried to see what had happened, but he was immobilized.

"Brett?" he heard Maddox's voice cry out from far away. His buddy appeared over him, but he was blurry. Brett tried to sit and wipe his eyes. His fingers touched something sticky. "Brett?" Maddox was shouting at him now. "Brett, say something!"

Brett opened his mouth but couldn't speak. His head prickled like he was going to faint. He glanced around, trying to understand what had happened—and if it might happen again. A shadow moved across his field of vision, someone in black. His eyes focused. The figure lurked across the street behind a neighbor's parked car. He raised his arm, trying to signal to Maddox, but the dizziness overtook him, and he slumped to the grass.

"Brett!" Maddox yelled in his ear. "Brett, buddy, don't fall asleep!" But Brett couldn't fight it anymore. He shut his eyes, his head throbbing so badly it felt like someone had driven a spike through his brain. He felt himself sinking, then, down, down, down, into a pit of darkness. The last sound he heard was the insistent dinging of Maddox's phone.

TWENTY-EIGHT

SENECA SAT IN a red plastic chair in a tiny, curtained-off cubby at the Dexby Memorial Hospital emergency room. In the bed, Brett lay with his eyes closed tight, though his lips kept twitching. An IV tube ran into his arm, and there was a blackish-purple bruise at his jaw and a lot of dried blood in his hair. Every time she looked at it, she felt a little ill. The coroner had tried to clean up her mom before Seneca saw her, but there had been a lot of dried blood on her, too.

The door creaked open. Aerin and Maddox walked in with cans of soda from the vending machine. "How's he doing?" Aerin whispered, handing Seneca a root beer.

Seneca shrugged. "He hasn't moved since you left. But the doctor came back and said he didn't have a concussion. They don't need to run any more tests. He'll be okay."

After the boys had gone to check outside, hair had risen on the back of Seneca's neck. What if Maddox was right? What if that voice she heard outside her hotel room door was real? What if it hadn't just been a mugger in New York? Was someone after them? She figured she was being silly, but she'd gone out to check on them anyway. When she'd seen Brett lying in the yard, unresponsive, and Maddox leaning over him, she first thought she was hallucinating. This couldn't be *real*. Someone couldn't *actually* be after them. And then she'd felt responsible. She should have taken Maddox more seriously.

There was a croaking sound from the bed. Seneca turned and watched as Brett's eyes scrunched closed, then opened. He focused on the figures above him, and his dry lips parted. The first person he looked at was Aerin. He tried to smile.

"Welcome back," Madison gushed, squeezing his hands.

"Just lie there, bro," Maddox added. "You're in the hospital."

Brett twisted and winced. "Someone hit me."

Everyone exchanged a glance. They'd pretty much deduced that. "Did you get a look at who it was?" Seneca asked.

Brett stared at the IV running into his arm. "Not really."

Aerin pulled open the curtain and peeked into the busy ER. "We need to call the cops."

"We can't." Seneca yanked the curtain closed again. "They'll want to know why someone might have done this to Brett. We'll have to tell them what we've been up to."

"Someone attacked him! We're supposed to just let that go?"

Maddox shifted, looking uncomfortable. "Aerin, what we found out about Kevin, the writing on the crane, even talking to Loren—not reporting it to the police might be seen as withholding evidence. We could be in major trouble. Someone threatening us could be a good thing if you think about it. It means we're close—maybe even right. Someone's pissed."

"I don't want anyone else getting their ass kicked!" Aerin cried.

Seneca chewed on her necklace. She agreed that the cops would have too many questions.

She turned back to Brett. "We have to stick to our story. When we brought you here, we told the doctor you and Maddox had been practicing *Ultimate Fighter* moves and things got rowdy. If a cop does happen to ask questions, you can't say anything more than that."

Brett winced. "Can we at least say I kicked Maddox's ass, too? I don't want them to think that this skinny guy put me in the hospital."

"Dude, I could totally take you," Maddox said, laughing.

"Can we skip the macho act?" Seneca interjected. She leaned closer to Brett. "So you don't remember *anything* about who hit you? No description?"

"All I remember is that they were in black. I saw them across the street. I tried to signal to you, Maddox, but you were concentrating on me."

Maddox raised his eyebrows. "The mugger in the city wore black, too. And was your attacker sort of medium height? Had a high voice? My mugger was—maybe it was the same person."

"What, like, a *woman*?" Brett looked horrified. "Hell no. A woman didn't hit me."

"Actually, I got a female vibe at the Restful Inn, too," Seneca said. She plopped back down in the plastic chair, feeling exhausted. "It's got to be Heath Ingram, though. We *visited* him yesterday. Asked questions about Helena. Maybe he was just disguising his voice...?"

Aerin tossed her can of Sprite in the small trash can by the curtain. "I just wish we had proof. *And* motive. Why would Heath whisk Helena to New York and then kill her?"

"Maybe she was cheating on him?" Maddox suggested.

"If only she'd told someone about Heath," Seneca mumbled. "A blog, or a diary." She racked her brain, trying to remember any inkling from Facebook, any hint that Heath and Helena were really together, but she couldn't come up with anything.

"The cops searched all of that stuff," Aerin said. "There was nothing."

A thoughtful look crossed Brett's face, and he propped himself up on the pillows. "Aerin. Didn't Helena say something about secrets to you the day she took off?"

Aerin furrowed her brow. "No . . ."

"You sure? You told Seneca you snooped in her room, and there was something else strange she said to you."

Aerin's gaze shifted. "*Oh.* I said that I missed her, and she said that we'd always talk but things just might have to be under wraps. Is that what you mean?"

Brett pointed at her. *"Yes."*

Seneca wrinkled her nose. "Aerin told the police that. It's nothing new."

Brett laced his hands behind his head. "Maybe she was trying to tell you something, especially if she was planning her escape. Maybe she was discreetly referring to a place you both loved to get wraps, as in sandwiches?"

Aerin blinked. "Huh?"

"Did anyone you know wear a head scarf?" Brett asked. "Or like . . . could it be referring to wrapping *paper*?"

Seneca snorted. "Brett, you are so weird."

"Ooh!" Madison squeaked. "Under Wraps is an app. Could that be something?"

Seneca whipped around. "It *is*?"

Madison nodded. "It's sort of like Truth in Truth or Dare—you post your secrets on it, and people rate them."

"I've never heard of an app called Under Wraps," Seneca said, dubious.

"It didn't take off. It had a stupid name, and there were a lot of other apps out there like it that had a better interface." Madison raised her eyebrows. "There was another feature where people whispered secrets privately. Couples used it to sext and post dirty things they were going to do to each other after school. Parents wouldn't know where to find the messages."

Aerin's eyes widened. "Oh my God. There *was* another part to what she said. *It'll have to be under wraps . . . like on our phones.* She might have been giving me a clue!"

Fireworks were going off in Seneca's brain. "So Under Wraps is a way for couples to talk to each other? Privately, untraceably, without using texts their parents would see?"

Madison nodded. "That's what I just said."

Seneca looked at Aerin excitedly. "We need Helena's old phone."

TWENTY MINUTES LATER, Seneca and Aerin returned to the hospital from Aerin's house with Helena's iPhone in hand. Though Seneca had told the others she'd wait before looking through it, she couldn't help but scroll through Helena's call list in the car. There were tons of calls to Heath. Texts, too. But maybe that made sense—they were friends. Also, the texts were all friendly and mundane, most of them recounting play-by-plays of *Walking Dead* episodes. On a lark, she looked up the contact for Katie, Helena's old rival. There was only one text from her, six months before Helena vanished: *thanks for nothing.*

Helena hadn't replied. What did it mean? Then again, maybe it wasn't worth pursuing—Katie had already been cleared.

She looked at Aerin. "Do you remember seeing Heath's name in Helena's file on the police server?"

"Sure, but it just said he was in Colorado. The interview was really short—the cops didn't question him about anything else." Aerin sniffed. "Maybe that's because the Ingrams helped fund the police station's luxury renovation that same year."

Back in the ER, Brett looked a lot stronger and was sitting up against his pillows playing *Candy Crush* on his phone. After a few minutes of going through Helena's old device, Maddox groaned. "*Under Wraps* isn't loaded on here."

"Are you sure?" Seneca asked, disappointed.

"I've looked everywhere. I checked in folders hidden inside folders, under different app names . . ."

"You can hide apps on phones?" Aerin's voice trembled. "I didn't know that."

"Damn it," Madison whispered under her breath. "That seemed so promising."

Then Seneca's phone beeped. "It's MizMaizie." She looked at the e-mail. *"I found no records of Heath Ingram in New York or Connecticut for the dates in question,"* she read.

Brett hitched higher in the hospital bed. "Really?"

There was more. *"There are hits for a Heath Ingram matching your age and description living in Colorado five years ago. He applied for a Colorado State driver's license on January 1 of that year. There's a marriage license, too."* She stopped. "Wait, what?"

Aerin blinked hard. "Heath *married* Helena?"

"No. He married someone named Caitlynn Drexler." Seneca showed them the picture attached. It was a dark-haired girl with wide gray eyes and a bland smile. Her hair was fixed in tiny braids. She also had a large daisy painted on her cheek—Seneca didn't *think* it was a tattoo.

"MizMaizie ran a report on her, too. Apparently, she's a recruiting member of the Church of the Spirit Animal." Seneca looked up. "Isn't that a cult that hippies join, and they take all your money? I saw a *60 Minutes* report on it a while ago."

Aerin rounded her eyes. "Do you think *Heath* was part of that?"

"That would be a good reason for making up a story about snowboarding and the Ritz," Seneca murmured. "When Heath came back to Dexby, did he immediately move in back home?"

Aerin snapped her fingers. "Maybe he had to. Maybe this chick stole all his cash for the cult."

"Think they're still married?" Seneca scrolled through the report. "I don't see an annulment. . . ."

"So Heath *didn't* kill Helena?" Brett said slowly.

"I don't know," Seneca answered. "Maybe not?"

Bzzt.

Seneca's spine straightened. She thought it was her phone, maybe another message from MizMaizie. But it was Brett's bed that was vibrating. Her breath caught.

It was Helena's phone. A call was coming in.

Everyone stared at it as though it was possessed. Aerin grabbed it, her hands shaking. "It's from a blocked number," she whispered.

The phone buzzed again. No one moved. Finally, Brett sat up and snatched it. "Hello?" he said weakly into the mouthpiece.

Silence. A wrinkle formed on Brett's brow. He blinked once, twice, and then said, "Yes. Yes. Okay. Thanks, man." He hung up the phone. "That was Loren."

"Drug dealer Loren?" Seneca squeaked.

Brett nodded distractedly. "He remembered the address for Helena. It just came to him, he said, out of nowhere, and he still had this number." His voice was amazed and trancelike. "She got deliveries at the building where John Lennon was shot. On West Seventy-Second and the park."

Maddox's eyes darted back and forth. "That's the Dakota."

Aerin drew back, her brow furrowed. "I don't know anyone who lives there. . . ."

"Loren remembered something else, too," Brett added. "The name on the account wasn't Helena's. It was *Ingram*."

Seneca clapped her hands. "So it *was* Heath!"

Maddox sank back on the pillow. "How could Heath be in Colorado *and* New York?"

"Maybe he went *after* he killed Helena," Seneca suggested.

"Or maybe he was going back and forth," Brett said.

"No."

Seneca turned. Aerin was standing slack-jawed by the door. "It's not Heath."

"But, Aerin, it *has* to be," Seneca pressed.

Aerin shook her head slowly. She looked like she was going to be sick. "There's another Ingram, one who definitely had access to a place in New York. *Skip* Ingram. *Harris* Ingram—*H.I.*" She clapped a trembling hand over her mouth. "I think Helena was with Heath's dad."

TWENTY-NINE

THAT ASSHOLE, AERIN thought numbly as she sat in the backseat of a New York City taxi. It was Sunday morning, and she and the others were speeding down Central Park West toward the Dakota building. They needed to get into Mr. Ingram's apartment, find some kind of solid proof.

That selfish, disgusting, fucking asshole. The words drilled constantly in her brain like a heartbeat. Mr. Ingram—she couldn't think of him as *Harris*, and definitely not as *Skip*—was totally the guy. He fit their profile. He'd *done it.*

He was scandalously older. Debonair. Cultured—a huge art collector. Aerin didn't remember him collecting Asian art per se, but that was because he collected *everything*—he and Aerin's dad used to go to auctions all the time, the way other dads attended sporting events. Her dad would come back with ugly abstract paintings and wooden tribal statues, all of which he hauled off to his hideous apartment downtown. Presumably Mr. Ingram had done the same.

Naturally Helena would have had to recruit Kevin Larssen as

her fake boyfriend to cover up an affair with a *married man*. And the apartment at the Dakota? Even *that* Aerin remembered, in hindsight— Marissa had prattled about it years ago. She didn't *want* Skip to get a place in the city, but they might as well get something fancy. The Dakota, she boasted, had one of the most difficult-to-please co-op boards in town.

And, oh, the billions of times Mr. Ingram and Helena were around each other in Dexby! The barbecues, casual dinners, lavish parties, the movies in their home theater. All the times Aerin had seen Mr. Ingram and Helena talking in the kitchen and thought nothing of it. She'd thought, *Wow, Helena clearly got the polite gene in the family, because I don't have a clue how to talk to adults.* And all the while, Mr. Ingram was checking out her sister's chest. It made her ill. Just their affair alone was a disgusting crime. Helena wasn't even eighteen. Mr. Ingram should have known better.

Still, Aerin couldn't picture Mr. Ingram *murdering* someone. At one of the first Scoops Christmas parties, the Santa they'd hired had gotten the flu, and Mr. Ingram had stepped in, donning the red suit and *ho-ho*ing good-naturedly. But even that curled her toes now—she'd sat on his *lap*. She wanted to go wash her butt right this instant, the memory felt so fresh.

How did Mr. Ingram get Helena to escape to New York with him? What had he said, in that baritone, Kennedy-esque Boston accent? *"Come with me"? "I can hide you in my apartment"? "I'll buy you beautiful clothes"? "But you can't see your family ever again"?*

And then, like an animal, he'd killed her.

Aerin's phone buzzed in her hands, startling her so badly that she nearly dropped it. Thomas's name flashed on the screen. *Hey, stranger. How are you? Eat any Cheetos lately?*

Aerin felt a swoop of guilt. She hated that she'd hacked into the police system using his password. She'd even gone back in this morning, too, to check out Mr. Ingram's alibi. He'd said he'd been on a business trip to Washington, DC. The dumbass cops hadn't challenged him.

She wanted to text Thomas back, but the moment she did, she feared she'd spill her guts. She turned off her phone and placed it in a zippered compartment in her bag.

Brett, who was sitting up front, an ice pack on his still-swollen face, turned to the cabdriver. "Uh, can you take the cut-through to Fifth?"

The driver gave him a strange look. "I thought you were going to Seventy-Second and the park."

"Let's cruise around a little. We can see the city."

The driver shook his head but did as he was told. Aerin swiveled around and gazed at the green sedan directly behind them. She caught Brett's eye. *Following us?* she mouthed.

Brett chewed on his already-bruised bottom lip and shrugged his shoulders.

Aerin's stomach hurt. On the way to the train station, Brett had directed Aerin, who was driving, to take the most circuitous route possible to lose any tails. They'd gotten off one Metro-North train and waited twenty minutes for the next because a woman was looking at them suspiciously. And then, just to be safe, they'd gotten off the train in Harlem, switched to the subway, and took *that* to Eighty-Sixth and then got a cab. What was normally a forty-minute trip had taken two hours.

After getting stuck in Fifth Avenue museum traffic, the cab took a cross street through Central Park and drove up Seventy-First. "Pull over here," Brett instructed, gesturing to the corner of Seventy-Second and Columbus, one block from the Dakota.

Everyone tumbled out, duffels over their shoulders. It took Brett a while to get out. Aerin wasn't even really sure if he should have been let out of the hospital; he still seemed pretty woozy. Maddox pointed to a coffee shop. "We'll change in the bathroom. Ready?"

The coffee in the shop smelled burnt. The place was bursting with parents and their sticky, dressed-up kids; an Easter Bunny sat at the back, handing out eggs. Aerin had blanked on it being Easter Sunday; it meant, unfortunately, she'd have to attend the Easter Bunny party later—her mother never missed it.

They made a beeline for the bathroom, which was littered in toilet paper. Inside a stall, Aerin changed into the pink scrubs they'd stolen from the hospital after Brett had been discharged. Madison stepped out of a stall in scrubs as well, but Seneca still wore the navy Calvin Klein suit they'd raided from Aerin's mom's closet. Her face was pale.

"I want to scrap this whole thing," Aerin said shakily.

Seneca shook her head. "We've come this far. We can't just *stop*."

Back in the dining room, a baby who had a face like a lumpy catcher's mitt had started wailing. Maddox and Brett emerged from the bathroom, changed into scrubs as well. From one of the duffels, Brett rummaged past cleaning bottles and tossed Aerin and Madison kerchiefs. They were going to be cleaners. Brett managed to coax out of Skip Ingram's personal assistant that Skip was in Dexby today, having Easter brunch with his family. The assistant had also given them the name of the cleaning person Skip used in the New York apartment.

Seneca called the cleaning lady and impersonated the assistant Brett had just spoken to, saying Mr. Ingram had decided to use another service and she had to turn over her key to the apartment. They agreed to meet at the Dakota at a quarter to ten; it was 9:40 now.

They stepped back onto the street. Aerin glanced at the busy thoroughfare, glaring at the looks people were giving her as they passed. Or did she just *think* they were looking?

Somehow, her wobbly legs made it down the block. An older, olive-skinned woman waited in front of the Dakota. When Seneca walked up, the woman stood. They exchanged a few words, and then the woman passed Seneca an envelope. Aerin couldn't believe it. The woman hadn't asked for Seneca's credentials. She scuttled off quickly, pulling her hood around her face.

Seneca ducked into an alleyway, opened the envelope, and held up a key. "Perfect."

They started toward the building, which towered over the park. Aerin studied its ornate windows and ironwork. A lot of families she knew had places in the city—her parents had even considered getting one before they split. Helena had put in her two cents, saying she'd love a brownstone in the Village, a loft in Tribeca. This place, in comparison, seemed so formal and conservative. Like Kevin Larssen—not her style.

Then again, why the hell did Aerin think she knew her sister's style anymore?

They headed through an open gate to a small security office to the right. Inside, at least ten video screens of various views of the property lined the walls. Two guards eyed the group suspiciously. "Is Mr. Ingram expecting you?" the taller, craggier one asked.

"We're Mr. Ingram's new cleaning service." Seneca held up the key. "He wants us to clean for a dinner party he's having tomorrow. You can call his assistant to check."

Aerin held her breath as the guards looked them over. Belatedly, she realized that they looked all wrong, from Brett's black eye, to Seneca's wild hair, to Maddox's golden-boy looks and Madison's sparkly silver eye shadow. *Don't call to check,* she willed silently.

"Go on up," the short, pudgy guard said after a moment, buzzing them in.

They were directed through a stone courtyard with a huge, sonorous fountain in the center. Wind chimes jingled. Benches were strewn around the fountain, and the air smelled clean. Madison touched Aerin's arm. "This is . . . nice," she tried.

Aerin glanced at her. "Are you trying to say it's better than her hiding out in a basement pit?" It was still disconcerting to insert Helena into this tableau. Sitting at the fountain, waiting for her love to return—*ugh*. Throwing pennies into the water, wishing for Mr. Ingram—*shudder*. Or maybe that was a crazy image. Helena had been all over the news—if someone had recognized her, Mr. Ingram would have been in major trouble. He'd probably told her to never leave the apartment.

Aerin balled up her fists, fury filling her again.

The building's public records said that Ingram owned apartment 8B. After an elevator ride, Aerin stood in front of it and concentrated, wondering if she'd be able to tell, somehow, if her sister had been here.

She felt nothing at all.

Seneca slid on a pair of gloves and jammed the key into the lock. The bolt clicked, and the door swung open. Light slanted across a front parlor full of thick, expensive furniture. Silk draperies hung from the floor-to-ceiling windows. The only sound was the swish of traffic.

Until the beeping.

It was shrill to the point of hurting Aerin's sinuses. She clapped a hand over her ears. Seneca's skin turned ashen. "An alarm system? Are you kidding me?" Maddox yelled.

"We don't have a code!" Aerin cried.

Seneca turned the envelope upside down and shook it. Nothing came out. "I—I didn't think we'd need one. This is a secure building, with a doorman."

"It's also one of the most exclusive buildings in the city!" Aerin screamed.

Brett slipped on gloves as well, ran to a panel on the wall, and lifted the little door to look at the keypad. "My family has this same system. There's a way to override it." He typed in some numbers. The beeping stopped, but the silence was actually worse. "Okay, we have about five minutes until the alarm company calls Ingram to advise him that there's been a break-in. But if we can get out of here beforehand, I can rearm the system and we'll be good."

"How are we going to find something in *five minutes?*" Madison wailed.

Aerin turned back to the front door. "We need to get out of here."

Seneca spun around, her gaze flicking from room to room. "We can still find something. We just have to think. Put on gloves, Aerin. Let's go."

She sprinted into a back room. Aerin and Madison followed, pulling on gloves, too. Aerin's skin prickled as she walked, as if Mr. Ingram was going to pounce on top of her from the ceiling, Spider-Man-style. She knew she was being melodramatic, that it didn't make any sense, but that didn't stop her from twitching around at every tiny noise.

The large back bedroom contained a king bed covered in a shiny silk comforter—Aerin couldn't help but picture Helena lying on it. Seneca raced to a bureau across the room and opened the top drawer, then the second one down. Shaking her head, she sprinted to the walk-in closet and flung open the door. Shirts and ties were hanging from hooks. Loafers, wing tips, and oxfords were lined up on the floor.

Madison made a face. "He has bad taste in accessories."

"Four minutes," Brett called out.

Seneca brushed past her through the kitchen; Aerin trailed behind like a shadow. Madison opened a cabinet and showed Aerin an *I Heart NY* mug. "Ring any bells?"

Aerin just shrugged.

In an office, the girls looked on bookshelves, but all they found were biographies and textbooks. Aerin checked a windowsill, hoping to see the glass dog figurines Helena liked, a bowl she might have made in ceramics, even another paper crane. Nothing. On a far wall, however, were three long swords with intricate handles. Japanese characters were etched into the blades.

She looked at Seneca. "Samurai swords?"

"I think so," Seneca murmured.

They looked all around the swords, hoping for some kind of clue of Aerin's presence, but all they saw were their own reflections in the shiny metal. Seneca slapped her hands to her sides. "This definitely suggests he's her Samurai Knight, but it's not enough."

"Two minutes, fifteen seconds," Brett said, glancing at his watch.

Aerin padded into the white-tiled bathroom and opened a medicine cabinet. There were pill bottles, but nothing interesting. Creams for dry skin. Tylenol, vitamins. Below the sink, she didn't find a single tampon or bottle of Proactiv or the Japanese blotting papers her sister used to treat her oily forehead. In the shower, there were bottles of Selsun Blue, shaving cream. Not even a pink razor. But why would there be? Helena had been here *five years ago*.

"One minute," Brett said.

Seneca stepped into the hall. "Anything, Maddox?"

"Nothing."

A sour taste welled in Aerin's mouth. "This is ridiculous. There's nothing."

Seneca put her hands on her hips. "What would Skip hold on to that no one would find?"

"A letter," Maddox suggested. "A book. A picture."

"Underwear," Madison called out. She glanced at Aerin. "Sorry."

Brett opened a hall closet filled with dark overcoats. "An umbrella?"

Seneca glanced at the alarm. "We have thirty seconds left. We should just go."

But Aerin stared into the closet, her gaze flicking over the coats on the hangers, hats on hooks. Something brown and floppy was shoved behind a derby and a zip-off fur hood on the top shelf. Aerin pulled it out, pressing her gloved fingertips against the soft suede. It couldn't be.

Brett was at the front door. "We have about twelve seconds before I have to rearm."

Maddox and Madison bolted into the hall. Seneca's gaze was on Aerin. "What's that?"

Aerin held the fedora gently, like it was an egg. When Helena came home with it from the thrift store, Aerin remembered wrinkling her nose. The hat was just so *odd*, nothing like anyone else their age would wear. It was like her sister had turned into someone she didn't know. Someone who wore weird hats, someone who dared to be different, someone who had delved into adulthood and left Aerin far behind. Aerin had assigned the hat way too much meaning, a symbol of just how far she and her sister had drifted. She'd hated the thing.

Until today. Because here the hat was, in Mr. Ingram's apartment, providing them with all the proof they needed.

THIRTY

LATER SUNDAY AFTERNOON, Maddox, Madison, Brett, and Seneca sat on the couch in Maddox's den, dazedly unwrapping Easter candy and staring at the TV. Aerin had gone home to be with her mom. Maddox pictured the two Kelly women watching the news in that huge house, all of its luxury useless in softening the blow of the dreadful truth.

Huge Break in Helena Kelly Case, read a headline on CNN. A reporter stood in front of the Dakota, her expression sober. "Information is still coming in, but sources tell me that a tip revealed that Ms. Kelly and Harris 'Skip' Ingram had an affair five years ago, around the time Ms. Kelly disappeared. Detectives searched his apartment in New York City, where they found several personal possessions of Ms. Kelly's as well as DNA evidence and blood. Testing has not been completed, but officials expect the blood to match Ms. Kelly's. Ms. Kelly's body was found in northern Connecticut only last year, and while detectives are still trying to piece together how it got there, linking Mr. Ingram is an enormous breakthrough for this unsolved crime."

The screen showed more images of the Dakota, and then the Ingrams' property in Dexby, which they were searching now. Maddox and the rest of the group had worried about how finding the fedora in Skip Ingram's apartment was going to go down. When they'd advised Aerin to drop the hat on the floor, leave the apartment, and call the police, admitting who she was and what she suspected, she'd shaken her head. "I can't reveal myself!"

"Yes, you can," Brett had assured her. "Say you remembered something. Just get them to search the apartment."

It was a risk—the cops could have laughed. They might not have been able to procure a search warrant. Aerin could've gotten into trouble. But everything had fallen into place.

Maddox turned to Seneca. "I can't believe they found blood."

Brett scoffed. "He was a sloppy, first-time murderer who knew nothing about forensics."

"Using bleach to clean up blood does *not* work," Maddox chanted, recalling the discussions on Case Not Closed. There was a chemical that cops used to override a bleach cleanup job, detecting even the tiniest trace of blood serum.

Now the news was talking about how Mr. Ingram had just confessed to having an affair with Helena. He could be charged for predatory sex with a minor, and he would face a gross misdemeanor charge of unlawful harboring of a minor or runaway *and* withholding evidence from the police. That was if he didn't get smacked with murder in the first degree. "Mr. Ingram avows that he did not kill Helena," a man identified as Skip Ingram's lawyer said to the camera. "He never even meant for Helena to cut off ties with her family. He was planning to leave his wife by a certain date, and he and Helena were going to return to Dexby after that. He maintains that Helena was the one pushing to move into the city. He was against it."

Seneca balled up her fists. "Then tell her *no*, dude. You're the adult in this relationship."

Madison snorted. "And what, he expected that he and Helena would return to Dexby and people would invite them to dinners at the club like everything's normal? The guy's cray-cray."

Maddox's phone buzzed in his back pocket, and he shifted to peek at it. *I need to see you,* Catherine had written.

Speaking of cray-cray. His head had been aching all afternoon, and he wasn't sure if that was because of what he was learning on TV or because of how many texts he'd received from Catherine in the past day. One hundred seventy-six. That had to be some sort of record.

He didn't know what to do. If even an hour went by and he didn't respond, she messaged him on Twitter. Or Snapchatted him. Or Gchatted. Or e-mailed or called. *Are you hanging out with that Seneca girl?* she kept asking. He swore he'd seen Catherine's car passing the house several times today, too.

Maddox felt completely trapped. If he did tell her they were truly over—which he desperately wanted to do, since he didn't feel anything for her anymore—would she really revoke his scholarship? He'd worked so hard for it. There wasn't time to apply to another school for next year. His mom would be devastated.

His attention snapped back to the TV, where police were leading Skip Ingram out of the Dexby Country Club. He was wearing an expensive-looking tan suit, and his shoulders were hunched. For a split second, he looked at the camera. His eyes were watery.

Maddox groaned. "Why do they always do the crying thing?"

"Mr. Ingram, do you have a comment?" the reporter yelled.

The camera turned to Mr. Ingram again. He opened his mouth as if to speak, then glanced at someone offscreen and shut his mouth.

Maddox turned to Seneca. "We got him. *We* found him. Isn't it amazing?"

Seneca's mouth twitched. "I don't know. It feels too easy. . . ."

Brett waved his hand, which was still bandaged, in a sore, jerky way. "Are you kidding? He's our guy for sure. Stop worrying."

"But we don't actually know if *he* killed her . . . or why."

"Who cares why?" Brett said. "Her blood was in that apartment. He did it."

Seneca stared uncertainly at the cross-stitched pillow she was holding to her chest. Maddox couldn't help but notice her hair half falling out of its ponytail, remembering the feel of that hair against his hands. He chuckled weakly. "So let me get this straight. You're pissed when you're wrong, but you're miserable when you're right?" He dared to flick her thigh with his thumb and forefinger. "You are impossible to figure out."

Seneca retaliated by halfheartedly tossing a peanut-butter egg at his ear. Snickering, he threw a mini chocolate bunny her way, and it bounced off her chest. Seneca's eyes narrowed, and she grabbed the Easter basket and dumped the whole thing over his head with gusto. "Hey!" Maddox squealed. But he secretly didn't care. He was just glad that she was paying attention to him again, finally back to her old self.

Madison, who was sitting at the end of the couch, made a big production of standing and stretching. "I have to get ready for the Easter Bunny party." She gave Maddox a sly smile.

Brett slowly and creakily stood, too. "And I'll, um, see what the weather's like outside."

They scuttled out. As a commercial came on TV for Kim's, a local restaurant, Maddox snuck a glance at Seneca. She gave him a cagey one back. "Was that planned?"

"*No,*" Maddox said honestly. "Though, um, I *have* wanted to talk with you alone. I wanted to tell you again that I'm sorry."

Seneca's brow furrowed. "You already did. And I already forgave you."

"Even for what happened on the balcony?"

"Yep. It's fine." She stared straight ahead.

"No, it's not. I can tell."

Seneca blew air out her nose and glanced at him for a split second. "We can't just pretend everything's normal again. Life doesn't work that way."

Maddox nodded, feeling a pinch of sadness. "I wish it did." He sighed. "I just want us to be friends again. You're different than anyone I've ever known. And by that, I mean *better.*"

She gave him a circumspect look. "You use that line on all the girls?"

Maddox shook his head. It wasn't some throwaway line to get into her pants. What he really wanted, he realized, was just *her*—being around her, hanging out with her, talking. Even if that meant they were just friends. "I really like you," he said. "I have since our first conversation online. I think you're funny and smart, and every new thing I find out about you makes me like you more." He cleared his throat. "Even about your mom. Even about how you screwed up at school."

Seneca made a face. "Thanks for compiling that flattering list of all my best attributes." But then she stared at the floor. "I have to say, you're full of surprises, Maddox. It threw me off at first. But maybe I don't mind it so much."

Maddox felt his cheeks grow pink, and he turned to look at her directly, eyes questioning. She was looking straight at him, her face open, vulnerable. Did she ...

The door slammed. Maddox shot away from Seneca, heart in his throat. It was just his mother, Betsy, in the doorway. "Okay, Maddy," she chirped perfunctorily. "You ready to go?"

Maddox blinked. "Go ... where?"

"Practice. With Catherine."

For a moment, Maddox was stunned. "I-is she here?" He pictured Catherine camping out in his front yard. Peeking in his window. Had she been watching him and Seneca?

His mother slipped on her blue Toms. Her gaze landed on the TV, and a strange look came across her features—they hadn't yet discussed Helena. "No," she said slowly. "She just called. She said you've missed a few practices, but she had time this afternoon if you wanted to play catch-up. I left you a note. You didn't see it?"

Maddox blinked. He hadn't seen any note.

"I have to drive you because I need your car to pick up some flowers to take over to Aunt Harriet's." She brushed her hands on her pants. "So let's go."

Maddox scrambled for an excuse. "I'm feeling kind of wiped out," he said weakly.

His mom put her hands on her hips. "It's important you keep to the schedule."

There was a huge lump in his throat. He had to get out of this. He couldn't see Catherine right now. But how could he explain that?

He looked at Seneca. She shrugged innocently. "Go ahead. I don't mind."

Maddox stood, feeling trapped. In the car, he couldn't think of a thing to say to his mom, not even about Helena. His emotions felt convoluted. He needed to face Catherine with a level head. And tell her—well, what exactly did he want to tell her? Could he really say good-bye to Oregon? On the other hand, did he really want to be trapped in her crazy web?

The rec center parking lot was empty save for only two vehicles—a blue van that seemed to always be there and Catherine's Prius. Maddox spied her sitting on the bleachers near the track, her favorite spot. His nerves started to snap under his skin.

Stay calm, he chanted silently, stepping out of the Jeep. *Just be honest.* As he approached her, Catherine rose to her feet, her eyes huge and round. Maddox took a breath, steadying himself.

"Catherine." Maddox was pleased to hear his voice come out loud and strong. "We have to talk."

THIRTY-ONE

THE KITCHEN HAD fallen dark around Aerin, but she hadn't turned on any lights. She sat at the table, turning an apple-shaped saltshaker over and over in her hands. The TV was off. The lid to her laptop was closed. The news was everywhere—on every channel, maybe even Animal Planet—but it wasn't like she needed it rehashed. It would start all over again, she knew. The stares. The questions. The whispers.

When she heard the engine in the driveway and a car door slam, she placed the apple back on the table and stared at the door to the garage. Her mother floated into the house like a wayward balloon. Her hands were shaking. There were bags under her eyes. She noticed Aerin and came to a stop in the middle of the kitchen, her arms drooped at her sides.

Aerin stood. "I tried to call you. Your line was busy."

Mrs. Kelly groped for the back of a chair. "I know. I was talking to Kinkaid . . . and then the NYPD . . . and then your father." She glanced at Aerin. "They're saying a source tipped them off about the . . . relationship. Was it you?"

Aerin's stomach was in knots. "Did the chief tell you?" Kinkaid, the chief of police who Aerin had spoken with, swore he would keep her identity a secret, but maybe because she was a minor parents didn't count.

Mrs. Kelly shook her head. "I figured it out." She shut her eyes. "You've been digging, right? This was why you went to Kevin's engagement party, wasn't it? And before all this broke, Marissa mentioned you stopped by yesterday, unannounced. But are you *sure*? Are you sure Skip . . ."

Killed her? Aerin silently filled in.

In brief interludes between hating Mr. Ingram's guts and wanting to murder him, Aerin did feel the teensiest bit of doubt, especially because Mr. Ingram had made an emphatic statement he was innocent and that he'd loved Helena deeply. What if he was telling the truth? A memory had come to Aerin a few hours ago: One summer, the Ingram family's cat, Pickles, had dropped a mouse at the back door, and Mr. Ingram had been terrified to even touch it. It had been Heath who'd carried the thing to the trash.

And speaking of Pickles, Mr. Ingram was crazy about that cat, paying thousands of dollars for expensive feline chemotherapy when she had bone cancer because he hated the idea of losing her. It was an Ingram family joke, actually—*Dad loves Pickles more than us.* Was that a man who beat his girlfriend so badly her bones still showed the trauma after five years of rot?

Of course, if she believed Mr. Ingram, she'd also have to believe his story that Helena had been the one who insisted she sneak out of Dexby and live with him . . . *and* that he was planning to bring her back to her family. She tried to picture Helena and Mr. Ingram working out the details, negotiating their plans. Could Helena have really thought,

I need this private time with this person, it will only be a few months, and then everything will be perfect? Didn't she consider how worried her family would be? Why hadn't she at least figured out some way to get in touch with them to assure them she was okay? Aerin had heard many times that love would make you do stupid things, that it was as powerful as a drug. But she couldn't imagine her smart, headstrong older sister actually falling for that bullshit. *Aerin* never had.

Aerin cleared her throat, aware that her mother was still staring at her. "I'm sorry it's him," she mumbled.

Mrs. Kelly drew back like Aerin had kicked her. "Don't feel *sorry.*" Her voice was sharp. "He hurt her. He hurt *us.* He should have known better. She was a little *girl.*"

Aerin's eyes filled with tears, and for a moment, they both silently cried. When she looked over again, her mother was watching Aerin in a tender, heartbroken manner Aerin hadn't seen in forever. "I work too much," she said out of the blue. "I pretend not to see things. But I do—I see what's going on with you, and I thought I did with her, too. Shouldn't I have seen this coming?"

"Don't be crazy."

There were tears in Mrs. Kelly's eyes. "But I had him in my *house.* I left them alone together! What mother does that?"

Aerin was about to answer, but then her mom collapsed. Aerin edged forward and tentatively wrapped her arms around her mother's shuddering body. Mrs. Kelly leaned on her so heavily Aerin almost tipped over. Her shoulder was instantly wet with her mom's tears.

She let her mom cry for a while until her sobs turned to whimpers. Then Mrs. Kelly raised her head, took a few cleansing breaths, and wiped her eyes. "Your father's coming in shortly. And there's a press conference tomorrow morning. I need you to be there."

Aerin sighed heavily. What did her mom think she was going to do—*not* go? "Fine."

"And we're going to the Easter Bunny party later, as a family."

Aerin sat back in the chair. "You've got to be kidding me."

Mrs. Kelly raised her chin. "We have to be strong. We have to go on with our lives. Even your dad's going to attend."

"*That's* what's important here? I think people would forgive us if we stayed home."

Her mother pushed stray hairs behind her ears. "I picked up your dress from the tailor. It's still in the car. I have a stylist coming at five. Let me know if you'd like her to give you a blowout."

Then she rose and glided to her room like some sort of deranged princess. Aerin stared after her, waiting for her mom to return and say it was all a joke. The shower water started. Food Network, which her mom always put on when she was getting ready for something, blared.

Aerin rose and walked up to her own room, flung open her closet, and looked at her shoes. They were all hideous. How the hell was she going to get into *party* mode?

She felt so scattered, and tense, and still very, very afraid. Wasn't she supposed to feel better, now that her sister's killer had been caught? And yet every movement she heard, she flinched. Every time her phone buzzed, she stiffened, anticipating something horrible. Meanwhile, all those buzzes were just nosy people wanting to know what she thought about Mr. Ingram.

God, she wished she had someone to talk to. She pulled out her phone and scrolled through her texts, eventually clicking on Thomas's name. *Had a grilled cheese for lunch and thought of you,* read another text he'd sent yesterday afternoon. And then, a few hours later: *At the grocery store and saw some borscht,* he'd written yesterday. *Looks delish if you ever want to have a picnic.* She smiled, thinking of the bags of chips he'd dumped on the coffee table for her.

She picked up her phone and dialed a number. "Dexby PD," Thomas answered on the second ring, his voice gravelly and familiar and heartbreaking. Aerin paused on the line for a moment, breathing rhythmically. "Hello?" Thomas said on the other end. "Hello?"

Aerin hung up and got her coat. She couldn't talk to him over the phone. This was something she needed to do in person.

THERE WERE BARELY any squad cars at the police station, and half the lights were off. Aerin pictured most of the cops home already, eating an Easter ham. Or wait. Maybe a lot of them were in a New York City office, talking about her sister . . . or else searching the Ingram estate. It was weird to think the whole freaking town was once again buzzing about Helena.

Aerin's watch said it was 6:00 p.m. The Easter Bunny party started in an hour. Her dress hung on a hook in the backseat, and her heels were in the trunk. Her mom's stylist had fixed her hair into a weird Barbie-doll style before letting her leave the house, and it looked particularly incongruous against her ripped Frame jeans and tight white tee.

It had started to pour, and she covered her head and sprinted from her car to the awning over the station's entrance. She knew from the many times she'd had to come here for interviews about Helena that the doors to the station were locked after five thirty; then you had to use a keycard. She wondered where Thomas's office was in the building. Should she call him?

"Aerin?"

Thomas stood behind her, half in the rain, holding a Starbucks cup, presumably from the store down the street. It was as though just thinking about him had conjured him up.

"H-hey," Aerin stammered, feeling unsteady.

Thomas stepped under the awning. "This Helena stuff... are you okay?"

She shrugged. "I don't know. Maybe. Or maybe not at all."

"Were you the one who tipped off the cops? How did you know?"

She shifted back and forth. The group had advised her never, ever to tell anyone they'd broken into the Dakota apartment. "I remembered something that connected her and Mr. Ingram. And I knew he had a place in New York City. It was a lucky guess."

He ran his hand over his wet hair. "I've been trying to reach you. I figured out it was Skip Ingram, too."

"You *did*?"

"I really scoured those files about your sister. There are security camera images of Helena from the days and weeks before she went missing—from grocery stores, ATMs, at school. The cops canvassed all sorts of things to get clues about her life. One feed was from outside Coldwaters Spa, from about mid-November. You know that place?"

"Sure." Coldwaters Spa was where girls in Aerin's grade prepped for their Sweet Sixteens. Her mother went there weekly, but Aerin found the silver tea settings and nonstop doilies too froufrou. "Helena was there?"

"The surveillance camera caught her getting into a car that wasn't hers. Someone was picking her up, but it wasn't your parents. The detective at the time didn't follow up on whose car it was—I don't know why. I did some digging for the make and model—it's a run-of-the-mill BMW, but it's got these custom rims and bigger tires. I guess my extensive car knowledge paid off." He shrugged. "Anyway, it belonged to Ingram. I was going to tell you . . . but it looks like you were one step ahead of me."

Aerin gaped at him. "You were going to tell me private police business?"

A clap of thunder sounded. Thomas glanced toward the sky, then back at her. "I thought it might be necessary. I knew you were looking around, asking questions. I wanted to make sure you were safe."

Aerin felt a shiver, and it wasn't from the damp cold. "Well, thanks."

"You're welcome, but it's not like you really needed my help, so . . ."

Across the street, Aerin caught sight of a single bright yellow daffodil poking up from the flower bed. It gave her a rush of optimism. Maybe this would be okay.

She smiled slyly, tilting her hips. "My mom's forcing me to go to the Easter Bunny party."

"Really?" Thomas looked surprised. "That seems . . . awkward."

"Right?" Aerin felt a rush of trust. She knew he'd sympathize. "Wanna be my date?"

Thomas smiled regretfully. "I have to cover the station. I just stepped out for coffee."

"You can't switch with someone?" She fluttered her lashes. "We could see if they still have that Cream of Wheat. And maybe we could ride in the squad car. I've never been in one."

Thomas walked right up to her. Aerin took in his well-fitting uniform and his chiseled face. There was a spot on his neck that he'd missed shaving. She wanted to touch it.

She tilted her head up and closed her eyes as he put a hand gently on her shoulder, drawing her close. The raindrops on the awning sounded musical. It was like the whole world was holding its breath.

Then she felt Thomas's muscles stiffen. "Sorry, but I'm in the doghouse—no shift switching for me. The chief thinks I gave out my password for someone to hack into the server."

Aerin's eyes sprang open. Thomas's smile had disappeared. "O-oh," she stammered.

He met her gaze steadily, his eyes cold. "I know it was you, Aerin."

Aerin recoiled. "I have no idea what you're talking ab—"

"The system tracks when we log in and what we look at," Thomas interrupted briskly. "The first login was right after you left my place the other night, and the only files opened were ones about Helena. The second time was when I was in a department-wide meeting, which is why Kinkaid knows someone else had my password. He thinks I shared it with someone willingly." He pulled out a keycard from his pocket, turned, and swiped it against the keypad. The pad beeped, and the door unlocked. "I also noticed that my Notepad app was open on my iPad after you left. The page with all my passwords."

Aerin winced. "Thomas, I'm really sorry."

He glanced at her for a moment, his face full of longing . . . and then disappointment. "Yeah, me too," he said sadly. He whipped the door open and walked through.

And then slammed it in her face.

THIRTY-TWO

SENECA'S HEART WAS hammering. She kept staring down at the marshmallow Peep in her hand and squishing his pliable little head. She hadn't moved from Maddox's couch, mostly because she was trying to process what had just happened.

Was she crazy that just for a moment, she'd thought about kissing Maddox again? Did he mean all those things about liking her? No guy had ever said anything that nice to her before. What was she going to do when he came back?

She felt a goofy smile spread across her face. Okay, so she liked him. Really liked him, despite everything. Her feelings surprised her, and the whole thing felt terrifying—it was difficult for her to get attached to anyone, she acknowledged that. But maybe liking him—and maybe going with it—meant she was growing as a person. Healing, even. Maybe she should give it a shot.

She watched more coverage of Mr. Ingram's arrest on TV. The media was focusing on Skip's story that he and Helena had allegedly planned to return to Dexby in the winter. It was probably a huge lie, right? Because if Skip had big, happy plans with Helena, then why did she turn up dead on his floor? It didn't add up.

Seneca heard the sound of an engine outside and jolted upward, certain it would be Maddox. When she looked out the window, a black sedan rolled past, not stopping. She frowned and slumped to the couch again. Who the hell had running practice on Easter anyway? That coach was a slave driver.

Bored and anxious, Seneca pulled up Google on her phone and then typed *Catherine + track coach + Dexby, CT* in the search window. Hits for someone named Catherine Markham appeared. Seneca clicked on the first one, a profile through the Dexby Rec Center. This had to be her. At the top was a picture of a muscled, sweaty brunette pulling ahead in a New York City 10K, and then another of the same girl on a medal stand, her arms in a powerful V. Seneca scrolled down and noticed a close-up of the woman, this time dressed in an oxford shirt with her hair down over her shoulders. She looked much prettier out of her running gear. And really . . . *familiar.*

It came to her almost instantly. Wasn't that Katie? The girl who desperately wanted to be on camera during all the reports about Helena? Helena's *rival*, according to Aerin?

Her head started to whirl. She remembered the text she'd seen from Katie on Helena's phone: *thanks for nothing.* How Aerin had said Helena had told her mom "absolutely not" when she asked if Helena wanted Katie at her birthday dinner. What had been going on between them?

Throat dry, she pulled up the number for Becky Reed, Helena's old best friend, who the group had spoken to several times already, and dialed. Miraculously, Becky answered.

"Was there a girl in Helena's class named Katie Markham?" Seneca blurted after she apologized to Becky for calling on Easter.

There was a long pause. "Uh . . . yeah," Becky said.

"And did she and Helena have a falling-out?"

"Kind of," Becky answered. "She dropped us. Seemed to hate us. I always thought it was just friends growing apart, though after that, she could be sort of creepy."

Seneca's stomach tightened. "Creepy how?"

"She'd show up at places she wasn't invited, send nasty texts, burn us on Facebook, that sort of thing." Becky made a noise at the back of her throat. "You don't think . . . ?" She trailed off. "She was cleared years ago. Besides, didn't you hear about that Ingram guy? He's the one who did it—it's all over the news."

"I'm sure you're right," Seneca said quickly, hanging up. The world felt upended. "She could be sort of creepy," she heard Becky say. "She'd show up at places she wasn't invited."

And now Maddox was *with* Katie. Did he know any of this? He couldn't—he surely would have said something. Why did she want Maddox to practice today? What did she know about Maddox and what he did when he wasn't running?

She has an alibi, Seneca told herself, but it wasn't comforting. Alibis weren't the end-all-be-all proof of innocence.

Fingers trembling, Seneca dialed Maddox's number, but he didn't answer. Her stomach started to hurt. She pictured that voice outside her hotel room door again. That raspy, angry, feminine voice: "Go home." Maddox had said his attacker seemed like a woman, too.

What if they were wrong about Skip? What if it was someone else they needed to be afraid of?

Seneca rushed to the driveway, drizzle blurring her vision. It was empty; even Madison's car was gone. Pivoting, she darted into the garage and wheeled out a red bike. The tires were flat, and the seat was set too low, but it would have to do.

THIRTEEN MINUTES LATER, now thoroughly soaked, Seneca cycled up to the rec center. She stuck the bike into the rack and took stock. There was a track around back. She rushed toward it and scanned the cars in the parking lot. No one was walking the track's outer rings in the rain. Breathing heavily, she dialed Maddox again. Voice mail. She tried Brett, Madison, and Aerin again, too—same.

She wheeled around, scanning the tennis courts, an empty sports field, and a huge building marked *Gymnasium & Natatorium*. She hurried toward it and pushed through a set of heavy double doors. They creaked open, revealing an indoor track and a bunch of basketball hoops. A man in a turban shot hoops toward the back. An older lady walked the track, talking on her cell phone.

A plaque caught Seneca's eye.

Directory, it read, and then listed names of people who worked on staff at the rec center. Halfway down was a Catherine Markham; her office was in room 107. A sign across the gym announced that offices 105 through 108 were through a hallway next to the women's locker room. Seneca hurried over, her shoes leaving wet marks on the gym floor. She knew she was being absurd, but she couldn't stop picturing Catherine tying Maddox up in her office, taping his mouth closed, telling him that he'd taken this investigation too far. . . .

The hallway of offices was lit by harsh fluorescent panels and smelled like socks. The concrete floor and walls intensified all sounds; Seneca could hear every raspy breath she took. Finally, at the end of

the hall, she noticed a light under a door. *Catherine Markham,* read a
nameplate next to the knob. When Seneca peered through the mottled
glass, she caught sight of two fuzzy shapes inside. Her stomach swooped
queasily. It had to be Catherine—*Katie*—and Maddox.

She tried the knob. It turned. She yanked the door open and stared
into an office filled with trophies. Maddox's back was to her. He was
standing, not bound and gagged, as she'd imagined. Catherine, who
faced the door, was next to him. Then Seneca did a double take. Actually, she wasn't just next to him; she was *kissing* him.

And Maddox was kissing her back.

Seneca must have let out a small sound, because Catherine raised
her gaze and pulled away. "Um, can I help you?" she said sweetly.

Maddox twisted around and clumsily shot up from the chair. "Oh
my God. Seneca."

Seneca tried to speak, but no sound came out. She felt huge and
obtrusive in the doorway. She gazed again at Catherine's slender legs,
her ample breasts, her pretty face. It suddenly made perfect sense. Tara
from track wasn't the only pretty girl in this town.

She spun around and walked out.

"Seneca!" Maddox called after her.

"Don't you dare leave, Maddy!" Catherine yelled at him. But
Maddox must have ignored her, because Seneca heard his footsteps
behind her.

"Seneca, *wait!*" he cried.

Seneca passed a cart of basketballs, contemplating upending it. Her
mind spun as she stomped over a big seal of the state of Connecticut on the gym floor. She heard the footsteps get faster, and Maddox
caught her arm. *Of course, can't outrun the track star,* she thought sourly.
She turned around, fuming. "It's not what it looks like," he gasped.

Seneca just glared at him and wrenched her arm from his grip. Behind Maddox, Catherine had emerged from the hall, too. Her hands were on her hips, and her face was red.

Maddox looked nervously at Catherine, but kept going. "We were . . . a thing, sort of," he said. "But I'd been trying to tell her I'm not interested. I like *you*. But then she was going to revoke my college scholarship if I dumped her."

Seneca gawked at him. "Are you trying to get me to feel *sorry* for you?"

"No!" Maddox cried. "Absolutely not! I told her I didn't care— Oregon wasn't worth it." He glared at Catherine. "I also said I could report her inappropriate behavior to her boss at the rec center. I have a lot of texts from her that are pretty far from professional."

Catherine snorted. "Like I'm afraid of *you*?"

"I'll just be going," Seneca said through her teeth. The last thing she wanted to witness was a lovers' quarrel.

"No!" Maddox turned back to Seneca. "I told her all this, and I was ready to leave but then she just . . . kissed me again. That's what you saw."

Seneca felt a sensation and looked down. Somehow, during that last part, he'd grabbed her hands. An hour ago, the sight of their fingers entwined would have delighted her, but now they filled her with disgust.

She pulled away. She felt stifled in this echoing gym, in her own body. "Actually, I only came because I worried about her hurting you, Maddox," she said smoothly and loudly, not really caring that Catherine heard. "Did you know she was Helena's rival in high school? Catherine hated her."

Maddox blinked. He turned and looked at Catherine, who'd frowned and stepped back.

"What were you doing, *spying* on me?" Catherine snapped.

Seneca ignored her, concentrating on Maddox. "But I guess she's not out to hurt *us*, is she? You seem fine. *Better* than fine." And then, with a tight smile, she turned away and walked calmly toward the exit. "See ya."

Maddox rushed toward her. "Wait! Are you angry with me?"

Seneca's first instinct was to scream, but she pulled out all her best tricks and managed to compose herself. "No," she said airily. "It's your life, Maddox. I'm just your friend from online. You don't need to explain yourself to me."

Maddox's jaw dropped open. *Whatever,* Seneca thought. As long as he bought her lie, she didn't care.

Outside, dusk had fallen, and the rain had stopped. The only sounds were Seneca's footsteps on the wet pavement. When someone grabbed her arm, she lashed out, assuming it was Maddox again.

"Whoa!" Brett materialized in front of her. "Hold up!"

"What are *you* doing here?" Seneca cried, her heart in her throat.

"You called me. Said you were going to the track, that Maddox is in trouble?" He looked at the door, then at the angry expression that Seneca guessed was on her face. "Is he okay?"

"He's fine," Seneca said coolly. "Just fine."

She walked to the tennis courts, lit up by huge overhead floodlights, then slumped down into a crouch, staring blankly at the nets. The door to the rec center creaked open, and Maddox stepped out and looked around. Seneca hunched her shoulders and hid her face, praying he wouldn't see her. After a moment, Maddox jogged off.

Brett slid down next to Seneca, his gaze on Maddox's receding form. "What an idiot."

Seneca gritted her teeth. "It's not worth discussing."

Brett drummed on his knees. "Okay," he said gently. "I gotcha."

His sudden mercy was too much to bear, and Seneca felt a wave of sadness and desperation. "It doesn't matter anyway," she said brusquely. "I'm due home tonight. I was planning to leave on a train in a few hours." It wasn't true: She'd actually been composing a text to her dad about buying a day or two more. She was glad she hadn't sent it.

"Well, don't let Maddox cloud what we figured out," Brett said. "We caught a killer, remember? That's pretty huge. I bet we changed Aerin's life." Then a thoughtful look came over his features. "If only we could help you with your mom, huh?"

Seneca felt a dart of exasperation. He was seriously going to bring up her mom *now*? Then again, maybe it was better than talking about Maddox. And in a way, Brett was also right.

"I'm really sorry again about ambushing you about all that in the café," Brett went on. "I just wanted to connect with someone who had gone through the same thing, you know? But it was selfish. If you'd wanted to talk about it, you would have talked about it. I get that now."

In this light, Brett's bruises on his face looked even worse, garishly purple and puffy. Seneca pushed her finger into one of the chain links in the fence. She'd never once asked Brett how he'd gotten through his grandmother's death. Her indifference seemed callous—maybe *she* was the selfish one.

"Do you think about your grandma a lot?" she asked.

Brett pulled his cap down low. "Hells yeah. Do you? With your mom?"

"Well, sure. Of course."

"You know what I'd love?" Brett stared at the silhouettes of trees. "One more day with her. Just an ordinary day—nothing even that special. We'd have breakfast, I'd go with her on her power walk, and out to see the horses. We'd read the paper, I'd watch her needlepoint, whatever."

Seneca laughed lightly. "Your fur-diva grandma was into *needlepoint*?"

"I just meant that as a generic example," Brett said quickly. "But you get my drift. Just one more day to hug her, tell her I love her, all that shit. I'd trade that for anything."

Seneca felt tears come to her eyes. She fantasized about the day she'd have with her mom, too. Ordinary would be fine. They could talk about nothing. Watch an awards show. Fold laundry. She'd make her mom her favorite dinner, linguine with clam sauce.

Brett leaned back on the fence with a *clank*. "Did they ever find out anything about your mom's killer? I don't follow her case on the boards."

Seneca shook her head. "Nothing. Nothing weird was going on at my house—even my dad attested to it. My mom hadn't been getting any weird phone calls, and there was no indication that someone had been following her. She wasn't even acting differently leading up to it, like she was afraid of someone. It was just . . . senseless." She breathed out. "Meaningless."

Brett pointed to her *P* necklace. "But at least you got that back to remember her by, right?"

Seneca's fingers closed around it. "That's what I tell myself."

Slowly, tentatively, she let memories of her mom flood her mind, particularly that last memory of her in the morgue. She'd been covered with a sheet from the waist down, but Seneca could still tell that parts of her mother weren't lying right under there, not hanging together like a normal skeleton. A few months ago, when she'd first logged on to Case Not Closed, she'd finally read her mother's coroner's report. The thing was so shocking, she'd never been able to return to her mom's file. Among other things, the report said that some of her mom's lower bones had been broken very badly—*shattered,* the coroner had written. Presumably from an act of violence.

She let out a whimper at the back of her throat, the pain too great. "It's okay," Brett said softly, pulling her in for a hug. "It'll be okay."

The hug was comforting, but Seneca still felt an empty, unsatisfied longing. There was a skip in her brain, something not sitting right, but it was probably the confusion of all that had happened today, the push and pull of too many emotions. It was also frustrating to realize that as much as she liked Brett, she wished the hug was from someone else. She glared at the road Maddox had taken home. *Stop wishing he was still here,* she thought angrily.

She had to be done with him.

THIRTY-THREE

AS THE RAIN poured down, Aerin sat in the back of the limo on her way to the Easter Bunny party. The dress she'd picked out months before, a black Narciso Rodriguez, had a halter neck that circled her throat like a noose and a bodice that constricted like a straitjacket. Her mother was at one window, clean and polished in an off-white dress, but Aerin could still see the drawn cords in her neck, the quiver of worry around her mouth, and the tremor in her hand as she lifted the champagne flute to her lips. Her father sat by the other window, dressed to perfection in a black tux, his hands folded in his lap. So they were a happy little family again . . . except not really. Her parents hadn't said a word to each other the whole drive there. Even the driver had been giving them odd looks, probably wondering why they were acting like they were going to a funeral instead of the biggest party of the year.

They pulled up to the Morgenthau estate, a palatial mansion on a wide swath of bright green lawn. Searchlights swirled in the front drive. There was even a covered red carpet up the front walk sponsored by *Dexby Living* magazine with the party's official name, the Morgenthau

Estate Easter Charity Auction and Gala, written across the green back-
drop. Guests emerged from waiting limos and sports cars, and everyone posed on the carpet for the photographers like they were actually
important. Aerin hated all of them.

Across the lawn, a few girls in bunny ears and skimpy dresses were
running tipsily toward the guesthouse in the rain. Colin Woodworth
and Reed Cristensen, two Windemere seniors, huddled under an
umbrella, beer bottles in hand. And there was Dax Shelby, who, as the
rumor went, got lab-quality ecstasy from his big pharma CEO dad—
Dax always staged an egg hunt, hiding plastic eggs full of pills around
the grounds. Last year, he'd sidled up to Aerin, shaking an egg tantaliz-
ingly, and said, "Wanna find *my* eggs?" Thank God Aerin had dragged
Thomas into the pantry. Everyone else in this circle was such a loser.

Thomas. She felt an ache, then pushed it away.

The driver opened the door for Aerin's family. Minnie Morgenthau, who had a long, horsey face and plumped, fake lips, was standing there with an umbrella. "Elizabeth. Derek." Minnie took Aerin's
parents' hands in hers. "My goodness, you didn't need to come, considering all you've faced today."

That's what I told them, Aerin almost said aloud.

Aerin's mom air-kissed Minnie. "We wouldn't miss it."

Then Tori and Amanda rushed to the car, pulled Aerin out, and
embraced her tightly. Both girls smelled vaguely of booze, and Aerin
noticed that Tori was wearing the four-carat diamond ring that used
to be her mother's until she traded it in for something bigger. "Oh,
Aerin, you're so brave," Amanda murmured. "We love you so much."

Aerin wriggled desperately out of her friends' grip. So she was
some sort of heroine now? It wasn't as if they knew she'd solved Helena's
murder. They were just enjoying the epic drama.

"I don't want to deal right now," Aerin grumbled, grabbing her friends' hands and stomping toward the guesthouse, not caring that her dress was getting soaked. She put her head down as she passed through the wide-open front door, but people were still staring. *Fuck all of you,* she thought rabidly, weaving around some more girls in bunny ears.

Amanda handed her a beer from an ice-filled trough in the kitchen. Aerin turned to thank her, but when she met Amanda's gaze, she looked a little afraid. Aerin turned away and downed the beer quickly, barely tasting it.

Then she heard the whispers from around the corner.

"*I heard he confessed to having an affair with Helena,*" one voice said.

"*Me too,*" said another. "*It's so nasty, don't you think? But he's saying he didn't kill her. I believe him.*"

"*You're an idiot, Frances. Of course he killed her. He probably got bored of her and just wanted to get rid of her.*"

"*No way. He plays golf with my dad all the time. He's really nice.*"

Aerin must have had a furious look on her face, because Tori stood and clenched her fists. "I'll kill those bitches," she growled, starting into the next room.

"Tori, no," Aerin said weakly, following her.

They walked through the archway and ambushed Brooklyn Landers and Frances Hamilton, two sophomores Aerin didn't even know, sitting on a long couch, gin and tonics in hand. Tori walked straight up to them. "You want to say that again to her face?"

The girls turned pale at the sight of Aerin. Frances grabbed Brooklyn's hand, and the two of them scuttled into the powder room and shut the door behind them. Tori looked at her. "Want me to shove a broomstick in the door so they're stuck in there?"

"That's okay," Aerin said, feeling as if she'd had six beers instead of just the one. Lobbing her empty can into the trash, she gestured to Amanda and Tori that she needed a second alone and wandered to the covered back porch. She slumped down in an Adirondack chair and stared blankly at the woods.

If she was really honest with herself, she saw Frances's point. Why would Mr. Ingram kill Helena? Maybe Helena had given him an ultimatum? It had also come out that Mr. Ingram sometimes smoked pot—maybe he and Helena had smoked together. Maybe they'd gotten into harder stuff, too, had Loren deliver them pills, something that made them crazy.

Her thoughts clicked back to the comment Helena had made about things being under wraps between her and Aerin. That app had seemed like such a good lead—it had all added up. Maybe Helena had downloaded it somewhere, just not on her phone? If that was true, though, had Helena been trying to say that Aerin should download it, too? If only Helena *had* downloaded it for her that last day. She'd been using Aerin's phone after all, checking the weather, seeing if it was going to snow more.

A light went on in her brain. Wait. What if Helena *had* downloaded it?

She must have gasped, because Chase Grier, a sarcastic varsity soccer player who was scooping ice cubes out of a big bucket nearby, turned and gave her a strange look. "You okay?"

Aerin's mind was thundering fast, but she managed to nod. "Fine."

Chase didn't move. All at once, she felt too visible. She darted around the side of the guesthouse, her shoes sinking in the wet grass. Once alone, she wrestled her phone out of her evening bag and clicked on the App Store. Then she heard a noise in the darkness. She raised her head, vision unfocused. A shadow lurked a few feet away, backlit by a spotlight.

"Hey!" she screamed out as the figure began to approach.

"Aerin, it's me!" called a voice. "What are you doing out here? Peeing?"

The figure stepped out of the light. It was Madison, resplendent in a candy-pink gown, her long black hair blow-dried ruler-straight. Aerin had completely forgotten Madison was coming to this. And then she realized—Madison was exactly the girl she needed.

She pulled her closer, her heart beating fast. "I have something to show you," she said excitedly. "Something you definitely need to see."

MADISON WAS EVEN more paranoid than Aerin was, so she grabbed Aerin's hand and led her through a footpath into the woods behind the Morgenthaus' property. The rain was finally stopping, but the trees and plants were covered with dew and smelled moldy. Aerin could feel the end of her dress getting soaked in the mud, but she didn't really give a shit.

She told Madison what she'd figured out. "I thought about the Under Wraps app. Helena didn't load it on her phone—she loaded it on mine."

Madison shifted her weight. "Why would she do that?"

"Because the police wouldn't look on my phone for clues about her. She could communicate with Mr. Ingram and no one would know. Helena was always misplacing her phone—or pretending to, anyway. She was always borrowing mine to do little things like check the weather or send a text. Now that I think of it, it happened daily. But she wasn't just checking the weather—she was on Under Wraps, talking to Mr. Ingram."

"Okay," Madison drawled. "But why didn't you ever notice the app?"

"Because it was probably hidden in a folder, like Maddox said. But just now, I went to the App Store and tried to download it. Apple told me it was already on my cloud, which means someone already bought it for me, on an old phone. I definitely never bought it. It *had* to be Helena." She tapped her screen to light it up again. "I'm downloading it on this phone now. I need you to show me how to use it, though."

"Sure," Madison said, sounding impressed.

A few seconds later, the icon for Under Wraps, a commingled *U* and *W*, appeared on the screen. With shaking fingers, Aerin clicked on it. *Welcome back, SamuraiGirl0930.* That must have been Helena's user name.

A password prompt appeared. Aerin's fingers hovered over the keyboard. "Skip?" she said aloud, typing it in. *Wrong,* read words on the app. She tried *Karaoke,* bands Helena liked, even *Kevin.* And then, her stomach turning, she typed in *HelenaIngram. Welcome,* a message said.

"We're in," she whispered.

A cheerful jingle played, then a navigation screen appeared. A bar on the right-hand side showed icons for *Received Messages, Sent Messages, Compose New,* and *Tell the World.* Madison clicked on *Sent Messages.* "Let's see what she was talking about."

A bunch of files loaded. The posts reminded Aerin of Instagram: first a picture, then a caption. Madison scrolled to the oldest message at the bottom of the list and opened it. A selfie of Helena sitting on her bed appeared—the room's decor exactly the same as it was now. Aerin reached out to touch the image on the screen. Helena seemed so alive.

I can't believe I'm really thinking about doing this, read the caption.

Nothing more. Madison tapped a button that said, *More Info.* Data popped up on the screen. "Only one account received this message," Madison explained. "HAR1972."

"Do you think that's Ingram?" Aerin whispered.

"Who else could it be?"

There was a lump in Aerin's throat as she scrolled through more of Helena's messages. In the next one, Helena had taken a photo of herself in her bathroom mirror. She was wearing a tank top and gym shorts that showed off her long legs. *All I think about is you,* read the caption—again, just to that one account. Others described how she dreamed about him at night, how she was so excited that they were together, or how all she thought about was their last meeting.

"These are from the summer and the fall," Madison reported, checking the time stamps. Then she clicked on a message halfway through the list. It was another selfie of Helena sitting on her bed, this time wearing a familiar purple sweater, a white overcoat, and that famous brown fedora. She had a determined look in her eye. *I'm ready,* the caption read.

"This is from the day she disappeared," Madison murmured.

But it wasn't the last message Helena sent. Next was an image of a red rose with the words *Miss you.* The date was from a week later. Then came a picture of a kitten batting an alarm clock accompanied by *Counting the minutes until you're back.* December 18. Aerin breathed in. So Seneca had been right. Helena *had* lived after that fateful day in December.

Red-and-white candy cane stripes served as the background for *Merry Xmas to us*; the date the message had been sent was December 26. Aerin bit down hard on her lip. Christmas. There were a few messages, too, that weren't sent to Ingram's account—weren't sent to anyone. *Are you there?* one said. And *Don't think I'm not thinking about you.* And then *I miss you, Aerie. But don't worry. I'll be back soon. February 2, to be exact—Groundhog Day!*

Aerin's heart stopped. Helena sometimes called her Aerie. So she *had* been trying to speak to her through this? And had Skip been telling the truth—they really *were* going to come back to Dexby? He was really going to leave his wife?

The only missive that featured Helena's photo after she vanished was the very last one on the list. It was of a close-up of Helena's face, her eyes wide, her lips stuck out in a pout, her hair longer and shaggier. It was hard to tell where she was—the photo was heavily filtered, the background blurred-out—but she looked sad, not scared. *It'll be okay.* It went to Mr. Ingram.

Madison pointed to it. "*What* will be okay?"

"I don't know," Aerin murmured.

Madison exited out of the sent messages and clicked on *Received Messages* in the navigation bar. Tons of images loaded from the same HAR1972 account. None of them were selfies of Mr. Ingram—thank God, Aerin didn't think she could bear seeing his face—instead the messages were superimposed over plain backgrounds or stock images. The first message was from early summer that same year. *I'm so happy, too,* he'd written. The next one: *You were so pretty this afternoon.* The next: *Thinking of you.* Aerin squirmed. Helena fell for this?

As it got closer to the date of Helena's disappearance, Mr. Ingram wrote things like *I know this is hard for you. I will support anything you choose.* And *I will love you always.* And *So excited about our future.*

Madison made a sniffing sound. "This doesn't sound like a man who plans to kill his girlfriend."

"Seriously," Aerin murmured. She scrolled on. In early January, four weeks after Helena disappeared, he wrote, *I'm ready to leave her*. She looked up. "Marissa?" She tried to remember Marissa's attitude around this time—could she have known?

"Check this out," Madison said, scrolling up. The next message was dated January 24. There was no picture, only a blank screen. For a caption, Mr. Ingram had written, *I'm worried about her. Afraid she'll do something crazy.*

January 24 was the date Helena had written *It'll be okay*. Aerin clicked back to Helena's composed messages, but the one on the 24th was her last. "Do you think this is when she...?"

Madison raised her eyebrows. "That's about when Loren reached out to her, too. If he's telling the truth, she wasn't calling him back. Something *could* have happened to her."

Aerin clicked back to Helena's received messages, expecting not to see any more from Mr. Ingram, either, but his next note to Helena was on January 30. *Please come back*. There was another on February 2. *Today was supposed to be the day. Why are you doing this?* February 6: *I will always love you. Wherever you've gone, whatever you need to do, it's okay.* February 8: *Just tell me where you are. I'm worried.*

Aerin gripped her kneecap. "What is he talking about? Why doesn't he know where she is?"

"Could she have run away from the Dakota?" Madison asked. "Skipped town?"

"Blood was found in the apartment, remember? The detectives are pretty sure it's going to match her type." But Aerin understood her question. "Why would Ingram write to Helena if he knew she was dead? Maybe he was just covering his tracks in case the cops ran across this?"

Madison wrinkled her nose. "On a super-secret app?"

"So then what's the other option? That he really didn't know where she was?"

Madison's eyes widened. "Do you think *she* had a key to his place in the city?"

"Who?" Aerin asked. "Helena?"

Madison shook her head. She pulled up the earlier message from Mr. Ingram again: *I'm worried about her. Afraid she'll do something crazy.* When Aerin met Madison's gaze, a cold, still silence settled inside her, a gnawing sense of uncertainty gone. "Marissa," she whispered.

Madison nodded, then glanced toward the Morgenthau estate. Color drained from her face. "Speak of the devil," she whispered, gesturing to a limo in the driveway. A door opened, and Aerin watched as an emaciated, black-haired woman wearing a long lace gown and dripping in diamonds stepped out and posed for pictures.

Holy shit, Aerin thought. That bitch was *here.*

THIRTY-FOUR

MADDOX SAT IN the dark on his front porch, feeling his phone vibrate in his palms. *Catherine,* read the screen. He squeezed his phone, tempted to chuck it into the trees.

An hour ago, he'd shown up at the track and blurted out a speech about how he wasn't going to let Catherine control him, blah, blah, blah. Catherine's eyes had gotten very big and watery, and she'd turned around and fled to her office. And what was Maddox supposed to do, *not* follow her?

Actually, in retrospect, maybe that would have been a good move.

In her office, Catherine had sat on her desk, taking deep breaths. But when she looked up at him, her features had morphed. "Fine," she said in a composed voice. She whipped out her phone and dialed a number. "Can I speak to Coach Leventhal, please?" she said after a pause.

Maddox's heart flipped. Levanthal was the Oregon coach. She was really going to do it.

Catherine glanced at him, an eyebrow raised as if to say, *Still time to back out!* But he'd shakily stood. "Go ahead," he'd said in an even voice, turning to go. "I don't care."

He'd started to walk out of the office but felt a hand on his wrist. "Maddox!" Catherine cried, dropping the phone, spinning him around, and planting a kiss on his lips. Before he could fight her off, Seneca appeared . . . and saw everything. Saw, and assumed, of course, that he was a big, fat jerk.

And then that stuff about Catherine being Helena's jealous rival? Maddox hadn't remembered ever seeing Catherine at Helena's house . . . but then, maybe she wouldn't have been there. She obviously didn't want him to know who she was, though: Maddox suddenly recalled, very distinctly, mentioning Helena during their second practice session, on the anniversary of her disappearance. "Did you know her?" he'd asked Catherine, and she'd gotten a vague look in her eye and shaken her head no.

His phone stopped, then rang again. Maddox contemplated slamming it on the front walk but then noticed a different name on the screen. *Madison.* Jesus. Had she heard about the disaster with Seneca? He wasn't ready for another lecture.

He heard an engine growl and looked up. A yellow taxi had pulled up to the curb, and Seneca was climbing out, along with Brett. Maddox stared down at the ringing phone and hit the ANSWER button. "Madison, why is Seneca at our house?"

"Because I called her," Madison answered in a hurried tone. "I told her to get you so you could all come here together."

"Come where?"

"The Easter Bunny party."

Maddox blinked. He'd totally forgotten that was happening.

Madison started talking a mile a minute. "You know how we

thought it was Skip Ingram? Well, it's not—it's *Marissa*—because we hacked into Helena's Under Wraps account and found all these messages from Skip and Helena and at the end he says he's worried about someone, and that was totally Marissa, and it all makes *sense!*"

"Wait," Maddox said. By now, Seneca and Brett were coming up the walk. Brett was pale and worried-looking, his hands balled into fists. Seneca was studying something on her phone and shaking her head.

He let the words Madison had just said wash over him. Marissa Ingram? It did sort of fit. If she'd found out about Helena, she'd certainly have motive. And maybe she'd been the person who was trying to get rid of them, too. He'd *thought* that mugger in New York was a woman. . . .

The images of Skip Ingram on the news flashed in his mind. "We put the wrong person in jail?"

"Yes," Seneca snapped angrily, clomping up the walk and grabbing Maddox's phone from him. "Is she still missing?" she said into the receiver. There was a pause. "Okay, okay. Well, keep looking. We'll be there soon."

She hung up and handed the phone back to him, pointedly not meeting Maddox's eye. "I *knew* there was something wrong about Skip Ingram. I *knew* it."

Brett touched Maddox's arm. "Once Madison and Aerin realized it was Marissa, they noticed her at the party," he explained. "And then, before Madison could stop her, Aerin took off after Marissa. Madison tried to catch Aerin, but she got lost in the crowd."

"Aerin's a ticking time bomb," Seneca said shortly. "We need to stop her before she says something crazy to Marissa that lets her know we know." She blew her bangs off her face. "I can't believe Marissa would *show up* there, after everything that happened today. She's got balls of steel." She gestured to the taxi, which was still waiting at the curb.

Maddox rolled his shoulders and dove into the back. Marissa Ingram wasn't the only one who needed to have balls of steel tonight.

TEN MINUTES LATER, they were at the Morgenthau mansion, which was dramatically lit by a series of white spotlights. At the top of the hill, the first thing Maddox saw was a group of people twisting and posing on a red carpet. Flashbulbs popped. The photographer instructed people to turn left or right. Maddox craned his neck, wondering if it was actually someone famous—a lot of Rangers players lived up this way, as well as some actors, notable CEOs, and famous writers. But all he saw were kids and adults he recognized from around Dexby.

There was a knock on his window. Madison yanked the door open, then spun around and headed into the house. "I've tried all the main rooms," she called over her shoulder. "But this place is like a maze. There's a whole back wing, an upstairs..."

"Do you think we should call the cops?" Maddox asked. "What if something happens to Aerin?"

Seneca shook her head. "Marissa might see the police cars and run off before we can prove it's her. I say we wait until it's absolutely necessary."

They walked into the main ballroom, which was swarming with people in fancy gowns and tuxes. Maddox felt kind of lame in his jeans and tee, but then again, everyone looked so stuffy and ridiculous in tuxes, too. Madison took a turn into a hallway that opened into another party room that was even more swollen with guests. Long tables were set up along the sides of the room with items for the silent auction on

display. Among a few of the things to bid on were an all-expenses-paid
trip around the world, a diamond necklace worth $24,000, unlimited
use of a Rolls-Royce limo (with driver) for six months, and a year's sup-
ply of breast milk from a woman who ate only locally grown organic
produce.

Madison was moving faster now, winding around bodies, finding
holes between groups, sliding past priceless auction items. Maddox saw
blond girl after blond girl, but never Aerin. His stomach started to knot.
What if Marissa had taken her somewhere? What if she was hurt? What
would all these guests think if they knew a murderer was in their midst?

In another room, a crowd started to roar. The hum of the crowd
in the main space grew louder. The lights dimmed, and techno music
began to play. "Welcome, everyone, to our annual Easter Charity Auction!" a voice boomed over a loudspeaker. The group swept through
too quickly for Maddox to get a look at any of the bachelors.

They passed a room with men smoking cigars, some guys playing
pool, a dark space where a couple was sipping wine. Madison held the
hem of her dress and climbed a set of stairs that led to another level
of party rooms. In one, guests lined up on a long divan, chatting. In
another, a bunch of guys were gathered around a golf simulator, taking
turns with a driver. This level looked down over the ballroom; Maddox
gazed at the dozens of sleek heads below him. A shiny trumpet used by
one of the band members in the corner caught the light for a moment,
casting an eerie, blinding glare.

They started down a dark back hallway. Halfway down the hall,
Madison stopped and cocked her head. Maddox could barely hear over
the din of the crowd, but he thought he caught Aerin's high, lilting
voice. Seneca edged forward and peered through an open door. Maddox
stood on his tiptoes behind her and looked, too. Inside was a huge

marble bathroom with three sinks and a separate door for the toilet. Marissa's reflection appeared in a round mirror on the wall. She was standing over Aerin, her eyes wide. It was unclear what was happening.

Maddox jumped back into the shadows before Marissa noticed him. The group exchanged glances. *"Shit,"* Seneca murmured, her cheeks flared red.

Madison looked at Maddox. "*Now* can we call the police?"

Even Brett didn't argue. Maddox took out his phone and dialed 9-1-1. "What's your emergency?" a voice crowed on the other end.

Maddox drew back. The voice was so loud, and his would be even louder. There's no way Marissa wouldn't hear. "Um," he whispered. "I'm at the Easter Bunny party, and I need help."

"What?" the dispatcher squawked. "Where?"

Maddox fumbled with his phone, and it tumbled to the carpet. He could still hear the dispatcher asking questions, but he didn't dare speak to her. He stared helplessly at the screen. Maybe he could text the 9-1-1 dispatcher? Send a Morse code?

Now Marissa was talking. "It really is such a shock," she simpered, stepping closer to Aerin. "I can't imagine what you and your mom are going through, honey. I've been crying, I've been praying. . . ."

And then she leaned forward and hugged Aerin tight. Aerin stood like a metal rod, her arms stiff at her sides, a vein in her neck bulging. Maddox glanced at Seneca and raised his eyebrows. Maybe this wasn't so bad. It seemed like they'd just run into each other. Maybe Aerin hadn't said anything yet.

Marissa pulled back and looked at Aerin from arm's length. "I heard your mom's here tonight, is that true?" Aerin could only nod catatonically. Marissa pressed a hand to her chest. "I'd love to speak with her, honey. I need to tell her . . . things. But she won't pick up my calls."

A strange, steadied look came over Aerin's face. She raised her head to look Marissa straight in the eye. "Maybe my mother doesn't want to talk to you because she knows you're a fucking liar."

Maddox drew in a gasp of air. Madison winced.

Marissa pulled her hand away. "Pardon me?" The words came out in a strangled choke.

Aerin narrowed her eyes. Her whole body was trembling. "I know what you did to Helena. I know who you *are*."

"Aerin," Seneca said, shooting into the room and grabbing her arm. "Um, we have to go."

Aerin shook Seneca off. Marissa swiveled around, eyeing all of them as they crowded into the room. A knowing wrinkle formed on her brow, and before Maddox could move, Marissa shot forward, sending him careening against the side of a sink. She slammed the door and stood in front of it, turning off the light. Brett shouted, and Seneca screamed, and there was the sound of breaking glass. Maddox fought his way to the door, scrambling to turn the light back on. A mirror lay shattered on the floor, pieces scattered everywhere.

A shard in Marissa's hand caught the light. Her thin arms were wrapped around Aerin in an almost hug, a piece of broken mirror pressed at Aerin's jugular. She looked at the frozen group, a furious look on her face.

"Do everything I say," she whispered hoarsely but firmly. "Or your friend's dead."

THIRTY-FIVE

PINNED AGAINST THE vanity, his body still aching from the attack the day before, Brett couldn't help but notice that the room now smelled sharply of sweat and Marissa's cloying rosy perfume. He watched helplessly as the woman pressed the piece of glass into Aerin's neck. He so desperately wanted to strangle Marissa—he bet he could, he *knew* he could, despite his injuries—but Aerin sent a quick desperate glance at them all as though warning them not to make any sudden moves.

Downstairs, music still thudded. People laughed. Brett heard the crackle of the microphone at the bachelor auction, followed by applause. How would anyone know they were up here over all that chaos?

Marissa's breathing was choppy. She kept readjusting the position of the glass against Aerin's throat. "Okay, everyone," she growled. "Drop your phones and kick them to me."

Brett did as he was told. Marissa scooped up the phones and placed them in her handbag. "No one can leave. You make a break for it, and you'll regret it. Understood?"

Shaky nods. Seneca cleared her throat. "You don't want to do this, Mrs. Ingram. You don't want to hurt us. You're not that kind of person. I can tell."

Marissa snorted. The lines around her mouth were as prominent as etchings in copper. "I'm doing what I have to do. I tried to get you people to quit it. I *warned* you so many times. You should've gotten the hint and realized you were in over your heads."

Brett felt a clench in his chest. So Marissa *had* been their stalker.

"But you didn't kill any of us when you were warning us," Seneca said in a soothing tone Brett was astonished she could muster. "You're not a monster. You just didn't want us to create any waves, right?"

Marissa pursed her lips. She seemed sort of in shock, maybe like she couldn't believe she was doing such a thing, or maybe that the trail had finally led to her. "That's right," she said in a resigned voice. "But clearly, that tactic didn't work."

"All we want is the truth," Seneca cooed. "We're not out to hurt you or come after you. We know you didn't do it. We just want to hear what happened."

Brett stared at Seneca. *"We know you didn't do it"?* What was she playing at?

Marissa's face softened a little, like Seneca's method was working. "You can tell us," Seneca coaxed. "You can tell *Aerin*. You've known her your whole life. She just wants to know what happened to her sister."

Marissa turned an inch, then lowered the piece of glass slightly. She gave Aerin a small, contrite smile. "I just wish this had never happened, honey," she burst out, like it was something she'd been holding in for years. "I'm just so, *so* sorry."

"Did you kill Helena?" Aerin blurted.

Marissa looked shocked. "I would *never!*" She sounded remarkably convincing. Her face crumpled again. "Look, I sensed something was going on with her and Skip that summer. I never caught them, never found any texts or e-mails or letters, but I just . . . *knew.*"

"Why didn't you say anything to my mom?" Aerin cried.

Marissa cut her gaze to the right. "Because I didn't have any proof. That's a horrible thing to accuse someone's daughter of. It would have ruined our friendship."

Brett felt sick. That was what she'd been most worried about? Their friendship?

"When Helena went missing, Skip was missing, too. For a whole weekend. I was frantic, but I told everyone he was on business—the police, your mom, other friends, everyone at the search parties." She looked at Aerin again, with purpose. "You have to understand, honey. I was still hoping that it was all in my head."

Brett balled up his fists. It was unnerving how Marissa kept calling Aerin *honey*, like she actually cared about her. He wanted to rip her apart just for that.

"Days passed," Marissa said. "Weeks passed. Helena was still gone. Someone *could* have kidnapped her, absolutely. Or she could have run away with someone else, or on her own. But as each day passed and she wasn't found, wasn't *anywhere*, I just had a feeling Skip had something to do with it." She looked tormented. "On Christmas Day, he said he needed to go to the office. My husband works a lot, but never on *Christmas.* That time, I tracked him with the GPS app I loaded on his phone. He really was in New York City, in the apartment. That's when I started to wonder if he was there with her. If she was alive, okay, and they were in some sort of . . . love nest." She made a face.

"So why didn't you do anything then?" Aerin asked.

Marissa looked lost. "I was trying to find the right time. I was trying to understand why he'd *done* it." She sighed. "In the end, I dropped little hints that I knew. He denied it completely, but I could tell he was lying. So finally, I went to the apartment. I unlocked the door. And that's when I . . ." She broke off and shut her eyes, making a troubled face.

Aerin's face paled. "You *what?*"

It took Marissa a few moments to speak. "I saw her, on the floor. She was dead."

A cold ribbonlike shiver ran through Brett's body. He watched as the others exchanged confused glances. He knew what they were thinking: That didn't correspond with the Under Wraps messages at all.

"Was Skip . . . there?" Aerin asked. "Had she been dead for a while?"

Marissa shook her head, her black hair flapping against her cheeks. "He was on a work trip for real this time. As for how long she'd been dead, I couldn't really look at her."

"Why didn't you call the police?" Brett asked.

Marissa stared at Brett as though this was the craziest question anyone had ever asked her. "I couldn't do *that.*"

Brett thought he understood why Marissa didn't call. She'd probably flash-forwarded the scene and saw the shame that would come upon her family once the story broke open. Skip's business would tank, his clients would go elsewhere, and a good deal of their fortune would be lost. It would ruin Heath's future, too—and he was already a screwup. And, most of all, it would change Marissa's life for the worse. She had a good thing going. She'd lose everything.

"So you cleaned it up," Brett said. "You were the one who took the body to that park upstate, weren't you?"

"Skip never even thanked me." Marissa tried to laugh, but it came out as more of a whimper. "It was the safest option, though, neither of us telling what we'd done. If we were ever questioned, we could legitimately say that he'd never confessed what he did to me, and I had never confessed what I did to him."

Aerin shifted uncomfortably. "It's just that I thought Skip thought Helena ran away. He wrote messages to her, saying he was so worried."

Marissa's head shot up. "Messages *where*?"

"On this app she used. They wrote to each other all the time. He said all her things were gone and that he just wanted to make sure she was safe. It seemed like he really . . . loved her."

Fury flooded into Marissa's face. In one quick movement, she pulled Aerin close to her and pressed the shard to her neck once more. "Are you saying you don't *believe* me?"

"I don't know!" Aerin cried. "I just . . ."

"Think before you speak," Marissa roared, her face close to Aerin's. "Because I can kill you, Aerin. I'll kill you right here, right in front of your friends."

"No!" Seneca cried out.

"I'll do it!" Marissa wailed.

"Stop!" Brett screamed.

There was a sharp cracking sound. Brett jumped away just as the bathroom door broke down. "Freeze!" a voice shouted. Several silhouettes appeared in the hallway. "Dexby PD! Let her go, Mrs. Ingram!"

Police officers flooded the room, guns all aimed at Marissa. The commotion caught Marissa off guard, and the glass slipped from her hands. Brett shot from his post at the vanity, scooped up the shard from the floor, and deposited it in the sink. As he turned back, a cop was tackling Marissa to the ground, and another straddled her legs. Shiny handcuffs glinted in the overhead light. Everyone was screaming, crying, sobbing with relief.

He glanced over at his friends. Seneca had fallen to her knees on the tile. Maddox was comatose by the sink. Madison had her hands pressed to the sides of her face and was yelling something at the cops about Marissa being guilty. Brett swiveled around the room and searched for Aerin, but at first he couldn't locate her in the scuffle.

And then he spied her. She was by the tub. Another cop stood protectively in front of her. It was a young dude, barely older than Aerin herself. Brett thought he'd seen the guy before—maybe at the country club? Hadn't Aerin been talking to him?

He started to move toward Aerin, desperate to throw his arms around her, hold her tight, whisper to her that he was so happy that she was okay—and that he was so *sorry*. Screw finding the perfect moment to kiss her—*this* was the perfect moment, and he couldn't wait any longer. He was going to press her to him and make her feel safe and secure. He'd keep her safe forever.

But something stopped him in his tracks. The young cop tipped his head back to say something to Aerin, and their eyes met. The smile Aerin gave him was unlike anything Brett had seen from her before—it was relieved, it was admiring, but it was also filled with something else. Appreciation. And love—*real* love, far deeper than the flirty, lustful looks she gave him.

"Holy shit," Brett blurted, though his words couldn't be heard over all the commotion. All at once, he understood. Something went very cold and still inside him.

He'd never been anything more than fun for her. He'd never been more than a joke.

THIRTY-SIX

AERIN MELTED INTO the corner of the bathroom and watched as the cops, Thomas included, hefted Marissa to her feet and read her the Miranda rights. "You have the right to remain silent," Thomas recited. His booming, authoritative voice was really sexy.

"Don't *touch* me." Marissa's gown was hitched to her knees, and her arms were forced behind her back into handcuffs. She twisted her neck and gave Aerin a piercing glare. "Tell him, Aerin. Tell him what I told you. I'm not the guilty one! I didn't do anything!"

Aerin felt a lump in her throat. She stared into her mother's oldest friend's eyes, trying to find some humanity, but all she saw were dark pupils, lined lids, false eyelashes. The story Marissa told her swirled and congealed in her mind, shocking and sickening and probably only half-true. Marissa didn't just find her sister's dead body in the apartment that day. She'd killed her. It was the only thing that really made sense with the rest of the evidence.

Maybe Marissa had managed to rewrite history in her head, a coping mechanism to help her live with what she'd done. But still, even if she'd convinced herself Helena's death wasn't her fault, she'd still buried Helena without telling a soul. Doing that and then facing Aerin's mother afterward, pretending she knew nothing, was positively monstrous. Suddenly, Aerin remembered Marissa coming by with a care package for Aerin's mom for Valentine's Day. "She'll come home to you, I can just feel it," Aerin had heard Marissa say. "She's going to be just fine."

Meanwhile, she'd *known*! She'd dug a hole and put Helena's lifeless body in it!

Aerin looked at the cops. "She's guilty."

Thomas and two other officers led Marissa out of the bathroom and into the hall. And then the bathroom was silent again.

Aerin fell into her friends and hugged them tightly. She could hear them murmuring things to her, but the words washed over her without sinking in. After a moment, Madison bent down and retrieved their phones from Marissa's bag. She passed them out quietly, her hands trembling. Aerin almost wished someone would start laughing to cut the tension—otherwise she might burst into sobs that never quit.

There were murmurs in the hallway. Aerin stepped out of the bathroom and looked over the railing. Downstairs, the Easter Bunny party guests stood agape, watching as Marissa, dress wrinkled and hair mussed, was led by three police officers to a waiting cruiser in the front drive. Someone had thought to turn the music off, but it had been supplanted by whispers. A news team had arrived already, and a cameraman started panning the mayhem. Kids had spilled from the guesthouse, looking disheveled and drugged. Elena Fairfield, who was in Aerin's grade, grinned at the camera, posing this way and that in her Easter Bunny ears, but then Mr. Fairfield swooped in and draped his blazer over her skimpy dress.

Aerin's legs were still wobbly as she started down the staircase and across the ballroom. Everyone was staring at her, including all her friends, but she barely registered their looks and definitely didn't hear their words. *Marissa,* rang a refrain in her head. *Marissa.* Her imagination was going crazy. She saw Marissa finding Helena, attacking her, murdering her there in the apartment. And then stuffing Helena's body in a garment bag and dragging it into a service elevator. Burying her in that park, then cleaning the mud off her boots with bottles of Evian.

And then . . . just living the rest of her life. Hosting parties, buying yachts. Ordering a custom trinket from her jeweler. Enjoying *her* child, because *Heath* was still alive, unlike Helena. Enjoying her husband, as much as she could while knowing he was a cheating, child-molesting bastard, all because she was too fucked-up to tell the truth.

Her stomach heaved, and she dug her nails into her palms, waiting for the feeling to pass. The last thing she wanted was to puke all over the Morgenthaus' floor. She glanced over her shoulder for the others. Seneca and Madison were huddled near the stairs, pale-faced. Maddox was already outside near the squad cars. She couldn't find Brett anywhere.

There was a bleating sound, and Aerin's parents cut through the crowd and threw their arms around Aerin tightly. "I was so worried." Aerin's mother pulled back and looked at Aerin in horror, then over her shoulder at where the cops were shoving Marissa inside a car. Her diamonds glinted in the whirling lights. She had to pick up the ends of her gown so they didn't get caught in the door. Once settled, she crossed her ankles, showing off her Jimmy Choo stilettos.

A strange, mournful look came over her dad's features, and Aerin felt so adrift that she laid her head on his shoulder, too tired to care that it had been years since she'd hugged her father. After a moment, she gave her mom a turn, burrowing into her chest. Before she knew what she was doing, she pressed her thumb into the center of her mom's palm. It was their old handshake, back when they were close: a thumb to the palm, then to the back of the hand. To her surprise, she felt her mom's palm wrap tightly around hers. Then came the three squeezes, as decipherable as a skip code. *I've. Got. You.*

They stood like that for a while, letting the crowd and the news cameras and the police stream around them. Then someone else cleared his throat, and Aerin looked over. Thomas stood off to the left.

"H-hey," Aerin stammered, straightening up.

There was a long beat where they just stared at each other. Her mother let go of her hand and nudged her toward him. Aerin walked a few paces, feeling shaky on her legs. "I was pretty sure no one was going to come for us," she murmured.

Thomas shrugged. "A 9-1-1 call came in of this guy whispering he was at the Easter Bunny party. The call didn't hang up, though, so the dispatcher was able to listen in as Marissa threatened you guys." He smiled. "We were able to record a lot of her confession."

Aerin glanced out the window to the driveway. "Are you going to have to go back to the station tonight?"

"Yeah. It's gonna be a long one—interrogations, booking paperwork—and you might need to be interviewed, too, though you won't be charged with anything. I promise." He winked.

Then he moved closer and cleared his throat. "And I understand," he said in a lower voice. "About . . . you know. The password. I shouldn't have given you a hard time at the station. I would have done it, too, if it was my sister, Aerin. I would have done the same thing."

He was looking at her so intently. Aerin's heart swelled, and she swallowed, hard. "Oh," she whispered. "Well, thank you." And then she threw her arms around his neck for a hug. She longed to kiss him, too, but this probably wasn't the right moment. She had a feeling, though, that there would be more opportunities. Maybe a lot of them.

She could only hope.

THIRTY-SEVEN

EARLY THE NEXT morning, Seneca stood on the southbound Metro-North platform and stared down the tracks. The train was late by twenty minutes, and the platform was clogged with waiting passengers. *I promise I'm at the station,* she texted her dad. *Coming home soon.*

She'd cracked and told him that she'd been at a party last night where a murderer had been arrested and that she'd needed to stay behind to be questioned. Her father had wanted to drive to Connecticut as soon as he heard, but she'd assured him that she was fine and would be on the first train in the morning.

She didn't want to leave, but she owed her father a talk. And maybe, if he let her, she would come back to Dexby soon. Aerin had already offered Seneca her bedroom. Mrs. Kelly, who Seneca had talked to for a long time last night at the police station, had said Seneca could come stay for the summer if she wanted.

Next to her, Aerin and Madison, who'd come to see her off, were peering at an online Connecticut society gossip page, which had posted pictures of last night's Easter Bunny party. "Oh my God, Amanda looks horrible," Aerin murmured, pointing to a dazed-looking girl in a dirty white dress. "And what's wrong with Cooper's eyes?"

"He looks stoned," Madison said wisely.

Then Seneca cast a tight smile toward Maddox, who was sitting on a bench a few paces away, checking his phone. "You can go if you want," she said tightly.

Maddox stood. "No way."

She shrugged and turned toward the tracks, but she could feel his gaze on her. He probably thought she was going to let the thing with Catherine drop just because they'd had a major victory last night, but she wasn't going to make the same mistake twice. So maybe Maddox looked especially handsome today in a hunter-green polo. So maybe she'd remembered a dirty joke he'd told her at the carnival about badgers and started laughing this morning in the shower. So maybe he'd written her a long e-mail saying that he'd canceled future training sessions with Catherine and told her never to contact him again. He also said that according to the coach at Oregon, his scholarship was still intact, but he wasn't sure if he was going to take it. It didn't seem worth it anymore. The only thing that did seem worth it was Seneca.

So maybe that was the most romantic thing anyone had ever said to her. But it still didn't matter. The door that had cracked open inside Seneca was now sealed. They could be friends again, maybe, but nothing more.

"Well, I'd say this trip was a resounding success," she said crisply, holding up her phone. A Google Alert had just come in for Marissa; this one was a dazzling recap of Marissa's arrest on CNN. Thanks to the 9-1-1 dispatcher recording Marissa's confession, the police were able to hold Marissa without bail. For the time being, the two Ingrams were in jail together, though most were saying that Skip would be released on bail later today based on the reasonable doubt Marissa's story had created that he'd actually killed her.

Last night, Seneca and the others had separately given statements saying that with Aerin's help and from hacking into an app Helena used before she died, they'd figured out that Marissa might have been aware of Helena's affair. The cops weren't charging the group with withholding evidence. In fact, they seemed quite impressed with their sleuthing. The Dexby chief had even jokingly asked if they'd like to solve other mysteries around town, though Seneca was pretty sure he hadn't been serious.

And best of all, Seneca and the others had gotten credit for their work. *Research by a group of three local teens and one girl from Maryland was key in leading to Mrs. Ingram's arrest.* The reporter had messed up on how many of them had been in their group, and he hadn't given any names, but Case Not Closed had been mentioned, which meant they'd get props from everyone on the boards.

Aerin crowded around Seneca's phone, and the two of them gazed at Helena's picture in the article. "That's a good one." Helena stood outside the Dexby Country Club, wearing the brown fedora, a fringe vest, and wide-leg pants. There was something about the light at her back and the angle of the camera that made her face look older, her hair especially blond.

Seneca peered at Aerin, noting the circles under her eyes, the languidness in her movements. She hadn't slept last night, Seneca bet. Aerin might have the truth about Helena now, but at a cost: It was eating at her, the reality perhaps worse than she'd ever imagined. How many millions of sleepless nights had Seneca had, after all, reliving seeing her mother on that slab? How many ways had she woken herself from a nightmare of seeing her mother being murdered? Was Aerin picturing Helena perishing on that polished wood floor? Wondering what her last words and thoughts were? Wondering if she'd suffered? Seneca wished she had some words of wisdom for her, or that she could offer some assurance that in time, those questions would fade. But that was the problem: They hadn't, for her. Maybe they never would.

A gust of wind picked up, shaking the trees and lifting the ends of Madison's pink scarf. A line in the new article caught her eye: *Mrs. Ingram asserts that she had nothing to do with Ms. Kelly's death, only coming upon her lifeless body after she'd been murdered.* She pointed it out for the others. "I'm still stuck on that. If Marissa didn't do it, that means Skip did. So what were his messages on Under Wraps about?"

"Marissa's lying," Maddox said, his voice full of certainty.

Seneca chewed on her thumbnail. It was just that Marissa had come up with the lie so handily last night. She hadn't shown any of the telltale signs that she was making anything up. Then again, maybe she should follow Brett's advice: They got their guy. She should stop worrying.

Then she peered down the platform toward the stairs. "Anyone know where Brett is? I texted him that I was leaving today. I figured he'd be here by now."

Aerin shook her head. "I haven't seen him since last night."

"He didn't ride to the police station with me," Maddox said. "I waited and waited, but he didn't show."

"Did he talk to the cops?" Seneca asked. "I didn't see him at the station."

"I'm sure he did," Aerin said.

Seneca pushed her hands into her pockets. Across the street, a bunch of cars pulled out of the Restful Inn. "It's crazy how sketchy I thought Brett was," she said, recalling that first train ride. "Goes to show first impressions aren't always right." Then she thought about her conversation with Brett at the tennis courts the night before. If only she'd thought to ask about his grandmother sooner. Their conversation had been therapeutic for her, too.

Then a tooth in the intricate clockwork in her mind caught. Something about last night hadn't sat right with her, and now she realized what it was. She turned to Maddox. "Why did you tell Brett about this?" She grabbed her necklace.

He squinted. "Huh?"

"Brett said to me, 'But at least you got that back to remember her by.' He meant my mom's necklace. But the wording was strange—like he knew how I got it."

Maddox blinked. "I would never tell someone something you told me in confidence."

"But there's no other way he could have found out."

"What are you talking about?" Aerin asked.

Seneca couldn't answer. A slithery feeling washed over her body. She switched over to the phone function and dialed Brett's number. She would just ask him, no big deal. The phone rang once, and then a recorded message blared through the earpiece: *The number you are trying to call has been disconnected.*

She stared at her phone as though it had transformed into a snake. Madison touched Seneca's arm. "You have the weirdest look on your face."

"*What's* going on?" Aerin said again.

Seneca sank to a bench. She was light-headed. "I'm sure it's nothing."

But it didn't feel like nothing. There was no way the thing about her mom's necklace could be public knowledge, even for people who had insider info. The coroner hadn't yet taken pictures of Seneca's mom when Seneca stole that necklace off her. As far as she knew, the detective on the case hadn't made a note of her mother wearing it, either—the necklace had been tucked under Collette's T-shirt, the chain and pendant hidden.

She hadn't told her dad. She hadn't told another friend. The only way someone could have known her mom was wearing that necklace when she died would have been if...

Seneca had a horrible, outlandish thought. *No,* she told herself. Absolutely not. She was being insane.

But maybe she should check.

She typed in a search for Vera Grady on her phone. A *Wikipedia* page came up featuring a picture of the heiress with her platinum-blond hair and furs. The woman wasn't so old—maybe only fifty or so. And a sexy fifty, with a taut, thin figure. Seneca then clicked to the picture of Helena from the CNN article she'd just looked at. A sick feeling welled in her stomach. She had the same white-blond hair. So did Seneca's mom, actually. Seneca had never made the connection before. Then again, why would she have?

All sound fell away. Seneca stared at the group, the tips of her fingers prickling. "Um, how did Brett know how to override the security system at the Dakota?"

Maddox shrugged. "He said his family had the same one."

"Doesn't that seem convenient?"

He looked at her crazily. "Huh?"

Seneca's mind couldn't stop. "And when we were interrogating Kevin, Brett mentioned a secret boyfriend stealing Helena away from Kevin and wining and dining her at his Upper West Side pad. But that's before we knew about the Dakota."

Aerin wrinkled her nose. "I'm not following you."

"Me neither," Maddox said.

More and more ugly bubbles rose to the surface. "And the call, from Loren, at the hospital. His number was unlisted, but Loren's cell phone had come up on caller ID. And Brett answered it—he was the only one who spoke. How do we know Loren called at all? And why did Brett keep pushing us to go to New York? Why did Brett, out of nowhere, bring up the paper crane to me in a text when I was leaving? Why was he the one who opened the closet where Helena's hat was? Why isn't he *here*?"

Madison blinked hard. "Where are you going with this?"

Maddox started to pace. "Brett's one of the best amateur detectives on Case Not Closed. Maybe he's half-psychic—that's how he knew about the apartment on the Upper West Side."

"Half-*psychic*?" Seneca cried.

"And as far as Loren, of course he called that day," Maddox continued. "I mean, what are you saying, Brett blocked his number and dialed Helena's old phone and had a conversation with no one? That he already *knew* Skip Ingram had a place at the Dakota in advance?"

"I don't know," Seneca said dazedly. Her throat felt wrapped in duct tape.

"Brett has access. He's Vera Grady's grandson. He could buy out the CIA if he wanted," Maddox said.

But Seneca wasn't sure about even that anymore. She looked again at the Vera Grady page. The site also included a family tree, complete with pictures. Sure enough, there was a grandson named Brett Grady. Only . . .

Seneca pressed the phone closer to her face, trying to make sense of the tiny image. Brett Grady had a beaky nose and dark hair. His eyes were wide-set, and he had prominent cheekbones. He had the doughy paleness of someone who never worked out. The page said that he lived in Cupertino, California, and worked for Apple.

"I'm confused," Madison said, seeing it, too.

"Um . . ." Seneca passed the phone to Maddox and Aerin. They read slowly. Color drained from Aerin's face. Maddox just looked angry.

"This has to be a mistake," Maddox said. "*Wikipedia* is wrong a lot, right?"

But he didn't sound so sure.

Seneca stared down the platform, a screaming sound rushing through her ears. How had she let this slip past her? How did Brett know so much? And who *was* he? She pictured him now, his broad, average face and squinty eyes, that sandy hair, those broad pecs and strong biceps . . .

Her brain clicked through the details of Helena's case as well as her mom's. Then she looked up, a new chill running down her spine. "Oh my God. Aerin. Your sister's bones showed very aggressive blunt-force trauma, right?"

Aerin blinked at her. "Yeah . . ."

"Meaning someone very, very strong beat her before she died, right?" Her voice shook. "Someone much, *much* stronger than Marissa. I mean, she could barely hold you still at the party, with that piece of glass."

"Okay, so then it *was* Mr. Ingram who killed her?" Aerin asked slowly.

Seneca shook her head. "I don't think so. I'm thinking that maybe . . . maybe it was a serial killer thing."

"Wait, *what*?" Madison squeaked.

"Seneca, what do you mean?" Maddox looked horrified.

Seneca felt a lump in her throat. "Helena's pelvic bones were beaten the worst, weren't they?"

A terrified look crossed Aerin's features. "H-how did you . . . ?"

Seneca understood Aerin's shock—that detail wasn't in the news. The reporters said some of Helena's bones showed very violent trauma, but they didn't reveal *which* bones. There was something perhaps too cruel and perverse about discussing a seventeen-year-old's pelvic region, the cradle of all her blossoming reproductive organs, the knobby bones that constructed her hips and butt, with the public. Seneca knew the truth, however, because she'd illegally procured a coroner's report a few years back, paying money on a questionable website to get it. At the time, her eyes had skimmed over the words *multiple fractures to the coccyx, sacrum, pubis, ischium,* the pelvic bones' scientific terms, without thinking much of it. But maybe there was a hideous connection. A serial killer's calling card.

Perhaps there was a cosmic reason Seneca had been so attracted to Helena's case. Like the universe was trying to tell her something. Like there was a horrible bridge between the two deaths.

She looked up at Aerin, her eyes full of fear. "My mother's pelvis was smashed, too. In the same exact way. And I bet if we look up Vera Grady's report, we'll find the same thing."

The train screeched up like a banshee, but Seneca barely registered its presence. She kept staring at Aerin, and she stared back, the eeriness and weirdness and utter wrongness of this washing over them. It was only after the train came to a full stop that Maddox dared to speak.

"Did we let him go?" he whispered.

Seneca could only nod. Maybe, horribly, devastatingly, they had.

AFTER

IT WAS RATHER nice being Brett Grady, he thought as he sat down in the diner next to the Restful Inn for one last cup of coffee. Brett Grady had gotten the job done. Brett Grady had tricked everyone, even Seneca, who acted like she missed nothing. In fact, he might as well continue to call himself Brett for a little while longer. Why the hell not? The name had clout.

And so, Brett Grady, real name not necessary, glanced at his reflection in the dingy window. He'd already cut his hair shorter in the hotel room, and he'd pulled off that ridiculous ball cap he'd been wearing all week. He'd put his glasses back on; it was nice to see well again, finally—contacts had never been his thing. He'd taken off the garish, thuggish oversized jersey and pants and replaced them with a striped button-down and khakis. Popped the button-down's collar. Slid on loafers. He'd turned back into the Connecticut Everyman—preppy, bland, unnoticed. The kind who blended in too well. The kind who women stared through instead of at.

It really, really pissed him off when they stared through him. And when he got pissed off, he got himself in trouble.

A train whistle blew. It was the southbound Metro-North, probably. *All's well that ends well,* Brett thought. He wasn't crazy about the wife taking the blame instead, but it was close enough. It was a comfort knowing Skip Ingram would be behind bars. Everyone knew now that he was a child molester. No more fancy party invites for him.

Still. If only people weren't so foolish to start with. If only people weren't such assholes, this world would be a better place. Bad things wouldn't have to happen.

"Want a refill?"

The waitress who stood over him was the dishwater blonde with the saggy boobs who'd waited on him every day since he'd come here. She never had a smile for him. Never laughed at his jokes. And yesterday morning, when she saw him come in? She'd *rolled her eyes.*

"That would be lovely," he drawled. And then, slowly, he placed his hand atop hers. "The coffee here is really quite good. What's your secret?"

The woman flinched. "Um . . . I don't know . . ."

She tried to move her hand away, but he pinned it there. Fear bloomed over her face. Finally, he lifted his hand as if nothing had happened. She shot away, cradling her hand like he'd branded it. When she peeked back at him over her shoulder, he gave her a bland smile.

Brett downed the rest of his cup, dropped a couple quarters on the table, and stood. Little did that woman know she'd skated on thin ice. Had she been a little prettier, had she been more his type, it could have gone very badly for her. He shut his eyes, savoring the delicious way tendons and tissue and bone gave way when you compressed a neck. That satisfying crack of the spine. That triumphant feeling knowing that his hands and his hands alone were the only things stand-ing between her life and death. *If I changed my mind about you,* he said silently to the waitress's receding back, *you would plead for your life, and I'd just laugh.*

But he would spare the waitress—he had a new victim lined up. A girl who'd rejected him even though he was perfect for her. A girl he'd gotten to know quite well, inside and out. A girl who wanted someone else, someone undeserving of her love.

Aerin Kelly, that cruel, icy bitch. Hell, maybe he'd go after her new little boyfriend, too.

He couldn't wait.

ACKNOWLEDGMENTS

THIS BOOK HAS been a long time in the making, and I have many to thank. First, to those brilliant minds at Alloy Entertainment: Josh Bank, Les Morgenstein, Sara Shandler, Lanie Davis, and especially Annie Stone, whose careful and thoughtful guidance turned this from a cool idea into a real story. Huge thanks, too, to the editorial team at Hyperion, Emily Meehan and Julie Rosenberg, and my copy editor, Jackie Hornberger. Much appreciation to the marketing, publicity, and design teams: Marci Senders, Mary Ann Zissimos, Seale Ballenger, Jamie Baker, Elke Villa, Holly Nagel, Maggie Penn, Dina Sherman, and Andrew Sansone; and thank you, Hyperion sales team, for believing in me and in this story. Also a big thanks to Andy McNicol at WME, and Romy Golan, Theo Guliadas, Elaine Damasco (who created the gorgeous cover), and Stephanie Abrams at Alloy for your confidence and support. Go team!

Thanks also to Michael, who suffered through probably the most of my angst in getting this book off the ground, and to my parents for many wine-soaked dinners. Thanks to Mike Gremba for your real-world insights on police records and bloodstains. And most of all to Kristian and Henry. I hope none of the things in this book happen to you—well, except for finding friends who truly understand you, and in that case I hope you find dozens.